THE MARRIAGE FORMULA

THE MARRIAGE FORMULA

MARJORIE DURYEA

DISCLAIMER

There are real people and places playing a part in this novel, but it must be read as a work of fiction. The voices of the characters and the details around their lives are a product of the author's imagination. Any semblance to reality is purely coincidental.

ACKNOWLEDGMENTS

Foremost I'm indebted to my editor, Kera Voigtlander, for her sharp eye, invaluable insight and dedication to the realization of this story. I am also indebted to Ricky Villane for his encouragement and advice reading the very first drafts of the novel. His feedback on character development and storyline were extremely helpful bringing the characters to life. I also would like to thank Amanda Evans for being a focus group of one.

For Arthur

and

For Ricky

We can only see a short distance ahead, but we can see plenty there that needs to be done.

ALAN TURING, MATHEMATICIAN

PART ONE

EROS RULES

CHAPTER 1

MEETING THE BEAR

I met Joe in 2001 on the day I had a flat tire on New Bedford Road, less than a mile away from the high school where I worked. I taught geometry and trig: to bored recalcitrants in the former and aggressive overachievers in the latter. I didn't know who was worse; those who slept in my class and did nothing, or those who harassed me if they got a B+ instead of an A. You would think teaching math would be more cut-and-dry when it came to grading compared to other subjects. It certainly is more so than teaching literature, according to my friend Paulee, an English teacher. She never saw the emotion and strong opinions that came into play teaching mathematics when I qualitatively evaluated computations with answers to determine a grade. Reflecting on that, I preferred the recalcitrants.

Unfortunately I wasn't creative enough to motivate my underachievers even though I liked them, and the teaching profession. Maybe the problem was I liked them too much and wasn't tough enough. When I was getting my undergraduate degree studying to be a math teacher, one of my professors in the education department said: more than half of the role teaching on the primary and secondary level is managerial. When I met Joe, it was too late in the year to change dynamics in my classes, there were only a few weeks left before summer. I planned to study managerial skills for the classroom on my break to find techniques to be more effective—inspiring recalcitrants and defusing AP students.

I was thinking about that when there was a bump, bump, bump on the road. I prayed—please let it be an uneven road surface and not what I feared. I am not a religious person, obviously no deity heard me. I was now on New Bedford Road with no shoulder, tired and irritable from a full day of teaching, with a flat tire. I am a member of an auto club and have been one since I got my driver's license when I turned seventeen. I was not faced with having to change my own tire, but there was a good probability the township police would arrive before the auto club—I was blocking the southbound side of the road. When a guy pulled up and asked if I wanted him to change my tire I enthusiastically said, *yes*. It was the best thing that had happened all day.

He was a bear of a guy—not fat but husky, with a full beard that made him look even more carnivoran. He was far from ferocious looking though, and with his baseball cap and glasses he reminded me of a big teddy bear. But strong enough to do the job and not hurt himself or sue me, so I accepted his offer. It was impressive how quickly he changed the tire too and I told him so. Had he wanted to return a compliment when he said, "Your trunk is very clean." It wasn't a great compliment but I shouldn't have been judgmental. The guy was only trying to be friendly, regardless of how lame his compliment was; it had not been necessary for him to reciprocate at all. I was anxious to leave—it made me critical, and when his compliment morphed into a lengthy discussion I grew a little irritated. He seemed enamored with the topic—not moving, like my car. He told me his sister's trunk was a mess when he changed her flat. It took him longer to find the spare and jack than to change the tire.

One would think he was a talker, which later I would discover was not the case; he was misleading on the day I met him. I appreciated his help but I wanted to scream, *shut up.* He wouldn't stop, and when he started to tell me how close his sister lived from where we were I had to interrupt him. I was afraid he was about to give me all the specific details—maybe even directions to her house.

"What can I pay you for your trouble?"

"Oh, I don't want your money, just give me a hug."

Without even a second's thought, I gave the bear a great big bear hug. When I stepped back he had a surprised and stricken look on his face—as though I had permitted him to sexually assault me. His reaction startled me. I hadn't felt uncomfortable when I hugged him because there wasn't even one sexual context that came to mind when I looked at him. It was his reaction and obvious distress which now made me feel uncomfortable. I needed to make amends; I owed him more than payment for fixing the flat. I quickly took out one of my math tutoring cards, a little business of mine in addition to my full-time teaching job, and thrust it in his hand.

"Look, just give me a call, and I'll buy you lunch if you don't want money, but I need to move because I'm blocking the road."

I then took off thinking I'd never see him again, not imagining in my wildest dreams—I would marry him a year and a half later.

CHAPTER 2

SCHOOL DAYS

I shouldn't say it, but it was true, some of my students were simply deadbeats. They didn't even try to do any work; I pitied their poor parents. I was good in all my subjects in school. My mother Agnes, who I've called *Agnes* ever since she begged me to move in with her after college, never had to worry about my grades. My strongest subjects were science and math, winning awards throughout middle school; I continued to excel in high school in advanced placement classes, but I was never called a nerd. Good thing; it was not fashionable to be called one when I was in school, and my looks simply took precedence over brains. Nobody thought of me as a nerd—I was a sexy, curvy blonde.

My mother's good friend Alice, who had been a big Marilyn Monroe fan, told me I had the same measurements as her: 35, 22, 35. Alice was a seamstress and made beautiful prom and wedding dresses. My mother paid her to make the dresses for my proms. When she took my measurements she always said, "Oh, look at this body, your girl is gorgeous, Nessie." My mother's reply was always the same, "Make sure you don't make the neckline too low, Ally."

I was shapely when I entered freshman year. I wasn't quite a 35D cup yet, but as the boys liked to say, I was *ripe for the picking*. I might have been but I was not stupid. I didn't let anyone pick me until I wanted to be picked. All my close girl friends lost their virginity in high school, but I was in my senior year of college; a ripe old age of twenty-three when I willingly gave it away.

I was not fast or easy, but I was a big flirt in high school. I admit it, and I knew the power my body had on boys. In all other areas of my life I acted responsibly—more mature for my age, but was extremely immature in the way I flaunted my body. I would tease with no regard to anyone's feelings. If I had been practicing courtesan arts in the 19th century it would have been acceptable—downright commendable, but as an adult I cringe at times when I think about how I behaved in high school. I don't berate myself too much though. Sometimes remembering my antics I even laugh at my teenage self. Everyone has things they are ashamed about when they reflect on their high school days. And after years witnessing the behavior of my students, I hadn't been that bad; my behavior was departmentalized, not universal.

I would always arrive a few minutes before the bell in my science and math classes so I could make an entrance. Everyone would already be seated before I walked in the door; they were serious overachieving nerds. They were also boring and geeky, although I did respect their brains. As an adult I think only kind things about them. They were more mature than most teens their age when it came to academics; their lack of maturity was expressed through their social awkwardness. I exploited it with my skin tight jeans and tops with plunging necklines. I was never outrageous enough to be sent home from school, but I had to wear different clothes from home (I changed in the girls' restroom). My mother would not have let me out of the house if she had seen what I was wearing.

When I walked into the classroom the girls always pretended to ignore me, but I knew they were staring at me with disdain and envy. I was hot, and I could never understand why they couldn't try to look better themselves. Forget about make-up, trying to cover pimples, or choosing more flattering clothes—some didn't even bother to wash their hair. But they were not my concern. I did not spend much time thinking about their lack of style, I was able to ignore them for real. It was the boys I wanted to entertain, and based on their reactions—I was successful in my mission. Every boy would turn his bespectacled head towards me with a gaping mouth; their eyes following me as I slowly, ever so slowly, made my way to my seat. If I was feeling very wicked, I would pull my top down a bit, just a little, enough so the lace of my bra showed. It was usually enough to create a stir, but if I smiled at someone the sexual tension in the room became thick. I was palatable and could make them drool.

I never knew if any of my teachers caught my act; I was never approached by any of them. Maybe they chose to ignore my behavior since I was one of their best students, and to my credit I stopped the taunting as soon as the class started. I was overlooked but it was hard not to notice me. I had been tangible proof that students did not have to have greasy hair, pimples or glasses to excel in their classes.

My grades were always excellent, but I did experience failure. I failed to make any friends in those classes and I regret that today. None of my friends and dates in high school were in advanced placement math or science. They were a wild crowd—making my behavior seem very benign in comparison. They were the deadbeats of their day and I thought they were funny—I was a fan. As a teacher I got big-time payback now for my past sentiments. Deadbeats weren't entertaining or humorous when I tried to teach them.

CHAPTER 3

DATE OR MEETING?

Friday was a half day before school was to end the following Monday for the 2001 summer break. Why they didn't end the school year on Friday had made no sense to me, but I tried not to get disturbed by the administration. They could be more frustrating than troublesome students. I chose to do what I was told and ignored them the rest of the time. Paulee on the other hand, was always running to the union rep with some complaint or problem. She was very passionate about teachers' rights, but that's why I liked her. I have always been drawn to passionate, sometimes downright wacky people. They excited me and gave me vicarious thrills—doing things I wouldn't have dared to do myself.

My best friend in high school was Dee. She had a pierced tongue, seven tattoos, and lost her virginity in freshman year. She got drunk every weekend, smoked pot, and stole prescription drugs from people she babysat for. My mom would often say to me, "I like Dee, but I don't like what she does." Dee was not unique though, all the kids I hung out with drank and did drugs—but not me. I didn't even try pot until I was in my twenties. I was the mature one in the group: the old soul and designated driver who could not be peer pressured. That's why it hurt so much when my mother accused me of being high. I had not even taken one sip of alcohol or had a single hit at the party. I brought Dee to our house because she was way too stoned and drunk to be dropped off at her house that night. My mother knew I did not drink or do drugs even if my friends did. I think she was just angry because Dee vomited a foul, watery reddish mess on her white rug in the downstairs bathroom. She had been angry at Dee and lashed out at me, knowing fully well I was never a victim of peer pressure. I was the one who always lectured Dee about drugs, drinking, and even the negatives of tattoos and sunbathing.

"You know you are going to look like a wrinkled prune when you get older from too much sun," was my frequent summer warning. And I reminded her every time she wanted to get a new tattoo how they looked on sagging skin when you're old. She finally made a good counter argument to that when she said, "Sarah, no one looks good when they get old, with or without tats."

She didn't change my mind about the dangers of too much sunbathing, but her words made me imagine what my breasts would look like after gravity did its damage. It changed my mind about tattoos, but it was not peer pressure that made me get the little rose tattoo on the top of my left breast. When Dee gave me a gift certificate on my birthday I imagined people's eyes being redirected, away from old drooping boobs to a red rose. My mother was shocked—"Are you mad, Sarah? Whatever possessed you to get a tattoo?" Her first reaction was less about my behavior and more about the possibility of my having contracted hepatitis B or C. I assured her, "the place was clean and they used disposable needles," and it was too late for her to intervene over the deed. That was what finally made her angry; she did not want me to be a repeat offender. I had to surrender the fake ID, another present from Dee. We needed them since we had to be eighteen to get our tattoos and we were underage. I never knew who made the ID's and Dee refused to tell me. It was not a problem; I did not want a fake ID. I had no desire to get another tat or do underage drinking.

My mother told me what I did was a rash and immature act but I disagreed with her when I was seventeen and still do. It had been carefully thought out; it was long-range planning—cheaper than a breast lift when I was old and sagging. And I never got addicted to the ink—I only have one. It was Dee's eighth to celebrate my seventeenth birthday and she continued to get more after that. I'm not sure if anything Dee did was well thought out. She was a character, and I had loved hanging out with her in high school.

This desire to be a voyeur of wild people was in me since childhood (it was not a product of rebellious teenage hormones). My earliest memory was when I was around eight, and I had a friend named Johnny who lived a few houses down the street from us. He grossed me out and fascinated me. One day he took his pet goldfish Herman out of the bowl and swallowed it. My mother was disturbed when I told her, but when he accidentally hacked off one of his fingers with his father's hatchet, she wouldn't let me go over to his house any more.

Paulee, who is one of my closest friends, doesn't have body piercings or tattoos. Nor does she swallow live goldfish or play with sharp objects. It's her exaggerated temper which characterizes her as a wild person. I always warn her that she is going to give herself an early stroke if she doesn't try to stop getting so upset, especially when driving. If someone cut her off or tailgated her she screamed and cursed like a banshee.

One memorable incident was being a passenger in her car when she gave some guy the finger in her rear-view mirror, in addition to a few choice words. He was still behind us when we stopped for a red light; he got out of his truck, not looking very happy, and was walking over to Paulee's car. It was our good fortune that before he reached us the light turned green. I shouted, "Go, go, floor it," and Paulee took off, laughing as hard as she had been cursing; I laughed too. It was often very exciting being with her, but after the red-light incident, I told her I was driving next time or we could travel in separate cars. That's why a couple of weeks after I met Joe, I drove to the movies in my car to avoid being a participant in another one of Paulee's road rage misadventures. As soon as I returned home and walked in the front door, Agnes told me *a man named Joe* had called and left his number.

"I don't know anyone by that name."

"He said you'd probably say that," and punctuated it with a laugh which made me slightly uncomfortable. I imagined my mother and this stranger exchanging amusing anecdotes about me. Before I could challenge her on that she said, "He told me to tell you he was the guy who changed your flat tire," That jogged my memory—it was *the bear.*

Apparently, he had not forgotten my lunch offer; I had completely forgotten about him. My mother continued, "He said you can call him as late as midnight." It was only a little after ten but I was not in a rush to call him back.

The next day I kept procrastinating calling Joe, and my mother kept asking me if I had returned his call.

"Why are you so concerned about me calling this guy back?"

"Well, I just don't want him to think I didn't give you the message, that's all."

To avoid hearing her ask me for the umpteenth time about this damn call, I got the note with his number from the table in the hallway and called him back.

It turned out he lived in the same complex in Jackson as Paulee. I could not believe the coincidence; not only the same complex, he lived in a townhouse in the alcove of her very street. I thought it would be easy to settle on a meeting place since I was familiar with his area. Paulee and I frequently went out to eat near her condo. She was into small, boutique restaurants; there weren't many but I knew where they all were located. I suggested the little cafe on New Friendship Road or the Italian bistro in the same strip where we could buy pastries and coffee; both places had outside areas where patrons could sit. That's when I learned choosing a place would not be as easy as I had thought—he was not familiar with either of them. He said if he went out to eat for a special occasion it was Applebee's on Route 9, "but any fast-food restaurant is good enough for me." I liked Applebee's, but would not call it or the meetup with him a special occasion, and I had not eaten at a fast-food restaurant since college—I did not want to start again. Fortunately, he agreed to the cafe and we made plans to meet the next day at 1 pm.

When I told my mother I was meeting Joe for lunch she said, "Oh, how nice, you haven't dated for a while."

"This is not a date, it's a meeting. I have no interest in dating this guy."

"Well, you are going out to lunch. It sounds like a date to me."

"Mom, (and now she knew I was annoyed because I called her *Mom* instead of *Agnes*), I am not attracted to this guy at all. This is not a date. It's simply payback for fixing a flat tire, okay?"

"No need to get so upset, Sarah. I'm sorry, it's a meeting, not a date. I hope you have a great time at your meeting."

CHAPTER 4

FIREWORKS

One of the first things Joe said was he wasn't much of a talker (which surprised me based on our first encounter) and he hoped I wouldn't mind. Reflecting on it, I did not find him to be unusually quiet or much different than other men I had known in my life. And it was impossible to say honestly if his quietness would bother me since we had just met. I was familiar with the premise that conversations are exponentially less frequent and shorter in length the longer a relationship. If our interactions changed after we knew each other it might affect my tolerance, but it didn't matter. I did not envision this relationship going anywhere. Besides, when I met Joe at the cafe the problem was not a lack of conversation. It seemed odd to me that he said he *wasn't much of a talker*—he was not a good judge of his own behavior. The problem I had with him was we shared no common interests.

He told me he sold air conditioner and heating units wholesale to large companies; another oddity. If he did not like to talk, why would he choose a profession that demanded it? There had to be another reason to choose this profession and I soon found out. The not loquacious Joe (according to him) did not hold back. He said the best part about selling high price ticket items was he only had to sell one or two a year to meet his financial quota. If he lived modestly after reaching it, he was able to substantially lessen his work load. He could then devote more time to his hobbies.

He loved golf; he asked me, "Do you play?" No; it was boring, but I omitted that. Other hobbies were collecting antique wooden golf clubs, and making model planes. He didn't suppose I made models; he was right, no again. I was not a crafty person. He said he also flew remote model airplanes; he belonged to a flying club in Robbinsville. He asked, "Have you ever seen an air show with remote planes?" No, no, no—three strikes and we were now out. And watching a remote plane airshow did not sound appealing to me at all, but he thought it was exciting. "Especially when they crashed—it only hurts your pocketbook though, nobody gets hurt."

I was not interested in anything he had to say until he talked about his two cats. I love cats, but my mother is allergic to them. When I moved in with her she said she would not mind if I got one but I had to keep it in my room or outside. I chose not to do either; I opted instead to buy toys and treats for my friends' cats and play with them; Paulee had three. Joe told me he took ownership of his live-in girlfriend's cat Ollie when she moved out and left him. He decided to get a second cat a few months later so Ollie wouldn't be lonely. He was often away from the house for many hours or traveling for work. He named his second cat Bear which made me laugh out loud.

"I know, it's not an original name, but that's what he looks like, what can I say?"

"Well, I agree; if an animal, or even a person, looks like a bear—it is probably the first name that comes to mind," and hopefully he hadn't been able to read mine. He extracted enough information from me without doing that—he asked plenty of questions.

Comparing the two of us, I was the more loquacious that afternoon but it was only because I was so busy answering his queries. He knew far more about me than I did about him after our first meeting. Maybe that was better than being with a person who was focused more on himself, but when he asked where I lived? I gave him the short reply—"with my roommate Agnes in Brick." I always knew immediately at a first meeting whether I wanted to befriend you or date you. If I didn't want a relationship, I gave the short reply. I didn't want to explain why I lived with my mother when I was thirty years old. If a relationship was dead-ended, not destined to progress—why bother giving all the details about my life?

Paulee told me I reminded her of Ellen Barkin's character in *Sea of Love* with Al Pacino. Paulee loves Al Pacino; she thought her boyfriend looked like him when he was young. I didn't think her boyfriend looked like a young or old Al Pacino. He was short and Italian and that's where the similarity ended for me. But I am also an Al Pacino fan so when she asked me if I wanted to watch her DVD, I agreed. We got comfortable with wine, pot, and popcorn to watch *Sea of Love* at my house. Agnes was out with Ally so we had the house to ourselves. We were able to take advantage of her absence; she still discourages my recreational use of grass today, and when I lived with her she made me smoke on the deck.

We were not forced out of the cozy living room that night and we drank and smoked way too much. Luckily before I got too wasted (preventing me from making a sound judgment) the scene where Paulee had drawn her opinion about me came on. I had to agree with her—the character Helen sounded like me when she said, "I believe in animal attraction, I believe in love at first sight, and I don't feel it with you. Nothing personal." Yes, yes, that's how it was with Joe; that's why I gave him the short reply when he asked me where I lived.

When I met Paulee I knew I wanted to befriend her—I gave her the long version of my living arrangement with my mother. I told her when my older sister Penny graduated from college and moved to California my mother freaked out. Penny assured her she wasn't trying to distance herself from the family; the job offer had just been too much of an opportunity to turn down. And my mother chose not to argue the point with her, but when I graduated from college she begged me to move in with her. "Like roommates, I promise. I'll retire from my mother role." She did not want to live alone: we could split the taxes and all expenses fifty-fifty, and since there was no mortgage on the house—it was very affordable. I changed my plans to go out of state for my masters, and applied to Monmouth instead. Where I did my graduate work hadn't been a big concern, and I knew I could always move if our arrangement failed to work for either one of us. That was how I became my mother's roommate. And it had only been a little awkward the first time I brought a male overnight guest into the house, but she was true to her word. She did not act like a mother—more like a nosy neighbor.

I did care what people thought when they found out that I lived with my mother at age thirty. It annoyed me when some had an inaccurate perception of me, based on what living with one's parents at age thirty often connoted. I had not thought of myself as being needy or immature, and it required more details and explanation for others to see an accurate picture of me. When I first told Paulee about my living arrangement she responded, "How convenient for you." It had nothing to do with my convenience—it was my mother's, I had to straighten Paulee out. She was a keeper and worth the effort but I could not say the same for everyone. I lived with my mother for seven years but only the people who were close to me knew it. It would be a while before I gave Joe all the details.

Joe seemed like a nice, easy-going person, and I did have a pleasant time with him. Still, when he asked me if I'd like to have dinner some night—I was direct and honest with him. There were absolutely no fireworks with this guy. I said, "No." He refused to take no for an answer.

"Well, not as a date or anything, just as friends, okay?" I wasn't sure we had enough in common to even make that work or if he was being sincere. To see if he was serious about "just as friends," I countered with my own proposition.

"Can a couple of my friends join us?" To his credit he didn't appear to give it a second's thought.

"No problem, the more the merrier."

When I returned home my mother asked me how *the meeting* went. I told her he wanted to take me to dinner, and I was going to ask Paulee and Anthony to join us.

"So what do you call a double date, a double meeting?"

"Sarcasm does not become you, Agnes."

"I am only asking what one would call that?" Right; she also had to be warned—she was starting to over-step her roommate role.

I had to keep repeating again and again, "I have no romantic interest in Joe. He's a nice guy—*it's nothing personal.*" Simply put there were no fireworks, but that did not deter my mother—she would not stop pleading her point of view.

"Oh, fireworks. That's make-believe, Sarah. An invention created for movies and songs to make them appealing to gullible girls."

How could she say that? Fireworks were chemistry, she was a nurse for heaven's sake. I minored in science, I knew those uncontrollable feelings: a heart racing, the warm sensation between your legs, the tingling feelings one got when they touched you—were all chemical reactions. Human beings had sex hormones which triggered desire. We were no different than cats or bugs, and I told her that.

"Well, I hope we are more than cats and bugs, Sarah. We can use our brains too. Of course chemistry exists, but love and developing trust with someone is far more important. That takes time to develop. It should also be what motivates us when we choose a mate, not fireworks."

I couldn't believe my mother, who dropped out of the University of Minnesota before her junior year to marry my father, did not give chemistry more value in a relationship. He was a math professor at the university, thirteen years her senior, and she always needed to make the point of telling people he hadn't been one of her professors; she met him at a faculty-student event. She wasn't even pregnant, when against her parents' wishes she married him at twenty. She gave up her career plans and her father threatened to disown her. Both didn't deter her, she got married and by the time she was twenty-three had my sister and me. She couldn't convince me it was less about fireworks and more about love and trust that grew over time. It hadn't taken her very long when I did the math. Her specious love and trust argument was not her only crazy idea either; she also had one about latent chemistry which I disagreed with.

"You know Sarah, chemistry can develop over time. Just like in that movie; the Harry and Sally one. You know what I'm talking about—where Sally can't even stand Harry when she first meets him, then she falls in love with him. You are at least saying Joe is a nice guy. Besides, where have fireworks gotten you?"

Another movie reference, now from my mother. Paulee at least had made an accurate observation about me; my mother's reference about chemistry developing over time had been ridiculous. That wasn't real; latent fireworks are only found in fiction. How often does one in real-life end up falling in love with a disastrous blind date or an online match reject—outside of movie plots and romance novels?

She had been right about my dismal dating history though. Fireworks and mutual sexual attraction had not reaped positive results—all my past relationships failed. The problem? My boyfriends were never attracted exclusively to me and we always broke up when they cheated. Or like literal fireworks, were short-lived—they dropped me as soon as it began to wane for them. I was always left hot and bothered (fireworks are not always extinguished simultaneously for each participant).

I agreed with my mother that I had not been successful so far at finding a perfect mate, but was perplexed why it had suddenly become an issue bothering her. Why had *Agnes* suddenly become agitated over my love life? Like a mother. The only reasonable answer was that the biological clock was ticking for her along with me. I knew she wanted to have grandchildren, and my sister and I were getting older. Adding my age to the fact that I had not been dating for a few months prior to meeting Joe was too much for her. It was probably why she grew anxious and fixated on him, but I was able to put her mind at ease. Not about Joe—about Chad.

Chad was a man I was romantically interested in. He was a social studies teacher at my high school who had started in January, when the permanent teacher Connie took her leave-of-absence. We had not dated yet so he was not on my mother's radar. At that point, there had only been surreptitious glances, smiles and innuendos in the faculty room, but I wanted to confront him head-on. Paulee and I planned to throw a party on my deck after school was out—an excuse to invite Chad. I had been so busy at the end of school before summer break I forgot to mention the party and Chad to my mother. It would have eased her mind— lessened her fear about me becoming a childless spinster. My parties also always necessitated a heads-up for my mother. She never stayed at home when I was having friends over because of the pot. She was afraid we'd be arrested and frequently said, "I would rather not be here when the police come, thank you."

When I told her about the party she admitted to having been anxious about my dating hiatus. She was very happy about Chad, not the pot, and planned to make an early exit as usual. It was a relief; I knew she would have talked about marriage and babies with Chad if she had stayed long enough—in spite of her having said she was less anxious. I don't know to what degree Chad really lessened my mother's stress, but I know he had greatly reduced mine. She stopped pestering me about *the bear*, and started acting like *Agnes* again. There had been plenty of fireworks with Chad too—no worries on that front. Chemistry did not have to develop over time.

CHAPTER 5

FRIENDS OR LOVERS

I told Joe we were only available on Wednesday night, that's when Anthony, Paulee's boyfriend was off from work. He agreed to the time and picked the restaurant which Paulee complained about: "Really? Can't we go somewhere else with better food?" It wasn't our place to pick since Joe had offered to treat; he was celebrating a big commission check he just got. I was elated that Paulee agreed to go out with me (I now owed her one), but I needed to be very clear: "If he's paying, he's choosing the restaurant, not us."

"Okay, okay. He must really have the hots for you if he's treating total strangers."

"Well, I sincerely hope he does not because it is not mutual."

"That's a problem."

I was glad to hear Paulee, unlike my mother, thought it was a problem. She did agree with her though that love and trust were important and took time to grow. Paulee had personal experience with time. She and Anthony were together since high school, but I sometimes questioned why they were together at all; they argued passionately about everything—often at a very high volume. It was usually never over an easily proven question of fact. Their arguments were always about value, like which brand of tequila is the best. There's no correct answer for those types of disagreements because it is a matter of opinion. Anthony thought he was an expert about anything concerning booze because he managed a bar. There really was no point having a debate with him on the topic and I questioned why Paulee tried. She always countered with, "what debate?" and insisted they weren't arguing—"we're just talking loudly, Sarah."

Fortunately, Paulee and Anthony were not *talking loudly* about anything that evening, and we all had a pleasant time. But it was very noticeable that Joe was different in a group setting—he was very quiet compared to when we were at the cafe together. The next day Paulee gave me her feedback: she thought he was cute and did not seem to mind that he was not much of a talker, but Anthony said he wasn't lively enough for me. He couldn't believe I was "going with him." I had to protest, but before I could she continued.

"I shouldn't tell you this, but he said what a waste of two gorgeous tits. He called you two *Beauty and the Beast.*"

"Oh, God."

"Sorry, Sarah. You know Anthony thinks you have an unbelievable body. You're the reason he wants me to get implants."

"That's not what I am upset about Paulee. Please assure Anthony I'm not 'going with' this guy, and you saying he's cute is irrelevant. I'm only friends with him." I surprised myself after I realized what I said—I was friends with him now?

I made excuses the next few times Joe called to meet up, but my imagination was maxing out, and it was hard keeping track of my fabrications to fend him off. If this party worked its magic and I started dating Chad, I could honestly tell him I was with someone. It would have been so much easier if he had taken no for an answer but it seemed like that word was not in his lexicon.

Paulee and I worked on the details for the party. We planned to grill and have all the usual summertime sides. She also volunteered to bring pastries from the Italian bistro on New Friendship Road (the one Joe hadn't been familiar with—ten minutes from his townhouse). I picked up the ice cream and watermelon—it's not a summertime party without them. And Anthony supplied the booze and pot. My mother got annoyed when I called him "my dealer," but he was the one I bought my grass from. I don't know what she called him; and speaking of calls, I made mine to Chad.

He was very flirty as usual, but he cranked it up a notch when I invited him to the party: "That depends, will you promise to show me your rose tattoo—the one everyone talks about? I know you have it somewhere that doesn't see sunlight. You won't be wearing your school marm clothes, right?" He would never have talked like that at school; we had to watch ourselves there if we wanted to keep our jobs, but who was *everyone*? No one had known about it except Paulee. She apparently had blabbed—which was not unusual for her and even understandable. The distance from Paulee's mind and mouth was very short, and my tattoo was often in the forefront of both because she was an English teacher. When I first told her about my tat she exclaimed, "Oh, like the Tennessee Williams play?" I had no idea; I was not familiar with the play. But I knew Paulee, and she had been the obvious explanation for Chad knowing about an out-of-sight rose tat. There had been no possible way for him to have seen it because I didn't wear clothes showing cleavage at work; although I objected to my wardrobe being described as marmish. I overlooked his derogatory remark; I chalked it up to a poor attempt at being funny, and made a note to thank Paulee for her big mouth. I was enjoying my conversation with Chad.

Just talking to him there had been a pleasant sensation between my legs; what a difference some hormones can make. So you can imagine my shock when he asked if he could bring a date—abruptly throwing me into a cold shower. I managed to recover enough to tell him it would be fine, and gave him my address—with newfound knowledge. Chad and I had different ideas about our relationship, and he had knowingly led me on; I was left hot and bothered. I needed a date with Georgio.

I no longer looked forward to the party. Chad had been the very reason for throwing it, and now he had thrown me. Paulee eventually convinced me we did not need Chad for an excuse to have a party. "The only good reason for a party is to have fun, Sarah." She was right, and I was determined to enjoy myself. I planned to get really stoned and taste every tequila Anthony brought. I also absolutely refused to wear a top that showed my rose tat (tough luck Chad).

I was a good hostess and suppressed my disappointment; I was very cordial when Chad and his date Amy arrived—then avoided them for most of the evening. I might have been able to keep away from Chad for the entire party too if he hadn't cornered me by the soft drink table.

"Hey, stranger, I'm enjoying your party. Great place you have here by the river. But I'm disappointed, where's the tattoo?"

"Oh, I thought it might be too cool tonight by the water. Need to cover up tonight. Where's Amy?"

"Oh, she's in the restroom, we have plenty of time. How about a private viewing? I'll keep you warm."

I smiled at the sleaze bag, but it had been more of a grimace. He was hitting on me while his date was in my mother's bathroom. He was not showing me any respect, and it was now obvious what the last eight weeks had been about for him. He thought I was easy.

I do not deny being a flirt and I realize some men can form misconceptions about me. It was the reason I never drank or did drugs when I was younger—I wanted to be in control. I was very careful, and in addition to keeping a clear head I never placed myself in a potentially sticky situation with a boy. As a grown woman I have continued the practice of safety in numbers. That's why I wanted to invite Chad to a party with a number of people. Paulee had suggested a drink—one to one. I counted myself fortunate for not having followed her advice.

I had been so wrong about Chad, and he was wrong about me. I didn't mess around with married men or men with girlfriends (even if the girlfriend was indisposed in the john). Men like Chad would have to cool their ardor by taking a dip in the Manasquan and forget about going behind the bushes with me. Chad would never see my tattoo.

I was strong in my resolve to reject Chad that night, but those pesky hormones of mine ignored my new insight about him. My mind did not rule my chemistry and once again with this guy, (the same as after the phone call with him), I was left hot and bothered. I had no complaints though; I was experiencing no pain. I was stoned and tipsy and confident that Georgio would hit the spot to satiate my hot urges—as long as the batteries kept working.

CHAPTER 6

TENACITY

When people asked me why I even started going out with Joe, and I felt particularly sorry for myself I said, "He just wouldn't go away."

A few days after the party he called me: "How was the fiesta?" My first reaction was to be amused—did he think there was a Mexican theme? My second was dismayed—he knew I had thrown a party, so I lied. I told him it wasn't a party—only a few teachers from work for a little informal get-together. I was embarrassed because I hadn't invited him. I was curious too; how had he found out about it? When he told me it was Paulee I wasn't surprised. She ran into him when she went for her walk in the woods. He had been outside his townhouse, which butted right up to a sixty-acre forest reserve. She opened her big mouth when she stopped to say hi.

· · · · ● ● ● ● ♡ ● ● ● ● · · ·

"Why did you do that, Paulee?"

"It just slipped out when he asked me what I had been up to lately."

"I wish you hadn't mentioned it. He knows we had a party and I didn't invite him."

"Why does it matter, you don't like him, right?"

"I never said I didn't like him. I said I don't want to date him, or be his girlfriend, okay? I feel awful, he treated us all to dinner, and he gets no invitation to our party? Aren't you embarrassed too?"

"Don't get me involved with this; remember why we were having this party, Sarah." But she had involved herself by opening her big mouth and I told her so. That only made her dig in deeper.

"Okay; a better recall is to remember where he took us. Flash frozen meat on a grill is not what I call a satisfying dinner; we did not have to reciprocate." She was not moving me; I continued to be visibly annoyed with her.

"Okay, sorry, I'm only kidding. You can take the unhappy face off. I never knew you liked those chain restaurants."

She wasn't kidding about the restaurant Joe had chosen and she was not sorry about speaking her mind. I was upset about not inviting him to our party and kept being reminded of it. Paulee was able to easily dismiss it all because it wasn't her that he kept calling for dates—it was me. It was hard to forgive myself or forget when he was constantly intruding upon my space.

But I held firm. I refused to see him every time he called and asked me out, but he just wouldn't give up. That's why he was probably so successful as a sales-man, and he finally closed the deal with me. He was not only tenacious, he had an ability to frame his sales pitch in a way that made me feel I had gotten the deal I wanted. He also was so sweet I never thought he was being manipulative.

"Look, I know you don't want to be my girlfriend. That's okay, we can be just friends." It sounded like his sentiments were due to more conversations with his neighbor Paulee, but I liked what he said and let him keep talking.

"I'm just at loose ends right now, and I don't have a lot of people to hang out with." He then stopped speaking. When the silence became too uncomfortable, I interjected and I asked him why. He told me after his girlfriend Maureen left he realized all the people he thought were his friends were really hers.

"They disappeared along with her when she left me."

I did not say anything in response and after another awkward pause he finally said, "I get it, you don't want to date me, but I like you and would like you to join me for a movie or a beer once in a while. I swear I'm not going to make a pass at you. I'll be a perfect gentleman."

He was an honest salesman. It wasn't a facade—he was a perfect gentleman. He only wanted friendship, and as time went on I liked him more and more. He became one of my best friends, the same as Paulee. The three of us started doing activities together: walking in the woods, going to street fairs and the movies, or out to restaurants. Paulee continued to complain about Joe's lack of adventure and imagination when it came to cuisine though. She wanted to change it up occasionally; we had dinner some nights at her place instead of going to one of Joe's restaurant picks. She loved to cook so she would experiment on us with new recipes. Joe loved her food, but no matter what the dish or how many courses, her last one was always pot and dessert. Joe refused to smoke but he didn't object to us indulging. Paulee hinted to me she might put some grass in the dessert one evening; "Joe might like it." I talked her out of it and convinced her that it was better if one of us wasn't stoned—the table would have never been cleared otherwise.

Shortly after the Friday dinners began, Paulee and I started to help Joe care for Ollie and Bear when he traveled for work. Paulee cared for the cats more than me because she lived right up the street from him, but I made up for it by attending to his mail and watering his plants. Joe showed his appreciation by always bringing each of us something back from wherever he had been. Maple syrup from Maine, or pecans from Georgia; sweatshirts from the Outer Banks and cowboy hats from Austin. His region was the northeast but he volunteered to go outside of it when no one else wanted to. He was always eager to meet his quota to free up his personal schedule, but I thought he was also lucky to have the opportunity to visit other places. I had expected him to have stories to tell us about the cities and states he traveled to when he returned. It never happened because he spent most of his time in his hotel room when he wasn't at the factory or company. He never took the time to check out the sights; it was all about work for him and he was very successful at what he did. Clients liked him—he engendered their trust, and he landed some big, lucrative contracts.

While he was comfortable and successful with clients, he did not always get along with his co-workers in the home office. Sales is a very competitive business with too much backstabbing and politics. It was a very stressful work environment, and I was amazed at the audacity of some people who complained when Joe landed a big contract. They were often the very ones who had refused to go to Utah or Texas. Joe took the assignment when nobody else wanted it, and there was no problem with him overstepping outside of his region—until he secured the account. Joe shared his office politics only with me, never Paulee. He made me his confidant and I became his advocate, which sparked a nurturing gene inside of me. I became very protective towards him, and I soon grew to love this sweet teddy bear of a man. I wasn't in love with him, nor was I sexually attracted to him—but I loved him.

When I told Paulee I loved Joe, she clapped her hands and smiled. "Why don't you make out with him, or let him kiss you at least? I have a pot blend that will increase libido too, Sarah. I can put it in his food." I vetoed that again and explained to her, "I don't love him in that way, Paulee;" nothing deterred her. "But you say you love him, Sarah. Just try a little kissy face, it might spark something. What do you have to lose?" His friendship. I had not wanted to lose that but I was also curious—*would it ignite a spark?*

The next night Joe and I went out for pizza and a movie. After we pulled up in front of my house, before I opened the car door, I told him he could kiss me if he wanted. My words were still lingering in the air when his lips were on mine and his tongue was deep in my mouth. There had been no need for Paulee's pot to spike his food that night, he took me by surprise. It wasn't unpleasant; his energy and obvious desire for me were a turn on. They fueled my own desire and made me complicit. I had no control. My body invited him to fondle my breasts and suck my nipples—they ached from being so hard and erect. I was lost in the moment until a brief thought found me—I remembered those geeks in math class with their gaping mouths. But the memory only lasted a second because Joe slid his hand down my panties. He started to finger me, making me wet. I heard someone whimpering and moaning—and I realized it was me.

CHAPTER 7

THE COURTSHIP

I could not believe it was happening. I had a leading role in one of those movie plots. A guy with whom I didn't even want to be friends with initially, I now could not keep my hands or mouth off. He thrilled me with his touch, and I ached during the day thinking about him. I was *Sally* and *Helen* in real life, and for the first time I was with someone I could trust. This man would never cheat on me; he loved me—and not just my tits, ass and face. I now understood what my mother meant, and the difference between lust and love.

That's not to suggest lust was not in the mix. Joe thought I was beautiful—he kept telling me that all the time. It was even tiring sometimes to hear: *my tits were better than ones he saw in magazines, my ass and stomach were so firm, and my legs were model's legs.* It was not new; I had heard this from would-be suitors for years. But Joe also added "I love your brains" frequently, which was something I never heard other men say. It was refreshingly original, but I did not need constant praise about my intellect or beauty. I didn't have low self-esteem. It was only when I gained some extra pounds that I sometimes questioned my appeal. I would catch myself checking my reflection in store windows when no one was around, and my stress increased along with pounds if I stood next to skinny Paulee, but it was short lasting. The extra weight never stayed on for long—I knew I was *a looker*. Anthony has called me that since the day we met, but he was Paulee's man. It was nice to have finally found a man of my own who not only agreed with Anthony, but also had no desire to cheat.

"Joe does not have a wandering eye—I have his full attention." I said that to Paulee and Anthony at a restaurant one evening. Anthony reacted as though I threw my glass of water in his face. He looked stunned like I had said something crazy or incomprehensible. And he is not one to stay down for long; he is always ready to get up and fight. He never keeps his thoughts to himself—no matter where he is or who is present. The entire restaurant had been privy to his verbal reaction to my statement that evening. Anthony never speaks quietly.

"Are you kidding me? Why would he have a 'wandering eye'? You are his trophy girlfriend. Not in his wildest wet dreams did he ever think he would be with someone like you. He should be thanking Jesus Christ, and kissing the ground you walk on."

I wanted to hide under the table, but I had to clarify my feelings to Anthony. I did not get a chance; before I could say one word Paulee told Anthony to "shut up." He then started yelling, "Don't tell me to shut up, Paulee." He was no longer thinking about me or Joe.

If I could have said something, before they started screaming at one another, I would have said Joe may be lucky to have me, but I was also lucky to have him—I was very happy.

I'm not saying our relationship was perfect; but when are things perfect? We were no different than any other couple. One irritant was Joe's avoidance to talk about general things, choosing primarily to focus on his problems at work. It was understandable. His work stressed him and I wanted to be supportive. But I would have preferred to discuss anything else once in a while instead of Joe's boss or his back-stabbing co-workers.

It was also no mystery why Joe did not like many people at work—it was old news, but I did make one new observation. There weren't many people he liked away from his job. It might have been an inaccurate presumption on my part but he never shared information otherwise to change my mind. Paulee and I were the only ones I ever heard him praise, and it was no surprise when he started refusing to do activities if Anthony was going to be there.

Joe thought Anthony was a *loud mouth*, and Anthony thought Joe was a *cheapskate*. Both were true. Anthony was loud and often crude—but he was funny, and I enjoyed being with him. Joe on the other hand irritated me when he under-tipped at restaurants. I usually put in extra money to cover for him, along with Paulee and Anthony, until Anthony finally refused. He opted out entirely from our group gatherings—making it a moot point that Joe did not want him to be present. I missed Anthony's passion, and especially the excitement he always brought to the table; the irritant undertipping was left in his wake.

Restaurants eventually became less frequent making tipping moot too. Paulee had finally spoiled Joe with her cooking—her food tasted better than at a restaurant and it was completely free. A perfect mix for Joe, and she planned the meals on evenings when Anthony had to work so they were free of him—how could Joe resist? I missed restaurants with Joe but not the tipping arguments. Paulee and I continued to go to restaurants together—it lessened my need to eat out with a boyfriend.

It was not a problem either when Joe started to prefer staying in to watch DVDs instead of going to movie theaters. Puns intended, it was more about in- than-watch; our sex life was solid and strong. It was one area of our relationship where I had no complaints and a public theater would have been problematic. We would always begin watching a movie only to end up doing it right on the couch or floor, not bothering to pause the DVD. One night I lost track of time at my place and my mother was mortified when she came home—finding us partially clothed in a compromising position on the couch. The next day she complained.

"Really, Sarah? No sexual attraction for this man? I'd hate to see when you are attracted to someone, I'd come home and find you completely naked—hanging from the chandelier. Please have a little consideration and take it to your room next time."

She knew sexual attraction was now a nonissue concerning Joe way before she walked in on us. We both had a good laugh but that's not to imply she had not been embarrassed. I promised in the future to keep better track of the time—like any good room-mate—and time was never usurped by passion again.

Our courtship continued without further note-worthy incidents until approximately one year later—Joseph Janak asked Sarah Larsson to marry him. It marked the first anniversary of Joe changing my flat tire—and I said yes again.

CHAPTER 8

THE WEDDING

As soon as I got engaged my mom began to gradually transform, assuming her proper role as a mother. By the time I tied the knot there were no traces left of *Agnes* to be found. She became so irritating that I started to count the days until I would move out of her house. I could have moved in with Joe before the marriage (it was the ultimate outcome she had to face), but I endured her change instead. I knew she wanted me to stay as long as possible, I stayed for her sake. She liked having a roommate because she was often fearful or lonely at night, but she never complained about my moving out. Her dread of me becoming a childless spinster was greater than that of intruders or sitting alone watching TV. She was thrilled about my marriage, and she thought Joe was a great guy.

Mom was married by a Justice of the Peace; her father had threatened to disown her so it was a no-brainer that he had refused to give her a wedding. She wanted me to have the one she missed—with the church and all the trimmings. Joe told me the venue was my choice, especially if it were a religious ceremony. He was raised Catholic but had not been to a church since he was ten years old; his family did not even belong to one. We weren't frequent parishioners ourselves but we occasionally went to First Lutheran in Wall (my grandfather was a member).

It was an easy decision; we chose Pops' church to have our wedding and he would walk me down the aisle. It was something he especially wanted to do since he regretted not giving away my mother, and I was happy he was doing it. I didn't even know who I would have asked if he hadn't offered. I was only four when my father was killed in a car accident on the Ford Parkway Bridge in Minneapolis; I didn't even remember him. When I was shopping for a car I told my sister in jest that was the real reason Mom tried to talk me out of buying a Focus. Penny became angry with me, as usual. I have annoyed my big sister for my entire life, but she was six when our father was killed. To him he was Daddy, not an unknown—she took my humor as a personal insult.

"How can you make jokes about your own father's death?" She was right, I was trying to be funny; it was about cars though—not our father. Penny has no sense of humor. Paulee, unlike my sister, knows a joke when she hears one but she wasn't her usual self. I needed to get her to lighten up a bit too when I was planning my marriage. Joe and I were fine—everyone around us had pre-wedding jitters.

Paulee was concerned about Pops: "He's in his eighties; will he be strong enough to walk you down the aisle?" She had never met him or even heard my mother say he had more endurance than her; he walked or rode his bike every day. He had been a fisherman and the combination of long, strenuous hours and being out at sea by himself prepared him well for his lifestyle. My grandmother Agna died of breast cancer when I was in my senior year of high school and Pops had been living by himself since then, but doing well.

My mother still worried, especially about his independent nature; he was too independent for her liking. Not only did he cut his lawn without help every season, she had caught him several times on the roof fixing shingles or perched on a ladder sawing tree limbs. I agreed with her about the roof and the pruning but he insisted he could do everything by himself. "I am fit as a fiddle."

"It's not your fiddle I'm worried about," was always her reply and his physical welfare was not her only concern. His lady friends over the years after my grandmother's death were also always a worry for my mother. One of her greatest fears when we were planning my wedding was that Pops would bring his current *friend* to the wedding reception—who was the same age as her. She kept asking me how she could keep her from attending without being too obvious. I preferred to stay neutral on the topic but reminded her that he was entitled to bring a guest of his own choosing. She told me I was "no help at all," and Pops' guest continued to be a stressor for her.

At least I eased my Maid of Honor's mind after I described Pops to her. She no longer feared he would not be able to make it down the aisle, and when she met him he charmed her. She was not surprised he had lady friends. "I can see why you're a flirt too, Sarah. It must be genetic."

···•••❤••••··

Ally made my wedding dress and gave it to me as a present. It was so generous, and I will always be indebted to her. She also supported me in the style I had imagined, doing her best to create exactly what I wanted. I was thrilled when I saw the dress at the first fitting—but not my mother. Admittedly, the dress showed a good amount of cleavage; I had wanted my rose tattoo to stand out—to complement my bouquet of little red roses. When my mom saw it she audibly gasped.

"Sarah, this is supposed to be your wedding dress—not lingerie for your honeymoon. And your wedding is in December, aren't you afraid of catching a chest cold?" I told her I was thirty-one years old and she was no longer allowed to dictate terms to Ally about my neckline. Ally tried to calm her but managed to freak me out doing it.

"Oh, relax, Nessie, it will be very elegant when I am done. I haven't added the white fur to the neckline yet. And let her enjoy her body now; after a few years and a couple of kids it'll be shot to hell. The only good thing about poor Marilyn dying so young is she will always be young and beautiful in our memories."

I overlooked references to Marilyn Monroe and aging, and I was glad for Ally's support. It was her statement concerning my body after pregnancy that upset me. Would it be shot to hell? Joe and I wanted to start a family immediately, and I had already stopped using my diaphragm to give us a kickstart. I was worried about my body, not my dress, when my mother tried to bring the conversation back to neckline measurements.

"What about Joe? Do you think he wants all the guys at the wedding staring at your breasts?" I laughed to myself then; Joe would not mind, he probably would enjoy it. Anthony was correct when he said I was Joe's trophy. Guys could look at his prize as much as they wanted, but my boobs belonged to him. I chose not to say that; I had not wanted to upset her even more. I was also still too busy being upset about my body being *shot to hell* to continue arguing with her. After I recovered from Ally's doomsday prophecy I told my mother to relax. I hope she took advantage of the opportunity. There would be more things for her to stress about on the wedding day. She would also probably be the first to agree, the low neckline of a wedding dress would be reduced to a mild irritation in comparison.

If I think about who was to blame for ruining my wedding the first person who comes to mind is my sister Penny. It's an emotional response, not accurate but it feels natural since we never got along. My mother says that's not true and insists we played together *all the time* when we were kids. I'm not sure how she measures time; I only remember playing with her when she hit me over the head with a plastic toy rake when I was five; I retaliated by hitting her with the plastic hoe. Nothing else stands out, and after we started school there were few opportunities to spend leisure time together. We hardly saw each other, due primarily to our two-year age difference; and from grade school on we had different friends. It was the natural order.

As teens, age disparities were not the only reason she avoided me. I had friends in high school the same age as her. I even went to her senior prom as a freshman with a guy named Carl. Penny disliked Carl and all my other friends because she thought they were wild; I was *tainted by association*. She shunned me and them. Being her blood relative was not a mitigating factor. She never extended any familial love in my direction. In high school we would pass each other in the hall and she would walk right by me, not even making eye contact. Dee would ask, "Isn't that your sister?" I always answered, "yeah, that was my sister."

Penny also went out of her way to be mean and petty. She would tell tales to my mother how so and so was suspended for drugs, or someone else smashed their parents' car leaving a party. "They were drinking, Mother," and "there were no adults present," she would add with a smug smile. She ratted out my friends to make trouble for me. She had to do it this way—I only vicariously experienced the antics of my friends. It was a round-about method but her machinations worked. My mom would respond by forbidding me from attending an offender's future party or even ground me—now *punished by association.*

As adults we no longer attacked each other with plastic garden tools and Penny didn't know any of my friends to gossip about them with my mother. Tantamount to that, we even talked to each other on the phone every couple of months, but we still weren't very close. At the time of my marriage I knew Penny was a marketing director in LA living with a room-mate named Vicky, but not much else about her life. So what did we talk about on these calls? Superficial news about family, and sharing the latest books we read or movies seen. Our conversations satisfied a need (Joe to this day has no interest in that kind of chit chat), but they never enabled me to know her any better.

And my call to Penny almost two decades ago about my wedding was similar to calling a friend that I've known only a short time. There was no intimate feel about it. This was not exclusive to Penny though, and I am not referring to guests my mother invited whom I had barely known. I was literally marrying a casual friend, with privileges. I knew very little about Joe before our marriage, aside from him being a great lay. My knowledge about him would eventually increase over years, but my sister remains a mystery (and I've known her my entire life). The irony is that she always knows my business; it hasn't changed since high school. That's why I wasn't surprised that day when I told her I was getting married and she already knew. The surprise was when she said, "I'm sorry, there is no way I can be your Maid of Honor." Who asked her? Mom; apparently she had thought telling her about the wedding hadn't been good enough.

It was a delicate situation and my mother's fault for this awkward moment, not Penny's. I did not say a word—why embarrass her? We were no longer kids trying to beat each other up, and it was my mother who deserved to be hit over the head with a plastic garden tool. I confronted her and we had a nasty argument—she was still not speaking to me the day before my wedding. If it hadn't been for Ally, who took on the role of a mediator, my mother might not have spoken to me on the very day of my marriage.

Of course if Penny had not been born it would have been a nonissue. It is the zero-product property: not being born is (a) which equals zero; mother would not have said anything (b) which equals zero; the product of factors. It was a wasted theorem of course, it wasn't math and no one asks to be born. I had to set my mother straight: "Penny would be the last person on earth I would ever ask to be my Maid of Honor, Mom."

I would have elaborated more about why, but she did not give me a chance. It would have been a waste of my time anyway. She has a blind spot about us, preventing her from seeing the reality of our relationship. When I tell her we aren't close she always responds, "How can you say that, Sarah? You have always admired your big sister." There is a difference between intimacy and admiration. Our mother can't see the distinction, and when I was a teenager I did admire Penny, but only in part. I disliked her personality, her wicked machinations and thought she and her friends were boring. But she had some characteristics I wanted to emulate. The walk from the door to my seat in my math and science classes I copied directly from her. She strutted down the halls in high school like it was a high couture fashion show. She did not have to wear tight jeans or low tops to get attention either—she was not even wearing the current fad. Penny ignored fads because she was one of the cool kids who set them. Her clothes expressed a sophistication well beyond her years, and at five nine with legs that did not stop—she looked like a runway model.

She would later become a model for real after graduating from high school. She worked at a top agency in NYC. She did runway modeling when she first started but later switched primarily to print work. She was able to pay her way through NYU Stern, getting her undergraduate degree in Marketing and her MBA; all admirable accomplishments. She looked great in a bikini too. When Joe said I had the best tits he ever saw, had he seen my sister in her tiny bikini in *Sports Illustrated*? I was looking forward to searching his face for signs of recognition when he met her. I saved all the magazines Penny had ever been featured in and kept them in a storage container wrapped in tissue paper. I would show all of them to him. I was proud of my big sister and was not adverse to bragging about her. But admiration did not equate with envy any more than it did with intimacy.

I was never in competition with Penny; she was the one who resented me because I had breasts when I started high school and she was flat chested. She became very angry if people pointed out that differ-ence between us (she didn't bloom until her senior year). Annoyance with my mother had churned up negative vibes around my sister and there was no reason for it. I had always been able to garner as much attention as Penny, and probably even more with the puerile set in high school. Boobs win over style when it comes to adolescent boys. But we were equal opportunity attention grabbers—we had our unique followers and she had disdained mine. I was never afraid of her stealing them from me. She waited until my wedding, when all eyes were sup-posed to be on me. That's the day my sister Penny chose to grab all of the attention, and it had nothing to do with beauty, boobs or hurt feelings about her not being my Maid of Honor. We remained in agree-ment about that. Our personal reasons for why were unknown and ignored by both of us, but I knew my reason had been a touch toxic—stripped of sisterly-love. My toxicity, along with my mother's faux pas for having asked Penny to assume the role of lead maid, unleashed a negative force which spilled over to my wedding day.

My sister and Vicky were late getting to the church because they hit traffic driving from the airport. The ceremony had started when they arrived at the church so they sat in one of the back pews—my mother was seated in the front. I saw Penny when we were making our way up the aisle to take our places in the receiving line. She waved her hand wildly, throwing kisses at me from her seat when we passed her pew. Since she was in the back it took her and Vicky a long time to get in the line which was slowly moving towards us and the exit.

One drawback with the church where we had our marriage was that people were unable to gather in the front because it was too small. After people shook our hands and congratulated us they left for the reception—including my mother (it was an afternoon affair from 1-5:30 pm). When my mother reached us she told me she was off to the banquet hall to make sure everything was in order, and to see if Penny had gone directly there. Before I could tell her Penny had arrived and was in the church, Aunt Elsbeth grabbed my face with her white-gloved-hands (she continued to follow fashion dictates for the well-dressed woman in the 1950's). She kissed me smack on the lips, and by the time I got my face and lips back my mother was gone. I had no idea it would cause a drama, but I did not consider how weddings heighten emotions. It is the only explanation I have for Penny, who was notice-ably upset when I told her Mom had left the church.

"Without waiting for me?"

"She didn't see you, and I had no chance to tell her you arrived because Aunt Beth got in the way."

My sister was not about to drop it and was holding up the line. Vicky prevented her from saying more and creating a bigger traffic jam when she said, "Congratulations to you both," and grabbed Penny by the elbow. She said something to Penny I couldn't hear, but whatever she said worked to keep her moving, and when they reached the door Vicky turned to us—"We'll see you at the reception."

At the time I thought Vicky's behavior seemed odd for a roommate (excluding my mother), but it soon made sense. I was there when Penny made introductions: "Mother, this is Vicky," and she responded, "Oh, your roommate?" Vicky's behavior in the church was clear immediately, not strange in the least when Penny replied, "Well yes, we live together, but she's more than a roommate—she's my partner." I now understood Vicky but I was dumbfounded by my mother. Was she trying to be obtuse or in the nascent stage of denial? Smiling, she chirped in reply, "Oh, she works with you too, how nice."

I wondered how long this cat and mouse game was going to continue when Penny, also smiling, put it to a stop. She took Vicky's hand and kissed it. She then held both of their hands up in the air, looked directly at Mom and said in an adamant tone, "No Mother, Vicky is my life partner."

My mother's face froze in shock. She stared at them with her mouth slightly open, not saying a word

(Penny wasn't as boring as I had thought). Their entire exchange did not last more than a few minutes but during that short time my mother expressed: surprise, shock, denial, grief, embarrassment and anger. Once she recovered from the shock, in an anguished voice—filled with grief and denial—she implied how it was impossible for Penny to be a lesbian. "You are a beautiful woman, how can this be true?"

My mother's remark not only expressed grief and denial, it had been indisputably stupid—all lesbians are women and many are beautiful.

When I was an immature, short-sighted teen I shared my mother's view, in a fashion. Penny was so beautiful I could not understand why she never had a boyfriend in high school. She had guy friends, and went out in mixed groups of boys and girls, but she never dated anyone as far as I knew. She went to her proms with boy buddies, not dates. In junior year she went with Charlie, her friend who was in student council with her. In senior year she went to her prom with Peter who edited the school newsletter. He was gaunt with hollowed-eyes and had a big Adam's apple; I asked her why she was going with him, "he's so homely, Penny." I knew they were only friends but it still seemed weird. It was impossible that he was the only guy she could find to take her to the prom. Beautiful, sexy Penny? She retaliated by saying, "You're so immature and superficial, Sarah—looks aren't everything, you know." I was wrong, but not about Peter's looks; in retrospect I had asked the wrong question. I should have asked—do you have a special girlfriend who can take you to the prom?

Penny was not daring enough in high school. It was good to see she had evolved—she was no longer afraid to be herself. My preference would have been that she had chosen a different day to come out but I was fine with it. I was ready to get on with celebrating my marriage—Mom did not share my sentiments.

"I hope you are not planning on telling people this, especially at your sister's wedding. What will your Aunt Elsbeth and Aunt Ida say? I'll be mortified." Anger and embarrassment had kicked in. Surprise, shock, denial and grief had not provoked Penny, but my mother's shame and displeasure irritated her into action. "If you prefer we leave, Mother, we will."

As soon as Penny said it Mom started crying and ran to the ladies' room. I would go to comfort her, but first I pleaded with Penny to stay. I did not mention where she and Vicky were seated at the reception. She probably knew already—she did not need a warning; and it clearly would not have helped me to persuade her not to leave. She was not listening to anything I said anyway and started heading to the outside door. It was Vicky who stopped her with whatever she said and led her by the elbow to the ballroom, throwing me a smile over her shoulder.

Vicky had been successful with Penny again but I couldn't persuade my sobbing mother to come out of the ladies' room. I finally gave up and left her, and when I walked into the hallway I was confronted with a distraught Paulee screaming at Anthony. I was about to ask her what was wrong on her end but before I could say a word she screamed at me, "Finally, we've been looking everywhere for you. The band guy wants you and all of the wedding party to make the entrance. Where have you been?"

In a controlled soft voice, I told her about Penny and that my mother refused to come out of the ladies' room. I had hoped my lower volume would have a quieting effect but Anthony did not follow my lead. He yelled in response, making everyone in the hallway (including Joe's sister and her husband) turn towards us.

"Your beautiful sister is a muff diver? I can't believe it. What's wrong with the Larssen girls? Another waste of a pussy."

Paulee told him to "cool it," but the damage had already been done. Everyone heard him and Joe's sister looked at me strangely. Perhaps the meaning of *muff diver* was unclear to her, or she knew what it meant and did not approve of Anthony's choice of words. I was humiliated, but not about his off-color words offending her; I was afraid she might misconstrue the benign ones. I did not want her to think I agreed with Anthony about wasting myself by marrying her brother. I was angry at Anthony for his remarks, and there was no defense for him even though Paulee tried, "He thinks you're too good for Joe, Sarah." It was also not the first time she had said that. She had also told me many times during my engagement—way before his crude outburst, how it pained him to see me marrying Joe. And I believed her when she said, "he's not joking." It was the only mitigating factor—at least Anthony was being honest. It forced me to be thankful he had held his peace during the ceremony in church. He should have also held it at the reception—it was a done deal.

My mother finally came out of the ladies' room to sit stony faced at the table with Penny and Vicky. Paulee told me later she did not even crack a smile when I danced my first dance with Joe to *Breathe.* Paulee wasn't sure if she even looked at us and she was the one who picked the song, Mom was a big Faith Hill fan. I had agreed with her choice because I could not make a decision and Joe complained about it for weeks. He thought the song was too long, but no song would be short enough—he did not want to dance. He had resisted until the day we chose our music tracks with the DJ, who told us he could fade it out. Joe accepted the compromise which was a good thing because I had not wanted to shun tradition. It had taken too many weeks of practicing a semblance of dance steps and placating Joe to forgo our first dance. Hours of effort and my mother did not even watch us—along with many other people. Joe and I did not garner most of the attention in the room. More eyes had been on my sister, and the focus went beyond our first dance.

There were ripples of whispers circulating around Penny for the entire reception—initiated from the just curious and from those with more toxic tendencies. A few senior people looked repulsed or made noisy exits from the room when Penny and Vicky danced their first dance. It wasn't even a slow number and there were many women dancing together during the song, but the word had gotten out—*as well as my sister.*

I am not sure if Pops knew the buzz about Penny. He was youthful in many respects but not when it came to his hearing, and he resisted wearing his hearing aids because he complained about them ringing. He knew something was up with his daughter though, he saw her unhappy face. Maybe he was trying to cheer her up with his announcement after he made the wedding toast. He said it would add cheer to this "happy day." It had not been a very "happy day" yet from my perspective so I don't know why I was surprised at the reaction that Pops' announcement got. He was marrying his girlfriend Marie. That had been enough to hear for my mother. She didn't look very pleased, so Pops tried a little humor. He stressed how his marriage would be beneficial for her. "A younger woman is going to help care for me, Nessie. You'll have more free time to rest." That's the day we found out Marie was a year younger than Mom. Pops' joke bombed. His attempt at humor and his wedding announcement failed to produce any positive effects. My mother started crying and retreated to the ladies' room again; Pops' sisters redirected their negativity from Penny to him, and I finally gave up all hopes for this celebration. I could not wait for the wedding reception to end.

Did I really blame my sister for ruining my wedding day? No; she had not made a premeditated decision to come out that day. It happened because she simply refused to hide who she was anymore, and she took a risk—kudos to her. Rather than blaming her I admired her more. She was now one of those daring people that I was attracted to, and I had hoped it would enable us to be closer.

I could not blame Pops for ruining my wedding either—like Penny, his risk taking was admirable. He ignored the protests from his sisters Elsbeth and Ida, and my mother. He planned to marry Marie whether they liked it or not. I also believe he had sincerely thought that his announcement was a positive one. It was, from his personal perspective obviously, but I am not sure why he had thought it would raise his daughter's spirits—the other contender to consider.

Should my mother be blamed for her histrionics? She seems the obvious best pick for the wedding-spoiler title but there were mitigating factors to consider. Suppressing her maternal instincts for all those years—forced to be *Agnes*, had been more difficult for her than we both realized. There had been warning signs during my engagement, but who could imagine how combustible my wedding day would be for her. She could not help herself—she imploded.

There was no one to blame for my dismal wedding reception but it did not change the reality of that day. It was not one of the happiest of my life. By the time the good-byes were over and we went to Joe's townhouse, the home we would now share together, I was emotionally drained. But I continued to have positive anticipation for an evening of lovemaking. I believed that the day could be salvaged in part.

As soon as Joe carried me over the threshold, I jumped out of his arms into a hot shower and let the hot spray pound all the tension out of my neck and shoulders. I sprayed my body all over with yummy scents, and put on a sexy black teddy trimmed in fur, like the trim on my wedding dress. I had bought it especially for my wedding night, and hopefully my mother would not have gasped at the plunging neckline if she had seen it (after all this was lingerie). But it was Joe's approval I was seeking, not my mother's, when I snuggled up against him on the couch.

Coquettishly, I whispered in his ear, gently biting his lobe, "Let's go upstairs and make love." Joe was not only emotionally drained, he told me he was really tired physically. Carrying me over the threshold was the most he would be able to do that evening. He also reminded me that we had to leave early in the morning for our honeymoon trip; I understood totally—I could handle this literally and figuratively. I began to zip his fly down, purring, "Just relax, I'll do all the work," but before I could bring my lips to his treasure he stopped me. He pulled me up and kissed my hands:

"Sarah, I really don't want you to do that." What man doesn't want a blow job? Before I could question him further he continued:

"I really don't enjoy doing it, so it just doesn't seem fair if you do it to me, right? I can live without it." I collapsed on my bum and he was peering down at me when he said, "Hey, come up here, baby, and give me a hug."

Was this a joke?

CHAPTER 9

MY HONEYMOON

I was tired and irritable the next morning. Joe's agenda did not help to improve my mood. He wanted to leave at 4:30 am in the morning to beat the traffic and we had to pack snacks; he did not want to make many stops. We were going to Vermont. I had wanted to go somewhere warm, but a vice president of a company to whom Joe sold a cooling system gave us his cabin for a week. "It's too perfect Sarah, a romantic remote cabin in the woods—and it's free." Visions of pumping water, chopping wood and using an outhouse kept running through my mind. I voiced my concerns and Joe assured me it would not be like that, and as soon as Mr. Vice President sent pictures I would see for myself. I don't know if Joe ever received pictures, but I never saw any so I was not looking forward to going to Vermont, to a remote cabin in the woods—in December.

It was a long trip by car, but Joe had told me it was not that far—did I forget he was a traveling salesman? The length of a drive can be relative and I had been so busy with handling wedding preparations I never checked it out for myself. Joe was in charge of the honeymoon plans so I could concentrate on the wedding.

It sounded like a good idea until it wasn't, especially after four and a half hours of driving. I was seven again in the back seat of my mother's car on family vacations. Those drives were not even as long as this one, but just as boring. Mom always told Penny and me before we hit the road we were going to have fun. We kept tormenting her for the entire drive singing over, and over again: *Are We Having Fun Yet? Yeah, yeah, yeah.* My poor Mother. I owed her a favor for being a pain in the neck and I had one of my own now along with tight shoulders and a sore bum; she had made more stops than Joe. In total it took eight hours of driving to reach our destination.

When we finally arrived it was pure joy to get out of the car. I was also happy to discover it was ridiculous to call this dwelling a cabin; several cabins could have easily fit inside of it. It would have been more apt to call it a complex or an estate. It was even a bit intimidating with its heavy castle-like front door and a huge brass lion knocker. No one was home and we had the keys but I had to try it just for fun.

The knocker had a deep resonance which matched the room we found ourselves in when we walked through the door—we were in an airplane-hangar size space. A stylishly decorated one, with an enormous marble wood burning fireplace. I hoped they had a good supply of stored wood, but if someone was chopping it was not going to be me. I found out later that my worry was for nothing, there was also central heating.

The walls were mounted with moose and deer heads and there was a bear skin rug in front of the fireplace. The moose and deer had once been alive but I wondered about the rug. Were there bears around here? If the rug was fake it was real high-end. Joe told me the owner used this place when he had guests; it was his hunting cabin. I hoped it was not a real bear skin; bears and outhouses? We could be attacked by one when we went outside to use a privy. Outhouses turned out to be another foolish worry though—there was an abundance of indoor plumbing. I counted five bathrooms on the first level alone. There were also eight bedrooms, and we chose the biggest one with a giant four poster bed. It had a fireplace and its own bathroom—the count was now six.

I had no complaints about where we were staying, but I was famished. I had skipped breakfast and had eaten only an apple, some peanuts, and a few stale crackers the entire trip. I needed a real meal and there was no food in the refrigerator—I did not care one iota about that. This was our honeymoon and if I could not call for room-service I wanted to sit down in a nice restaurant. That was problematic.

Joe was right about this place being remote—we could not find a single restaurant. The only business near us was a little general store that sold hunting supplies, beef jerky, and marshmallow fluff. The proprietor said we needed to drive about an hour southwest to get to a town where we would find restaurants. More driving.

It seemed longer than an hour ride traveling on empty country roads for miles. We did not see a single house or another car along the way. Driving into town was like emerging from the wilderness, and this was no busy metropolis. There was only one restaurant; it was more diner than fine dining but I wasn't fussy, and they were still serving lunch specials. I was so hungry the meatloaf tasted like gourmet cuisine.

The town had several small businesses in addition to its one restaurant, and there was a small grocery store. After our meal Joe suggested that we buy food for the week. He was not driving here every day to eat. I told him I sincerely hoped he was not expecting me to cook on our honeymoon and he smiled at me. My honeymoon was turning out to be as dismal as my wedding day and Joe seemed to be enjoying himself.

"Absolutely not, baby. I will cook for you every day." His words were a pleasant surprise. It was not what I expected him to say, but I don't know what I expected: *you woman, me man, you cook*. If he had said that I would have moved to another bedroom. There were plenty to choose from in the cabin.

We bought food for the week and Joe made dinner for us later that evening. The grilled trout and salad were good, and for the first time since our wedding night I was looking more kindly towards him. Cooking for your mate is not a gendered task-strategy apparently—it not only works for men; it's an effective aphrodisiac for women too. It warmed me up. I imagined a romantic evening making love in front of the wood-burning fireplace in our huge four-poster bed, but when we went to our bedroom the fireplace was gas. It was still romantic even if it looked like a prop (I grew up with a real fireplace—I was biased), and it created a soft warm glow in the room. I could almost hear the crackling of wood even if it was only in my head (the four-poster bed was real).

The scene was set and I was in the mood but it took Joe a long time to get settled. When he finally did I climbed on top of him. To be more accurate—almost jumped, I was eager. I thought that's why he frowned until he said, "You know Sarah, it really doesn't work for me when you are on top."

"Since when?"

"Since always."

"You never voiced any opposition to it before." I was annoyed and his behavior the night before was too raw to ignore this—I had to air it all out. "And what about oral sex? You never seemed to dislike that before we were married. What is happening? We were sexually compatible, now suddenly we're not?"

He did not respond, and had this dumb look on his face. Like a big, stupid bear. I waited for him to say something but he remained as silent as the bear rug in front of the marble fireplace, and I finally lost it. I screamed at him in frustration.

"I know marriage is for better or for worse, but I would have preferred if you had at least given me a warning about the worse before we got married."

Now his face was puzzled as though he did not have a clue as to why I was so upset. Finally, in a soft measured voice, like he was explaining the facts of life to a child he spoke:

"People do things when they aren't married that I don't think they should do once they have tied the knot, okay?" I had no idea what he was talking about. I was about to ask him to explain when he continued.

"Before people get married there's no guarantee they're going to stay together. But when it's for the long haul, you need to be honest about what works or not. I don't understand why you're upset Sarah, don't you come every time we make love?"

Why had he not been more honest before we *tied the knot* was a better question, but it was true I always had an orgasm up to this point in our relationship (but there had not been any restrictions). I would go mad with these new rules of his or if our sex life wasn't imaginative. But I could compromise, that's why I asked him, "What if we do it doggy style? You can still be on top, Joe."

His face had changed so many times in the last five minutes I was starting to become confused myself. And it suddenly grew very troubled after I asked my question—like he realized for the first time he had married a sexual deviant. Using that damn voice again, like he was trying to impersonate a wise old prophet, he calmly said, 'We are not dogs, Sarah."

So much for my attempt to compromise—Joe's mind was closed. He also made it clear that he did not want to discuss oral sex again and the missionary position was the only one he was comfortable with as a married man. My mother did not have to worry about us falling off chandeliers in our marriage. Joe's ideas about sex worked for him, but not for me. When he started to make love—fondling my breasts and sucking my nipples—I did not get excited. I had to smoke a joint to relax.

"I wish you wouldn't smoke, Sarah."

"I'm sorry, Joe, I need to relax." He offered me a massage instead; and he knew how to give a good one, but when he started fingering me it was uncomfortable and hurt—his fingers seemed rough and scratchy. I told him I needed to pee. When I went to the bathroom he didn't see me grab my little purse (the one packed with my joints). I had only taken a few tokes when Joe called from the other room asking me what was taking so long. I answered that I'd be out in a minute or two. It took longer though—it usually does. I got on my hands and knees on the soft fluffy rug in the bathroom (because I knew Joe would not approve) and got myself going until I was wet and panting like a dog. When I was ready, I went back to bed with Joe. When he entered me it didn't hurt. I concentrated very hard on the rhythm and the sensations pulsating through my body to push away the intruding thoughts—*I had made a big mistake*. I should have never married Joe. I knew this to be true even though with each thrust— my body kept telling my mind differently. It was a heated debate I was unable to control.

CHAPTER 10

PRENUPTIALS

Eight weeks after marrying Joe was a marker: I realized I truly loved him—like a best friend. It was also when my mother finally convinced Pops, who was still hell-bent on marrying, to get Marie to agree to a prenuptial.

My mother could not believe a woman in her fifties would be honestly interested in a man in his eighties—for anything but his money. While Pops lived in an area where there were many wealthy people, he wasn't one of them. He only had modest savings and his social security benefits, and a mortgage-free house (a small cape he had built himself). Mom told me I was really naive: "his small house is worth more than you think due to its location."

The value of the house was secondary; she was more upset that her childhood home would most likely be razed if ever sold (that's what was happening to many of the older homes in Pops' neighborhood). She was not stressed about any modest assets Marie might receive if the marriage ended, but disturbed by visions of a divorced Marie awarded the house and seeing it torn down. Mother believed it should stay in the protective hands of the family when the marriage terminated by death or divorce. She was determined to convince her father to get Marie to sign a prenuptial.

"You can provide for her in your will, Dad, but if she loves you like she says—she should willingly sign a prenuptial." I was at Pops' house with her when she presented her argument—rolling her eyes at me every time she spoke of Marie loving him. Why had she done it so openly? Pops was hard of hearing but his eyes were okay. Whether he saw it or not was not clear, but my mother finally persuaded him to approach Marie about a prenuptial.

It's hard to be objective, and maybe even a little uncomfortable to look at your parents and elder family members in a sexual context, but I was trying to see Pops the way Marie might. If it was true she loved him and had no mercenary motivation, what did she see?

I came to the realization—Pops was a fox (and not just for his age). He was more pleasing to the eye than Joe, who was fifty years younger. My opinion about Joe was influenced somewhat by my marital discontent at the time of the comparison, but it was still true—Pops was quite handsome. He was fit, pretty toned, and had all his hair. He also had a long-lasting tan which continued to be visible all winter from being outside most of the summer—biking, walking or sitting on his back porch. Some people think Norwegians do not tan easily but they are wrong (at least in our family), and Pops was a sun-worshiper with not many wrinkles to show for it. Maybe I was wrong in high school when I warned Dee about sunbathing. If Pops was a typical result of being out in the sun for years it was not as harmful as touted. He looked great; but Dee had also been wrong—getting older does not necessarily mean one will not look good—Pops shattered that myth.

I believed Marie could be in love and sexually attracted to Pops. When I said that to my mother she wrinkled her nose up like I had offered her spoiled food. I told her I understood that it might be hard to accept someone thought Pops was sexy, but why was she acting like it was disgusting? I annoyed her, and she retaliated by calling me an "unrealistic romantic." If memory serves she was the one who had been so keen on my dating Joe. Who was really the *unrealistic romantic* in the family? We continued to disagree politely about Marie. And my mother never stopped questioning Marie's motivation for marrying Pops. But it was not a problem for her, as long as there was a legal safeguard—she could live with her suspicions.

When Pops and Marie agreed to the prenuptial my mother offered our time to do some research for them. She wanted us to knock out some details before they went to the family lawyer. I don't think she fully trusted them to go ahead with the whole idea; she was determined to keep the process moving, and I did not mind helping—it was a learning experience. Prior to doing the research I thought prenuptials were only for protecting your assets. I was surprised when I discovered a prenuptial can address other concerns—like power of attorney if a spouse becomes incapable of caring for themselves. More importantly, that implied divorce did not even have to be a factor. It was an intriguing concept if correct. If divorce did not have to be a factor, and assets were not the only area where a prenup could be applied, was it possible to have one addressing behavior? Could I have asked Joe for a prenup about vacations, restaurants, movies, and oral sex?

I knew Joe was tight with his money before our marriage, but I never knew the distance he would go to save it until we tied the knot—*the depth of a large dumpster*. One night I went with him to Lowe's after closing. He wanted to check out their dumpster. He was looking for *free* wood to build a rack for his antique golf clubs. I was to serve as a lookout—to alert him if I saw police or security. I was not surprised at his desire to save money. I was surprised he was doing something which seemed quasi-illegal, and he was the son of a retired policeman.

Joe always worried about money, which is understandable since he is paid solely by commission. He makes far more money that way than on a salary basis but there is no guarantee of any income at all to depend on. It's one of the few risks he takes in life. That was why I was surprised he would dumpster-dive, chancing bodily harm or arrest.

I also knew Joe was not big on vacations prior to our marriage but it wasn't until the eight-week marker that I learned how much. That's when he told me that our honeymoon would probably be the last time we took a trip together. "When I get time off I want to stay home. I'm sick of traveling for work." I did not bother to ask, *how about taking a trip for your wife?* I figured it would not achieve anything since I could not even persuade him to travel to a local restaurant or movie theater.

Joe's argument against restaurants was based on one fact that he simply could not get past—it's cheaper to eat at home compared to the cost for a meal out.

"Sarah, it's ridiculous what a breakfast costs if you compare it to how cheap a dozen eggs are."

His argument against movie theaters was broader than financial concerns, encompassing comfort and cleanliness. But money was always his first objection, based on ticket prices and the "outrageous" concession stand.

"Sarah, do you realize my mother used to pay fifty cents to go to a matinee at a local theater?"

"Wasn't that in 1960, Joe?" He agreed it was a long time ago but continued to moan about the prices being too inflated, the dirty theaters, and the too small seats. He preferred to stay home to watch a movie.

"It's so much nicer to watch a DVD at home. You can relax and drink a beer. You can even watch the movie in your underwear if you want."

Evenings removing our underwear in front of the TV were over; we did not have to worry about pausing a DVD. Joe would have probably liked to do that but I was not interested. I kept my fingers crossed that the movie would hold his interest, but sometimes it failed to do so. He would start kissing and fondling me. I'd watch him kissing me and sucking my nipples with his eyes closed, and I had the sensation of gazing down from the ceiling at him—as though he were doing it to someone else. I felt nothing. I was Joe's big rubber dolly sex toy, and as dry as one when he touched me. I started to wonder if there was something wrong with me, but when I masturbated there was no problem. There was a simple explanation—my hormones no longer flowed with Joe.

My hormone issue did not change the frequency of sex. Even subtracting couplings in front of the TV, we continued to match the rate set during our courtship. I had to continue my rituals to achieve this though. I always needed to smoke a joint and masturbate before going to the marital bed. My sexual problems were positive for Anthony. He made a lot more money selling grass when I dramatically increased my use. It cost a bundle too, and Joe complained. I proposed two classic mood-enhancers to replace the pot—candles and music. Joe vetoed both, but nothing is black and white.

Joe never wanted a candle burned anywhere in the house if we were not paying full attention to it—that included sexual distraction. He was afraid one of the cats might knock it over. We could have closed the door to keep them out of the bedroom, but Ollie would often make noise batting at the door if it was closed and Joe did not like to stress him. I wanted to ask, *how about my stress*, but dismissed the candle idea in favor of spraying herbal scents in the room. They failed to turn me on sexually but the room smelled nicer.

What was more frustrating was the lack of music. I fought for that concession until Joe explained why he could not have music playing during sex. "I can't focus with music on, I won't be able to hold back. I'm waiting for you, Sarah." I did not fully understand what he meant. He did not have problems with premature ejaculation, and we always came almost simultaneously—he did not have to wait for me. But I was willing to forgo the music if he needed that in order to be satisfied. I had to be fair; he should be able to get something out of it. I always ended up with an orgasm, he should be afforded the same opportunity.

At the same time I felt abused—I had to get stoned and masturbate to have sex with Joe; yet I also felt so magnanimous taking him into consideration. But altruism had not been enough to remove my discontent, or knowing that many women would envy me over the orgasms. That was a sore point with Paulee, but I had very little agency in my sex life—making it a less rewarding experience even if I climaxed every time. She would often say when I complained, "You know Sarah, a lot of women are not as fortunate as you are." She was partially right; I was familiar with the research that said—*fifteen percent of women have never experienced an orgasm*. Paulee sympathized with me about vacations, restaurants and movies but she told me I was damn lucky in my sex life and to have a husband like Joe.

Paulee never understood or appreciated how I was thinking of Joe, not only myself when I had complained. My lack of desire had been detrimental for both of us. He deserved to have someone who could love him fully. He showed me consideration in so many ways. He would get up to bring me a glass of water in the middle of the night and give me back rubs and foot massages; and when he was annoyed with me—he never raised his voice in displeasure. He gave compliments, opened doors, bought flowers—but nothing helped. I simply was not sexually attracted to him, and I could not do anything about it. The chemistry was gone.

I preferred to use Georgio for my sexual needs. It was less stressful, took less time, and Georgio always scored a homerun too, with an advantage over Joe. I did not have to chastise myself over not being sexually attracted to my vibrator. I loved Joe like a best friend, nothing more. That's why after eight weeks of marriage, I had been ready to ask him for a divorce—then I found out I was pregnant.

My advice to those who are engaged—*get your prenups and wait to start your family.*

CHAPTER 11

PREGNANCY AND THE PLAINTIFF SPEAKS

The pregnancy abruptly altered my plans. The baby did not pick the best time to take root but Joe and I had been the gardeners, and I was happy this new life was growing inside me. I rationalized my situation: there are women who ask their best friends to father their babies. Was it so awful that we were having a baby? No, if you dismissed this fact: one week before I found out I was pregnant I planned to ask Joe for a divorce.

I hadn't told anyone I was planning to ask Joe for a divorce, not even Paulee; she would not have been objective. When I grew unhappy after my marriage she assumed a role akin to that of a defense lawyer for Joe. If I had told her she would have listed all the reasons why Joe is a good man and how I was a fool to even think about leaving him. I never said he wasn't a good man. He was truly a sweet man too— but odd. She agrees about him being a bit eccentric, but thought eccentricity could be tolerated if it didn't interfere with one's life too much. That was where we had a major disagreement. Joe's eccentricity might have been amusing for her on the level that she inter-acted with him but it interfered with my life way too much. I was tired of his peculiar sexual ideas turning me into a damn pothead for one. Paulee had the audacity to say in response to my complaint, "At least he doesn't cover you with a sheet when you do it like some orthodox Jews." I objected on the grounds it was a stupid defense: "Paulee, we are not orthodox Jews, and even if we were Joe would never cover me with a sheet; he likes to play with my tits too much."

Returning to her major defense—*Joe is a good man*, I tried to elaborate more to make myself clear. My complaint about his poor communication skills for example—was not whether he was bad or good. I told her she was applying an artificial distraction to obscure the nature of the problem—a basic theory in mathematics. "I teach English, Sarah." She played dumb with me, she understood perfectly. She coached a debating team and was familiar with the fallacies of logic. "Joe being a good man is a red herring, Paulee, okay? Do you get what I'm saying now?"

Goodness had nothing to do with it. I wanted to live with a man who discussed a variety of topics besides—his problems at work, whether the cats needed their claws trimmed, or why the water bill was so high. I might have been exaggerating, but it was hard getting him to talk about anything that did not affect us in a direct or immediate way. The one exception—the immediacy of asking for driving directions. Joe would drive miles lost to save precious words.

He denied that he had a problem asking for directions and made the excuse that he simply preferred to figure it out for himself; "I can always find the direction we're traveling by checking where the sun is, Sarah." A plan that worked as long as we were travelling during the day, and when I pointed that out he said he also knew moon navigation. Only an oddball would say things like that (but I digress), and I was not even sure moon navigation was real. If it was, how had Joe learned it? And would it have been a waste of my words if I had asked how one managed when it was cloudy and one couldn't see the sun or moon? The only reason to keep pursuing the topic would have been to keep Joe talking. Looking back, I should have; sun and moon navigation would have been more engaging than our water bill.

Asking for directions is sometimes a real necessity and Joe refused to do it, so it was not surprising that he refrained from what he called *idle talk*. High on his list would be a discussion about a movie we had seen. He simply did not understand the objective, unless you are a movie critic. I wondered what kind of defense Paulee would have made for one of her students in her literature class if she asked them to discuss the symbolism in *The Scarlet Letter,* and got the response—*what's the point?* That was exactly how Joe behaved when I wanted to talk about a movie. "We already saw it, Sarah, why do we have to hash over it again?"

Of course it was not like he hadn't warned me about his taciturn nature. The first time we went out he said he was not a talker and hoped I wouldn't mind. Why would I mind? I never thought I would marry him when he said it; I wasn't prescient. Sounds analogous to being ignorant of the law, and more fodder for Joe's defense, but an advocate for him would even have more. If Joe believed there was a clear, sound objective for talking—he talked.

When I told him I was pregnant I could not shut him up (triggering the memory of the day we first met). He was filled with ideas about turning the office into a nursery, and suggestions for baby names. He spent hours researching and wanted me to do the same. His plan was we would research separately then share our findings to choose a name. That was how our long discussions started. There were many considerations when you were choosing a name: origin, meaning, cultural implications and emotional impacts on a child. I was surprised to discover that in some states there were even laws to consider when choosing baby names. Joe told me I was wasting time when I tried to share that information with him: "We are not going to name our kid a number, Sarah." I was not implying that, and my findings were excellent trivia facts, which he had a penchant for, but apparently not that day.

I found the whole idea of laws concerning parents' autonomy over children's names fascinating even if Joe thought it was a waste of our time. He was just *being Joe* and I did not complain. He was engaged with the baby topic and it was endearing. For a brief time I regretted having thought about divorcing him. But it was not long lasting or a mitigating factor for Joe's defense as a spouse.

When it came to our sex life—he was a damn dictator. If he had afforded me even one iota as much agency in bed as he did picking out baby names I would have been thrilled, but he never considered my wishes about what worked for me sexually. I had been seduced into this marriage then left powerless. The argument that I always achieved an orgasm when we had intercourse was irrelevant. According to Paulee and Joe that was the only goal of sex for pleasure. True, if it was sex with a prostitute, but not in a relationship with your husband.

It was now my turn to cross examine their orgasmic argument: "Why do we even need men at all, except for procreation?" We don't need them for orgasms. I determined that when I was fourteen using my fingers or the Magic Clit Puff I stole from Penny. Next, I narrowed the broad implication of the first question specifically to my case—why was Joe necessary for my ultimate sexual satisfaction?

Joe asked me the same question one night (he had finally figured out why I took so long in the bathroom before coming back to bed). "Do you even need me, Sarah?" I knew he was talking about orgasms so I should have answered, *no*. I did not need him or any man for that but I said, "yes." I said yes because I needed him for a relationship, while he thought achieving a climax was the only goal in lovemaking.

It should encompass more with your spouse—like developing intimacy and having fun. Orgasms should not determine whether the marriage is good or even if the sex is good—that's how I judge the value of my toys. Our sexual relations did not bring us closer, and simply put—it wasn't fun going to bed with Joe.

It was not entirely his fault because I knew the hormones were partly responsible, and that made me feel less harshly towards him. But it did little to change how dysfunctional our sex life was. Paulee had no idea how uncomfortable it was, even how creepy it could feel—due to a lack of chemistry and zero sexual attraction. Our couplings sometimes were how I imagined what being molested was like. There was a disconnect between my head and my body. I wanted him to stop but I responded. What my head wanted was usurped— my body made me complicit and ashamed. It was also terrible having such awful thoughts about Joe.

Our marriage was dysfunctional but my feelings toward Joe improved during my pregnancy. The baby played a big part in it. Joe could talk hours about a variety of baby-related topics lessening my grievances towards him, and there was a change in our sex life. Once it became too uncomfortable with Joe on top—we stopped having sex entirely. And I can't lie—I was relieved. I did not want to continue smoking grass while pregnant, even though I had dramatically reduced my usage, and the Magic Clit Puff was more satisfying than lovemaking with Joe. It had been unkind of me to think like that but it was not a cognitive choice. I was not choosing a toy over him out of some retaliation for his rules over me. The fact was—my life was better when we stopped.

Not having to sleep with Joe reduced the stress on my body and pocket book—two plusses. I no longer had to be high to have sex and the cost of batteries was less than buying grass. There was an additional plus; I no longer worried about how long it took masturbating while Joe counted the minutes waiting for me in the marital bed. Even more valuable was the lessening of guilt. I had felt bad preferring the Magic Clit Puff (6th-generation and my favorite toy) over him. The little shame remaining creeped into my mind sometimes but it never lasted long. I reminded myself—I would have been more than willing to go on top if Joe had allowed it. He simply refused to change his position on the subject.

CHAPTER 12

ROSIE

We named her Rosalie. We both liked the name and Joe's favorite grandmother's name was Rozalie. I preferred the French spelling with the *s*, so we compromised but our discussions on it had been unduly spent. We called her Rosie from the time she was a baby; she had the cutest, chubbiest, rosy little cheeks.

The first night she was home Joe and I stood in her room staring at her while she slept in her crib; we were mesmerized by her—frozen in wonderment. It was the middle of the night and she hadn't woken or cried but we just stood there tightly holding hands. We were not compatible and there were problems in our marriage, but there was no denying the fact—Joe and I made a beautiful baby.

By the time she was three months old she had a head full of blonde curls making her look like a cherub—all she needed were little wings. Joe's mother Jean told me Joe had blond curls when he was small but his hair turned dark when he got older. I never knew he had been blond, and he kept his hair so short there was not even a hint of a wave. I hoped Rosie's hair stayed curly and did not change color. I liked its contrast with her eyes; she was not a blue-eyed blonde like me. She had Joe's big, brown eyes but it was clear she was a combination of both of us. No one would question her parentage.

She might be ours, but she was a daddy's girl right from the beginning. I warned Joe he was going to spoil her by picking her up all the time. He believed it was impossible to spoil a baby, but that's not what my book said. And he was probably right when he responded, "that's only one book." Which philosophy was correct—always pick them up when they cry or let them cry it out? We were not prescient to know the answer when she was young, but I was afraid that Joe's overindulgence would make her a spoiled brat. Joe told me I worried too much, "why do you have to be a doomsayer all the time," was his usual response to my warnings. It was true, I was unable to predict the future, and when she was young the only thing that was evident was the strong bond between them. If she woke up crying from a nightmare or a tummy ache she wanted only her daddy. He always came running like a big Papa bear to wipe her tears away or slay the monsters under the bed.

I never fully appreciated their bond, growing up without a father. Nor did I appreciate the active role Joe took when Rosie was a baby. I thought all fathers behaved like him until I talked to other mothers. Some told me I was very lucky—their husbands hardly helped at all. That's when I first began to see how unusual Joe was—he even did the middle of the night feedings when Rosie was an infant. One mother I met in our neighborhood playground questioned me on that. "How does he help, you're nursing, right?" She was correct to ask, I was breastfeeding but Joe was an integral part. I would pump milk ahead of time before I went to bed and put it in the refrigerator; Joe got up in the middle of the night to prepare the bottle when Rosie cried. My sleep was never disturbed when Rosie was an infant—not even once. Papa bear was in charge; mama bear slept. When I met my friend Liz and told her what Joe did she was shocked. Even with twins her husband never helped. I realized Joe was apparently better than your average father; maybe better than your average husband?

One might presume my growing appreciation of Joe would make our sex life better. That did not happen because it continued to be non-existent, and my sex life was satisfactory (the only drawback was having to frequently replace batteries). I was not privy to Joe's sentiments or practices, but I am sure he was accommodating himself because there was no shared sex between us for thirteen months. I would tell him my breasts hurt, or I was exhausted, or use the classic excuse—a headache. Joe finally stopped making overtures. I told myself it was not only about preferring masturbation, I resisted him because of Rosie. I needed to smoke pot or at the very least have a couple of glasses of wine to have sex with him, and I was breastfeeding. I did not want to hurt my baby.

I never gave any thought about hurting Joe. Paulee warned me.

"You're gonna lose that man if you're not careful. Aren't you afraid he might cheat on you?"

I knew Joe would never cheat on me, but I told Paulee if he did—maybe he would find someone with whom he was more compatible—and I'd be very happy for him.

"Yeah, that's what you say now, Sarah."

Paulee shamed me enough to confront what I was doing, but even without her admonishments I would eventually no longer have the heart to keep denying Joe sex. When I weaned Rosie I told Anthony to put me back on his active client list. Paulee said she was glad I was finally thinking about Joe, but he wasn't the main reason. I missed smoking pot, and I had always planned to stop nursing around seven months. I was not a weirdo like Bev.

Bev was a woman I had met in Belmar who breast-fed her son until he was three. She told me he would stand close to her and lift up her breast with his two little hands sucking away as though it were a bottle. She smiled when she said, "He was so cute, I wish you could have seen him." I was relieved not to have seen him; just imagining it was not appealing.

Rosie was napping, on the Sunday afternoon I made my sexual overture to Joe. I only smoked one half of a joint and I was totally looped. I was not sure why; was it because I hadn't smoked for a while or had Anthony sold me stronger stuff? Whatever the reason there was no need to do anything else to feel ready to have sex with Joe. I was not even turned off after I asked him if he wanted to make love and he replied, "Are you doing drugs again, Sarah?" His question made me sound like I was a heroin addict, but he did not hurt my feelings (I was too stoned to care). It also became obvious pretty quickly that my pot use was not going to stop him from enthusiastically accepting my invitation.

I was stoned for the entirety of the sex act but I was not impaired enough to miss the revelation that afternoon. Joe enlightened me. I realized it was his enthusiasm that had been missing since we got married. He behaved now exactly as he had during our courtship. He stoked my desire.

I had focused too much on myself—not enough on him, and the missing chemistry was not my isolated problem. After he released his animal power—I wanted him just as passionately as I had during our courtship. He was almost ravaging me; sometimes his force was painful. It did not make me pause—it excited me even more. I also had no complaints that he was the top dog and there was no licking. I was more than willing to give up my agency; we both came quickly—faster than usual. I was satisfied and content like a little pussy snuggled on a sunny window sill.

It was not long lasting. It only took a couple of days until we were back to our old routine—the one we had established on the second night as man and wife. Was the solution to our sexual dysfunction to have relations once a year? It's unlikely Joe would have agreed to annual sex so I increased my pot use and resumed the practice of *peeing* before we had sex. I came as usual, but there was no sense of well-being or release. Instead, I was filled with an overwhelming sadness when I climaxed. I wanted the beast to return and I did not know how to get him back.

CHAPTER 13

BEV

Water has always been a positive force in my life. I grew up by the Manasquan River, and memories of hearing its sounds and feeling the breezes blowing in from the sea are probably etched into my synapses. One of my earliest memories is being on our deck sitting on my mother's lap. It's in the morning and I'm munching on a breakfast bar while she tries to teach me my numbers by asking how many boats I see. I wished that I could count boats that summer.

When I complained how I missed living by the water, people laughed at me. It was warranted; Jackson is close to rivers, lakes, reservoirs and the ocean, but those laughing people had to admit to another fact. I needed a car to get to any of those waters—I could not simply walk out my back door. I missed that and I have always had an affinity for water. The reason I ultimately chose the college where I got my BA was the large lake on its campus. I often read or studied at the picnic tables peppered around it. The geese had been very familiar with me; I had fed them crusts saved from my breakfast toast every day.

It scared me after I had Rosie that water no longer gave me the same pleasure, but few things did. I continued to enjoy hearing Rosie laugh, and she was a real cutie clapping her chubby little hands when Joe played with her. It was fortunate I continued to be a voyeur by nature, I was too tired most of the time to participate. I had been content to watch Joe doing pattycake with Rosie or pushing her on a swing instead of doing it myself. I slept well at night so it was a mystery why I was so tired much of the time. Every afternoon when I put Rosie down for her nap, instead of reading or doing house chores, I'd take a nap too. I loved Rosie very much but my love for her was not enough to ignite a spark in me.

I started smoking cigarettes to get a little boost. I had smoked in college but kicked the habit after graduation. Now I was lighting up again, but not often in the house (except for pot, that smoke is therapeutic). Cigarettes are harmful so I was limiting myself to only three or four a day. I hoped when I was ready to stop it would not be too hard.

I was sitting with my cup of coffee, smoking my cigarette on the boardwalk in Belmar across from The Best Grind; Rosie was in her stroller, gumming on a piece of bagel. A woman who was sitting nearby came over to me with her toddler.

"You're not supposed to smoke here you know."

I told her I was not aware of that, but before I could say another word she said, "Didn't you see the sign?"

She annoyed me; if I had seen the sign I would not have been smoking, even though I had seen other people doing it on the boardwalk. If she regularly came to this beach she must have seen them herself. Obviously there are people who ignore signs but I wasn't one of them. Was she implying I blindly followed people, breaking rules? Never.

Dee tried to persuade me to shoplift with her when we were in high school. It was a sport for her. I refused, but I enjoyed seeing the things she pilfered spilled out on her bed for display. She never stole expensive items: lipstick, gum, a candy bar—the value was not important. It was a fun-filled challenge according to her. The object was to steal something and not get caught. I preferred more mundane activities for fun and thought she was stupid to shoplift. I was afraid she eventually would get caught, but I continued to reap a vicarious thrill from her doing it. For my part I chose to be a law-abiding citizen as a teen—and as an adult. Joe laughs at me when I say that, "yeah, except for smoking dope."

I don't know why my using grass has always upset him; I never smoke on the street, and pot is beneficial. I should not be faulted because its benefits have not been widely accepted yet, but smoking joints was irrelevant. This lady was upset over cigarettes, and expressed her displeasure with a superior attitude that was hard to take. Her tone was disapproving and harsh—as abrasive as any cigarette smoke might have been.

She reminded me of someone but I was not able to envision anyone specifically. I was pondering that and trying to decide where to put my cigarette out when she rudely interrupted my thoughts. She abruptly told me to go over to the ramp where I was allowed to smoke. What a bossy bitch. There was only a little coffee left in the cup so I dropped my cigarette into it. When I saw the look of disgust and displeasure on her face I knew who it was—she acted like my sister when we were teenagers. It hadn't been clear before due to the dramatic difference in appearance. My beautiful sister and this very homely woman did not resemble one another physically one iota—but they were soul sisters in temperament. I bet this bitch would rat out someone like my sister did too. Memories of Penny and our teen years were flicking through my mind like flash cards until I stopped on one—and I remembered. It was not true I had never stolen anything. I never shoplifted, but I stole something from my sister; the same day she told my mother Dee was suspended from school.

Our gym teacher Mrs. Ivy caught Dee giving Alex Lopez a blow job behind the bleachers and she was suspended for three days. Penny was not trying to hurt Dee when she tattled to our mother about the suspension—she wanted to hurt me. Dee and I had planned to go to the movies that weekend, but after Penny ratted her out—my mother vetoed the idea. My mother also declared Dee off-limits for several weeks. I was not allowed to spend any time with her outside of school.

I was in essence being grounded indirectly since Dee was my best friend (and I didn't even like Alex).

I was really angry at Penny, and when she went out with her friend Barb to the mall I went into her room. My retaliation-plan was to steal something she'd be very upset about losing. I would eventually return it, but I wanted her to suffer searching for it in vain. That's the day I found her box of sex toys. A business card was taped on the inside of the lid for a mail-order company called Secret Pleasures that sold *marital aids*. There was a brand new one too, never used, in its plastic package—the Magic Clit Puff.

A couple of days later Penny asked me if I had been in her room. In the most innocent sounding way I could muster I replied, "No. Why?"

"I'm missing something." I asked her what she was missing but she refused to say and screamed at me. "You better stay out of my room, Sarah."

I knew she would not complain to our mother about me stealing something from her because Mom would have asked—"what did she take?" If she told her about the Magic Clit Puff it might have opened up a Pandora's Box, along with the one I had opened. Our mother was a devotee of Dr. Ruth, but we were never completely sure of what her reactions would be when it came to our sexuality in application. Acceptance of sexual theory espoused by a sex therapist had nothing to do with your own daughters masturbating or fucking.

Mother was never told and I never gave the toy back to Penny. On the contrary, I started using it. I had not only successfully retaliated, I discovered a whole new world. Penny deserved to lose the Magic Clit Puff for being a rat—always trying to hurt me. She was a spiteful blabbermouth, using the antics of my friends to orchestrate punishments for me. It was only fair she should play a part in mitigating my distress to make amends. I'm pretty sure she knew I stole her toy which also gave me great satisfaction, and I've never regretted not returning it.

I often think I should thank her for ratting out Dee. I would have eventually found the joy of sex toys on my own but Penny indirectly expedited the discovery. They have given me much pleasure since I was fourteen (thanks, Sis).

I imagined this annoying Penny-like woman, who I later learned was named Bev, would have no problem flagging down one of the seasonal police officers hired for the summer. They patrolled the board giving out fines for petty infractions, like smoking and parking violations. She would probably feel that it was her civic duty. It would not have even been too surprising to find out Bev made citizen's arrests herself. What surprised me was after I put the cigarette out I expected her to leave—she did not budge. Instead of returning to where she had been previously sitting she sat down next to me. Did she want to be friends after our altercation, or had she stayed to make sure I would not light up again? I didn't know, but I had no stamina to move myself; nor did I care that she was pontificating on the values of breastfeeding and homeschooling. It was stark proof of how numb I had felt most of the time—that day was no exception. Bev had only been able to make me feel alive for a brief time by annoying me. I was able to tune her out with very little effort. I stared at the ocean in a daze.

CHAPTER 14

THE WHOLE IS GREATER THAN THE PART

Did Joe need help? Did I need help? Did we both need help? Should we go alone? Should we go together? Too many questions. Joe had certainly needed help—it was obvious. His abrupt shift in sexual preferences—where had that come from? People do not suddenly change unless there is something wrong with them. One major difference between us had been that I had not abruptly changed.

When people asked "why don't you leave him?" I behaved as I always had depending on my relationship with the person asking the question. If it wasn't a close one I simply said—"I can't leave because of Rosie." She was a reason, but not the outstanding one. It was more my malaise—the lack of strength and will to make the effort to leave that kept me with Joe. I was not forthcoming about that unless you knew me better. Paulee knew.

Paulee was also aware of all the contradictions in our marriage, like during the thirteen months I had refused to sleep with Joe. I dreaded having sex with him but welcomed other touches. I asked for back rubs and was happy to reciprocate. I also liked to cuddle with him or hold his hand when we watched TV. Paulee had called me a "cock tease," and I was not able to convince her otherwise.

"Well, what do you call it, Sarah? You are teasing him or you regressed into your grammar-school sexuality. Either way, I don't think you're being fair to him using sex toys instead of sleeping with him." She had been wrong on both counts. He never complained about holding my hand or cuddling with me (and I did not use sex toys when I was in grammar school). I did love him; I just had not wanted to have sex with him.

It was a complicated situation. The thirteen months when we weren't having sex had been the happiest months of my marriage. I was sexually satisfied using toys and emotionally satisfied cuddling with Joe. It probably had not been the greatest time for him, but I was never trying to tease him. I was indebted to him for the way he took up the slack caring for Rosie and the house during that time. I was ashamed about neglecting my responsibilities. Not so much about Rosie—he was her parent just as much as me, more over the dirty dishes and general untidiness of the house. When I apologized to Joe he replied, "Not a problem, I cleaned the place before you moved in. I'm used to it."

And I continued to deny him sex. He never expressed any irritation towards me. His great guy persona shined throughout the thirteen months while I did it. He was a kind man, even if sexually unimaginative.

What had that said about me? Had I needed help or a lover? If someone had heard my complaints, they might have suggested an affair in lieu of leaving him. There are women who stayed in dysfunctional marriages for the sake of their children and looked for sexual satisfaction with other men. But those women obviously did not have inertia along with discontent, and even if I had had the get-up-and-go, I would never have had an affair. It was out of the question; I would not have been able to live with myself if I had cheated on Joe. An affair was not the same as leaving a sink full of dishes for him to wash.

The only infidelity I experienced was through the actions taken by other people. It was downright scintillating when Paulee started cheating on Anthony, at the very same time I was denying Joe sex. I thought she was being a tad sanctimonious at the time for berating me, but she was positive Anthony was stepping out on her with Carla (a server with fake tits who worked at the bar he managed). Paulee cheating got me really horny; hearing her stories made me masturbate twice a day, but they had no effect on my sexual relations with Joe.

When Rosie was almost a year-old, I was no longer subjecting Joe to sex deprivation; we were now in the throes of dysfunctional sex. I was not happy but I continued to lack the spirit to do anything about it, or to determine who needed help or how to get it. But what was clear: chain-smoking cigarettes, using lots of pot and having very little desire to get up in the morning suggested that I was the one in distress, not Joe. He was working, taking care of the house and Rosie, and seemed to be filled with vitality. When I compared the two of us, I had to admit—I needed help, but I lacked the drive to find a counselor or therapist. I was only able to muster up enough steam to peruse the self-help section at our local big chain bookstore.

I was amazed at how big the self-help section was and that alone had made me feel better before I looked at a single book—apparently I was not the only one who was miserable. I started grabbing books so quickly it looked like I was in a timed-shopping spree contest. I finally had to ask one of the workers who was straightening merchandise in a nearby aisle if she had a box because I could not carry any more in my arms. She gave me a plastic container; it was big enough for what I was holding and I continued to put in more books until it was filled.

By the time I checked out I looked like a woman on the verge of a mental break any minute by the sheer number of self-help books in my container. The cashier did not say a word to me nor did she look at me directly, but I caught her doing it surreptitiously. Two large bags and three hundred and seventy-five dollars later I walked out of the store. It was no more expensive than seeing a therapist two or three times, and it was better than doing nothing. It was also the only thing I had been able to do at the time.

The first book I read was filled with exercises. Exercise A instructed the reader to write down one thing they were thankful for each day—no matter how insignificant it might be. Put it down—even if it was for a light turning green or the sunny-side up egg not being runny. After a month, look at the list: "You will see that you have many things to be grateful for in your life."

I started my list; number one—*I appreciated Joe for being such a good daddy.* When I simply couldn't move, he would bathe, dress and feed Rosie. He was also the one who usually walked her in the stroller and took her to the little playground in our complex to push her on the swings. And because she was like most children her age and loved animals, when Joe wanted her to have a greater experience beyond our pets, he took her to petting zoos in the area. After we had gone to all the local places he did not even hesitate to travel a distance. This counted as an additional positive notation on my list—*willing to go somewhere* (a true out-of-character behavior for him) in addition to being a good daddy.

There was also an additional double credit that I gave Joe. He deserved kudos for comforting Rosie when she was teething and saving my sanity. I had tried massaging her gums, applying teething oil, and giving her teeth toys. No matter what I did she would not stop crying and I was going mad. Nothing worked until Joe started making faces at her or sounds to make her laugh. Sometimes he would carry her around, lifting her high over his shoulders when she started fussing. At his height, she had a pretty high perch; I hope it wasn't fear that had stopped her crying but she had seemed to enjoy looking at her world from a new perspective. And at night if she was fretting he would carry her in his arms crooning to her until she stopped. I laughed; she wasn't afraid of his singing either and it was pretty scary. Joe is not a singer, but Rosie had not been frightened nor was she a critic—she fell asleep in his arms.

After a month there had been many things on my list, but what stood out was shocking—most of the things that I had noted were connected with Joe. It was hard to accept because he was the cause of my angst. But then I remembered something from a math class—Euclid's theory of the whole being greater than the part. My marriage was the sum of its parts. Clearly what this list showed me was there were more parts that I liked about my marriage than not, but it was with the acknowledgement that all parts are not equal to one another (another common notion in Euclid's theory). Sexual satisfaction and compatibility are not equal to driving to petting zoos.

The list was still instructive even if not conclusive. I needed to put more effort in improving the parts that bothered me in our relationship—with a new perspective. I had been using my time to lament too much about what I did not have, and not enough appreciation for what I had—Paulee had said the same (it took a mathematician to make it clear as opposed to an English teacher).

I had thought of my marriage as an inflexible fixed whole, but rather than fixed—my marriage was a sum of flexible parts. This insight made my purpose clear, which in turn gave me vitality and I stopped smoking— these books really worked. Next, I planned a strategy to address the weak parts of my marriage with a new understanding—they did not represent my entire relationship with Joe. I outlined a schedule of attack in the following order: vacations, communication and our sex life (there had been no point in starting with the most difficult).

I asked Joe if we could take a little vacation, just the two of us; we had not done that since our honeymoon. I would have been satisfied with a long weekend, and my mother had already said she'd watch Rosie for us. He had no problem with me taking a vacation but he refused to go.

"You know I'm sick of traveling. I don't want to do it when I'm not working and don't have to. You can go on vacation with Paulee, I'll watch Rosie."

"But I want to be with you, Joe."

"But you're with me right now, why do we need to go on a vacation to be together? Is it me, or a vacation? If you need one, take it. I won't hold you back."

He just didn't get it, but he was true to his word and he never complained when I went on a vacation without him. The first trip was to the Bahamas after Rosie was weaned, and it was the beginning of a tradition: Paulee and I taking vacations together while Joe stayed home with Rosie. I have a photo album of pictures from all our trips; we always took a picture when we were leaving. The theme was always the same—Paulee and I next to our car waving before driving away, or at the airport or train station when Joe dropped us off. There were also pictures of Joe and Rosie. In the very first one she is all bundled up to keep warm because it was a cold day in March and Joe is waving her little hand telling her, "Say good-bye to Mommy." In the last vacation picture Joe is standing next to a sullen pre-teen Rosie sticking her tongue out at me.

I was able to take vacations, and I was fortunate. I had the money, the time, and a husband who had not complained about me going off with my friend without him to wherever (not everyone was so lucky). My list expanded over the years, and there were so many things to add that I needed to purchase additional journals. But the one note I was never able to write: *Joe took a vacation with me.*

My next concern was about the quality of our communication.

"Joe, I'd like us to talk more."

"We do talk, Sarah."

"I don't want to talk about only mundane things or trivia. I want to talk about macroscopic things, metaphysical things." He didn't say anything—he just looked at me with an expression on his face which clearly read he thought I went bonkers.

That's when I asked myself: was it even necessary to have theoretical talks with a practical guy like Joe? Paulee loved those kinds of discussions. She was able to fill in for Joe again, but she was not able to be a pinch hitter in our sex life. I do not have my sister's inclinations.

I could not put it off any longer, I had to finally look at our dysfunctional sex life. I decided to share my revelation with Joe about his lack of enthusiasm when making love since we got married. I hoped he could turn it up a notch. It was true, I was not naturally attracted to him; his big hairy body did not make me swoon (even his beautiful brown eyes did not do it for me). I could not change my impulses, but it was also true during our courtship it was hard to keep my hands off him. And after my imposed sex deprivation when we made love—he turned me on. When I was dating my great Aunt Beth always asked, "did he knock your socks off?" She was definitely not talking about intercourse but her sentiment was applicable now. Joe most certainly knocked the socks and all other clothing off me after my imposed famine. There was no denying that he got me hot and bothered that afternoon. Something changed and it was worth a try to get the something back.

"I wish you could be more enthusiastic when we make love, Joe"

"What's that supposed to mean, Sarah?"

"I don't know, more pep; try going faster or something."

"Go faster? I'm always waiting for you to catch up. I can get to where I want way before you, Sarah."

"Well, don't wait next time. Let's see who comes in first." I was so smug too, but he laughed at me and said it wouldn't be a fair race. I wasn't clear why he said it at the time, but after much pestering on my part he finally agreed—only he set some ground rules. There would be *no waiting to start or dope allowed*. Both were a problem for me, and I broke the rules. It was not a fair race. Maybe that's why he performed as usual, so I didn't mention his lack of enthusiasm.

The sex part of our marriage was the largest value in the whole. My discontent over our sexual dysfunction was a driving force that led me to the self-help aisle. I had to keep working more on that area if I hoped for overall improvement in our relationship. One night I took advantage of an opportunity that arose, in a manner of speaking. I was awakened by Joe's snoring; he was lying flat on his back, naked with the sheet and blanket tossed off looking like a beached whale. This whale was very much alive though—making very loud sounds. I was about to nudge him to make him turn on his side when I had an idea. I moved very slowly, not to wake him. When I reached my destination, I began to stroke and lick his family jewels—going up the shaft until it was firm enough for me to get down to work. Joe responded but I knew he wasn't fully awakened until he abruptly sat up in bed. I could see him well, there was a full moon and light was coming in through the window. He looked stunned and his eyes were two big saucers.

"Oh my God, I was having a dream I was being raped. Sarah, I told you I don't want you to do that." He had the nerve to say that to me when I could still taste his cum in my mouth.

I was not totally discouraged. The first book helped. It had given me things to think about and some direction; but I was soon back to smoking cigarettes, using too much pot and feeling lethargic. I had regressed, but I remained hopeful. If I found direction and purpose once—I believed I could find it again. And I had twenty-four more books left to read.

CHAPTER 15

LIZ

I was in front of the Best Grind with my coffee when I got my first glimpse of Liz. She was across the street on the boardwalk talking to Bev. Having known Bev now for over a month, I knew she was doing most of the talking. It was even wrong to call it talking when Bev was present—that suggests equitability. There was never a back-and-forth conversation or equal exchange of ideas with her—she was always proselytizing. I could ignore Bev, but empathized with this woman she had ensnared who obviously was not familiar with the territory. It only took one encounter meeting Bev for most people who frequented the boardwalk with their kids to avoid her. They went to other playground areas to dodge her pedantic rants. Liz was an unknowing newbie. I had planned to finish my coffee at one of the tables outside of the Grind, but I decided to take it over to the boardwalk. I wanted to help the newbie.

It was a good move; I liked her. She was very animated like Paulee, and similar to many friends I had when I was younger. The familiarity drew me to her immediately; I continued to have an affinity for certain personality types. When she talked she was very descriptive and had an ability to arouse a listener's emotions. My outlook improved being around her after only a short exposure; her positive mood was contagious. I had a very low supply of passion when I met Liz. Maybe it was self-preservation that made me feel she was a keeper the first day we met. I instinctively knew she could rescue me with a much-needed transfusion.

Liz told us she was a singer, and she was working on a new song. She could not stop talking about it, but she was not a bore. I was in awe of her. I wished I had a song that I could feel so enthusiastic about. Not literally, I never played an instrument or sang in a choir, but hadn't she simply been expressing her joy in life and being alive?

The song was not her only topic of conversation. She was enamored with her husband and very involved with her children. I envied her for the former, and shared her sentiments on the latter, even though my love for Rosie was never enough. I was probably a bad mother to feel that way but I could not pretend. Rosie could not make me happy most of the time or compel me to fully embrace my life. Sadly, I was attracted to Liz because I was only able to feel alive by vicariously experiencing her zest for life. I had very little zest of my own.

Studies say that we are drawn instinctively to attractive people. Liz was a beautiful woman, so maybe there was also more to my attraction. But beauty never drew me closer to my sister; they were very different though. Penny was cool and Liz was hot—exotic looking, with long straight black hair and a fringe over dark eyes. My sister is a blonde Nordic beauty who stared at you with boredom and superiority from the pages of fashion magazines. Liz's eyes were inviting; not judgmental.

Liz told me she was Armenian and Jewish, but she looked like an Egyptian princess. She also had a great tan, yet insisted she hated sunbathing; she even disliked going to the beach. She swore her tan was from a family vacation she had taken with her parents to Puerto Rico when she was in high school. It seemed hard to believe if it was true and I knew sun-worshipers who would envy her. I suggested if she wanted to adopt a stage name *Cleopatra* would be a good choice. It sounded more like an exotic dancer than a singer though. Perhaps that's why she seemed upset when I said it. She sounded a little abrupt when she replied that she preferred to use her name—Liz Bennetti. I certainly was not trying to insult her. But it might have been my imagination because she recovered quickly after the exchange. She continued talking as she had before my blip (if indeed it had been one).

She wanted to have a full-time career singing jazz and the blues. She said she'd do anything short of murder or prostitution to be able to sing, but it was very difficult to have a singing career with two toddlers and a husband who was not very supportive. The whole time she was talking Bev was rolling her eyes and making these little *umph* sounds—as though she were adding audible punctuation marks to Liz's sentences. I had no idea what her problem was. Annoyed at not monopolizing the conversation as usual was a possibility, but she managed to interject her opinions into the mix. At one point, in that haughty tone of hers, she said it was so unrealistic for anyone to think they could be a professional performer. What audacity to say that aloud, and I was happy when Liz quickly responded to her remark. She told us she just finished a job singing and was paid quite well. Bev umphed in response and I commented, "I see your husband supported you with that," and she responded with a no. Her husband never knew she had done it.

For the three months "of her gig," her husband thought she was taking a course in New York City at The New School. She was either a little bit wacky or fearless, and I was in awe. I could never imagine doing that myself. I would have never lied or deceived Joe like she had done with her husband, even though my circumstances had been different. If I had ever told Joe I wanted to sing in a club he would have probably said, "If you want to do that, honey, go for it, I'll support you," but he would never come hear me sing. He would not have given me total support, the same as with vacationing.

Liz did more for me on that first day meeting her than I got from completing every exercise in the first self-help book. It's no hyperbole to say meeting her was life-changing, and it was so simple. She reminded me that I once had a passion like hers. One that had belonged to me alone. I had lost track of it after I married and had Rosie, but thanks to her I found it.

For as long as I can remember I've wanted to be a teacher. But I decided not to return to the high school after Rosie's birth, even though I was up for tenure that year. There had been no guarantee I would have received it. The principal liked me but my department head and I often butted heads. I had also wanted to breastfeed Rosie, so I quit. After meeting Liz—I realized how much I missed teaching.

She awakened my desire to teach, but I was not sure about returning to the secondary level where managerial skills were a main focus. I was not very effective at managing myself at that juncture. That's when I remembered: the same professor who said managerial skills are needed the most when teaching primary through secondary, also said knowledge of your subject area was more important teaching post-secondary. I held a masters in mathematics; I could teach in a college. It was a little late to start applying for fall positions, but there was often a scarcity of math and science teachers. I had nothing to lose submitting my resume. I had time to apply to a hundred schools if that had been an option. But since there weren't a hundred schools in the area I applied to several community colleges. I had found a direction. It took the edge off my problems with Joe—I had something else to focus on in my life—and it belonged only to me. Or at least that's what I thought at the time.

· · · ● ● ● ● ● ♥ ● ● ● ● · · ·

Liz never knew how meaningful she had been in my life by any direct communication. I never mentioned it, but she knew I valued our friendship. At the end of the summer when she started singing lessons in New York I took care of her twin boys. I was happy to help her in this small way if it enabled her to get a little closer to achieving her dreams.

Liz would drop them off at my place every Wednesday early in the morning and return around 3:30 or 4:00 pm. Joe was usually in North Jersey most Wednesdays and would not return until the evening, and Liz's husband Rocky went to the gym after work. She complained, "Why does he have to go to the gym to work out? We have a home gym in our house." She told me his reason was that he liked to be around people. It was very ironic; Joe was the exact opposite. He did not like to be around people and had weights in his workroom on our upper level. I was always encouraging him to join a gym.

"Why do I need to join a gym, Sarah? I get a good enough workout right here at home and it doesn't cost a cent."

Our husbands did not seem to have a lot in common, other than both being gone on Wednesday afternoons; and when Liz came to pick up her boys there was no rush for her to leave or for me to start dinner. We would take the kids out in their strollers or to the playground, and afterwards have some wine and smoke pot (only one glass and we shared a joint—Liz had to drive home).

We continued this way until the summer ended and fall began. In October we experienced a very hot resurgence of summer temperatures. Liz said, "It's perfect weather to have a summer picnic, and you never saw my house." I was curious about her home since she brought her boys to my place when I baby sat, but I also suggested that we could have a picnic at a park; we both could bring food. She did not want to do that, "it's my turn to provide refreshments for a change," so I enthusiastically said yes to her hosting a summer picnic. Technically summer had already ended, but it was perfect weather for an outside gathering. That would not be a positive factor for Joe. I doubted that he would want to attend no matter how beautiful the weather might be, but I was confident my going without him would not bother him in the least. It was always okay with him if I went alone to parties or events. I could hear him already, "You go, I'll stay home and watch Rosie."

CHAPTER 16

THE PICNIC ROCKED

Joe surprised me, he was going to the picnic. When I told him Liz's husband liked to golf it *sealed the deal*, as Joe was always fond of saying. The only disagreement we were having was over our dog. I wanted to leave her home and Joe wanted to bring her with us.

"But it's a picnic, Sarah, we'll be outside," was the only argument he made. He must have been deluding himself since he never lied. I knew the real reason for bringing her was he hated using the cage. We used crate-training but were often inconsistent due to his objections. That was probably why she was not completely house broken and prone to having occasional accidents. I refused to hassle with him about the cage or to bring her along so I told him we could gate her in the kitchen. I promised to clean up if she had an accident, and I would have done it, but figured Joe probably would. I had no regret about that either since he was the one who bought her without my input or agreement.

We had talked about getting a dog, but I was surprised to see one in my house when Paulee and I returned from the Bahamas. I would have also preferred something smaller but Joe explained after researching he found that small dogs were not always good with children; that's why he chose a lab. It was a good choice on the side of caution but bigger dogs made bigger messes. We should have waited until Rosie was older to get a dog. It was past being debatable on the day of Liz's picnic, but Joe purchasing Sadie was a fixed memory.

He chose her name, and asked if it was okay with me. *Sadie* had been one of his baby-name picks. I vetoed it for our daughter but when he proposed the name on the day I first saw the dog, I screamed, "I don't care what you name your dog." Probably too loud because he thought I was angry about him buying her; it wasn't true. I only wished I had been a part of it. I shared a life-long desire for a dog just like him. It was impossible due to Mom's allergies to dogs and cats. Allergies were not the reason for Joe and his sister growing up without a dog. His parents simply preferred to shoot or eat animals rather than to indulge or elevate them to a higher status. The only animals that were allowed in their home were dead—mounted on walls or sizzling on a plate.

Their mother finally relented and agreed that they could get a pet if it was kept outside. Jean bought them a rabbit, and Bunny Boy was confined to a cage in the backyard. Jean permitted them to open the top for feeding and to pet him, but he was never allowed out except for cleaning purposes. Joe and his sister found a way to skirt around their mother's rules. "Bunny Boy had the cleanest hutch there ever was," according to Joe. He still was not much of a pet being confined in a cage for most of his life and that's my guess why Joe had a dislike for cages. At least Bunny Boy was allowed to die of natural causes, unlike all the rabbits and squirrels Mac shot in his backyard from his kitchen window. Joe's father likes to brag about how many he "bagged."

Joe's father is fond of killing animals and talking about it even if he knows you are uncomfortable hearing it. When Rosie was five or six he was telling us about one of his *hunting trips*, and Rosie started to cry. Joe tried to get his father to stop.

"Dad, please. She's just a little girl. She doesn't like to hear about animals being killed." His father as usual was not put off at all and responded, "Oh, yeah, well how the hell does she think she got that hot dog she's eating?"

I don't know if she understood what her grandfather was saying about her lunch that day. When she was small she thought the mounted deer heads and the taxidermied birds and animals Jean decorated the house with were plush pet toys. When she got older she understood they were dead animals her grandparents had killed—she was not happy about the decapitated Bambi heads.

Mac will never be stopped from shooting or talking, and Joe took Rosie out of the room that day. I was lucky Joe did not take after his father. If that had meant a disagreement about caging a dog it was a small sacrifice and preferable to living with a man like Mac.

After the dog question was finally put to rest I started to look for something to wear for the picnic. It was really hot and muggy so I chose a sundress of rather sheer, light material. It had built-in cups and was designed to be worn without a bra—that was okay with me. It was too hot to wear one, but I was unsure about the dress—it was flimsy. I put it on and checked myself in the full-length mirror. It looked good, and I would definitely be cool if I wore it, but I wanted a second opinion. I asked Joe if it was okay, and he said, "You look great, Sarah."

Sometimes I was not sure if Joe paid full attention to me, and after the party I would ponder this reflecting on my dress choice and Joe's approval—but I didn't give it a second's thought then. That's why I ultimately chose the pale blue sundress, but later would regret my decision—and question Joe's common sense.

Dress on, hair combed, and makeup applied—I was ready; and Joe put Rosie in her car seat—we were off to Liz's home. She lived in a large house in Belmar—six blocks from the beach. What I would not give to be that close to the ocean, and she was not a beach fan—which made me ask: why is the universe so arbitrary? It can take sadistic pleasure at times playing with our lives. Liz living in Belmar, while I lived in Jackson, was not a serious life or death example but it still spoke of how unfair life can be. She lived near the beach and didn't care; I craved the ocean and was stuck in Jackson.

I liked the townhouse in Jackson though, and when I asked Joe if I could redecorate he had given me free rein. He was only generous with his permission; I paid for everything. I didn't mind because it had been my idea to redecorate. I didn't realize it was foreshadowing the monetary aspect of our life together. I was thrilled when he said, "Do what you want. It's just a place to hang my hat." That had been obvious based on his furnishings. His townhouse was filled with cast-offs from his parents' house, furniture from thrift stores, and stuff he had found off the curb.

I did have fun playing interior designer; it was my first opportunity to decorate a living space, having only lived in dorm rooms and my mother's house. I threw things out, replaced rugs and drapes, bought new furniture, and decorated with abandon during the months leading up to our marriage. I sound like a sappy greeting card but it was true: I turned a mere house into a real home (I had only wished it was closer to water).

Liz's house was so large I marveled how she found the time to care for it; she did not have a housekeeper. I hoped she hadn't spent hours cleaning in preparation for the picnic, but she hadn't struck me as an obsessed cleaning nut. It would have really been unnecessary in this case since most of the activity would be outside. And I was happy to see she didn't look like she had been scrubbing floors when Joe and I walked into her house. She was cool and beautiful; there wasn't one hair out of place in her sleek, straight black tresses. It was me who looked like I had spent hours scouring every surface of her huge house. My face was beet red from the heat and the material of my dress was clinging to me from perspiration. My hairstyle was *a la scarecrow* which surprised me since I had worn it very short that summer. To my dismay the wind had still managed to blow it out in haphazard directions.

I had forgotten that the air conditioner in Joe's car hadn't worked for a couple of years when he said, "Why don't we take my car, yours needs gas." If I had remembered, I would have said—*no way.* His busted air conditioner and refusing to have it fixed was another example of his penny-saving ways. When I had the misfortune to be in his car in hot weather in the past he'd always respond to my complaints with, "Open the windows; it'll feel like we're riding in a con-vertible." It wasn't true then or now, and I was more uncomfortable in his car than at any previous time.

I was melting; but it was Joe who opened all the windows which allowed the wind to create my hideous hairstyle. He was only trying to help and I should not have screamed at him, "Why did you do that Joe? Look at me." He sheepishly replied he had just wanted to cool me off; and it was not his fault I had forgotten to put a comb in my little cloth purse. It had been embarrassing nevertheless to think Liz and her husband might assume my hairstyle was intentional, and reflecting on the evening—I find it surprising Liz never said a word to me about my hair. For Rocky and me there were explanations why it was overlooked the entirety of the picnic. I was flustered, and he was too focused on other parts of my body to notice a hairstyle.

When Joe and I walked into Liz's kitchen, she was so quick playing hostess I didn't get a chance to ask her for a comb and where her powder room was. She flew over to me with a hug and introduced herself to Joe before I could say one word. It was the first time she was meeting him and she patted his arm instead of shaking hands; he was holding Rosie. She told him he could put her with Miles and Mattie in the playpen she had set up in the shade outside. She then asked me if I wanted to see the house but warned, "it's not decorated like yours." She said that often, and I thought she was exaggerating—she wasn't. Her house had very few paintings, decor pieces, mementos, or even family photos—the rooms themselves were almost empty. The small sofa and end tables were dwarfed by her large living room. Liz's Steinway in the room didn't even help much to fill the space. Her dining room was also empty and a bit bizarre—she had turned it into a big playpen. It was gated off from the living room and kitchen area, and there were several playpen mattress pads scattered on the floor along with toys. The only thing resembling a dining room was the chandelier hanging from the ceiling. She had not removed it; perhaps when she no longer needed a giant playpen she would restore it to its intended purpose. Looking around her rooms in the lower level of her house made it clear—it was not very difficult cleaning this part of the house. There were very few dust-catchers in it, and I mused on what the rest of her house would look like. But before she could show me more empty rooms, I heard a man's voice calling her from outside.

"Liz, can you come out here? Mattie is crying." Liz turned to me and said she'd show me the rest of the house later. I was about to follow her out to the backyard when a man walked into the kitchen.

"Oh, this is my husband Rocky, Sarah."

As soon as I looked at him a charge of electricity went through my body, but it didn't stay grounded. It traveled to him and bounced back and forth between us—a mutual attraction. It was chemical. Our baby blues were locked in a primal dance driven by hormones. The connection was only a few seconds but it seemed to last forever.

He broke the hold when he asked me if I wanted a beer; he told me that's what my husband was drinking. I said "yes," and I don't like beer. What I really wanted was a joint, but I never would have asked him if he had grass. I didn't know if he even smoked. Had he known his wife did? I knew he was a state trooper and she told me he "was not very conservative like they tend to be." But that had not necessarily equated to an admission of them sharing joints together, and based on my own relationship with Joe, she might be the only one who smoked. Joe never tried to out-and-out stop me but he never condoned it or shared a joint with me.

He especially would not have liked to hear I had been smoking at this picnic after he found out what Liz's husband did for a living. Joe was overly concerned with its legality. He obsessed over his father, who was a retired policeman from Staten Island, discovering my penchant for the herb.

Our biggest hassles over my pot use had occurred most often before we had sex. The second was when we were preparing for a visit to his parents. Just like it had been a must to ease my sexual tensions, I also had to smoke before I went to my in-laws, eliciting Joe's Pavlovian response: "He's gonna smell it on you, Sarah." To which I always responded "so what Joe, is he going to arrest me?" I did not have a clear idea what Mac thought about me. I knew he did not hold much respect for my political views, but the way he ogled, there seemed to be a real appreciation for my boobs—but why take the chance? So even though I thought Joe overreacted, I followed his lead. One afternoon he asked me to change my clothes before we left for his parents' and I did, but I smelled nothing. Am I immune to it? If the sweet fragrance is floating around in the air I notice, but I have never been aware of any smell left on my clothes or hair; it's not cigarette smoke. But after Joe told me he smelled pot: I changed my clothes, brushed my teeth, and sprayed so much perfume on myself I smelled like a floating funeral parlor. A morbid metaphor, but more than apt since I hated going to Joe's parents' house—viewings were less stressful.

Rocky handed me a beer, and our connection was reestablished. My face, neck and chest flushed; I put the cold bottle against my cheeks and was about to place it on my chest but caught myself. I did not want to bring any more attention to my breasts than what they were already receiving. And I kicked myself for wearing that dress. It showed my boobs way too much. I became angry at Joe for letting me wear it. Why did he say it was okay? Once he even told me a dress I had chosen for his mother's birthday party was "hot"; what's that all about? Why would a husband want his wife to look *hot* in that context? I had promptly changed that day, but I had read his *okay* as meaning my sundress was appropriate for Liz's picnic. I should have followed my own first instinct.

Rocky and I were in the kitchen no longer than five minutes. Time kept playing tricks though making that hard to determine, but it was long enough for Liz to come looking for us. When she walked into the kitchen she made me jump—like she had caught us screwing on her kitchen floor. She started to chat away telling us how Joe was so good with the kids and how he was even able to amuse Mattie. She acted as though there was nothing unusual going on in her kitchen. What had been wrong with her? Didn't she feel the heat bouncing back and forth between her husband and me? Didn't she smell the lust?

For the rest of the picnic I tried to avoid direct eye contact with Rocky if I could help it. I sat close to Joe and would lightly place my hand on his thigh from time to time which surprised him. This was not normal behavior for me after we were married. He finally quietly asked, "Are you feeling okay?" No, I wasn't okay; everything was slightly off. Why was my normally taciturn husband being very sociable, and especially with Rocky? He was downright gregarious as I recall. He even seemed eager when he went in the house with Rocky to see a new tennis racket; new golf clubs I could understand but Joe did not play tennis. I could not wait to leave and go home (usually it was Joe who wanted to exit parties early).

It was 9:00 pm when Liz said she forgot the cheesecake, and each of us had to have a piece before we left. I was about to ask if we could take ours home and Joe said, "That's great, I love cheesecake, but I gotta make a pit stop first." He followed Liz into the house to use the bathroom and I was left alone with Rocky. I needed to think fast—I asked Rocky if he would mind getting me a glass of wine. I had enough wits about me this time to ask for wine instead of beer, and I figured Liz or Joe would return before he completed his hosting duties. It worked. I was happy to see Liz coming out with the cheesecake but no sooner than putting it down on the table she said, "Oh, I have to get a different knife to cut this." She went back in the house the same time Rocky came out. Joe was nowhere in sight.

When Rocky handed me the glass of wine he lightly brushed against my breast. I wished again I hadn't worn this dress. The material was too thin, I knew he saw my nipples get hard. Had he even felt them when he brushed against me? Thinking this made my heart start beating fast and I had an ache between my legs. Luckily, he couldn't hear or feel the chemical reactions inside my body, it was impossible. Yet I was sure he was aware of what he was doing to me, and he looked right at my breasts when he sat in the chair across from mine. He did not even try to pretend he wasn't looking at them—this guy was a creep. When his gaze finally found my face I smiled. It was a bilateral response, part uncontrollable and part calculated—but I wasn't sending a signal to encourage him.

The uncontrollable kicked-in first, like all the other responses humming in my body on high—it just happened, sensory responses are out of our control. It's similar to an allergic reaction; I can't control them either. In this particular case, unlike a sneeze or a hive, I smiled—without thinking. I was still following a primal rhythm, but I had to use logic and not be led by my primordial instincts. I may not be able to control an allergic reaction, but I can remove myself from an allergen. That meant I had to engage the calculated part of my micro-facial dynamic, and use my cognitive skills.

With the most nonchalant voice I could muster I returned his gaze, "Like my tattoo?" I lowered his heat using my facial expression and voice. I pretended to not be bothered at all by him. I sent the message that I thought he had only been looking at my tattoo—instead of undressing me with his eyes. I was convincing, but my temperature hadn't cooled one iota. I had to get away from him immediately: "Well, I am going to check if your wife needs any help."

I fought to maintain control, and saying *your wife*, and not *Liz*, was a cognitive deliberate choice of words. I then stood up and quickly walked to the house but I had the sensation that he was following me with his eyes, and I was right. When I was near the backdoor he called out, "I like it, a lot." So much for effective pretense and lowering anyone's heat. His behavior was disgusting. Poor Liz. I couldn't deny it though—I felt excited and alive. Poor me.

The one thing I know for sure—not only are hormones uncontrollable, they are also selective—choosing to turn on with certain people. We can't choose, and it was not natural with Joe—even if it worked sporadically with him. I wished it wasn't that way because Joe was a decent man and I loved him. I did not want to get hot over a man whom I hardly knew (and what I knew about Rocky I didn't even like). My hormones ignored my plight; I was burning for Rocky, and instead of walking into the house I had really wanted to take off every stitch of clothing, walk naked back to him, and press his face into my breasts. Hormones have no brains.

After the cheesecake was eaten and the goodbyes had been made several times, we were still standing in the kitchen. Joe, who could remain silent easily for an hour and a half in a car drive, would not shut up. I finally reminded him about the dog.

"Oh, yeah, we have a lab puppy. She's only about seven months old and we have to take her out." He also had a bitch in heat standing right next to him who wanted out of this house.

Finally, I was sitting in the car, and Joe was putting Rosie in her car seat. My face was on fire, and when Joe got in the car he looked at me. The driver's door was still open with the ceiling light on and he asked, "Are you okay, baby, your face is all red?" I smiled at him. I was glad he was not aware of the cause—aftereffects were not dissipating. My smile also had nothing to do with gratitude for his concern or how I liked it when he called me, *baby* or *honey*. I was so keyed up from my encounter with Rocky that Joe could have ignored me and I would not have been annoyed; he did not need sweet endearments that night to woo me either. He could have called me *dog face* and it would have turned me on. We had only been driving on 195 for five minutes when I started stroking the inside of his leg; he started to get hard.

"What the hell are you doing, Sarah? You're gonna cause an accident. Were you smoking dope at the picnic?"

"Of course not, Liz's husband is a state trooper."

"So, what's that supposed to mean?"

I kept my hands to myself for the rest of the drive. When we got home, I put Rosie to bed and Joe took

Sadie out for a walk. When he returned we put the TV on and settled down on the couch.

I once told Paulee that sometimes I imagined myself as a hole in a knot of wood and Joe was getting off on me. I still came; she looked at me in wonder.

"You can think you are a knot in wood and still come? I have to fantasize about Brad Pitt. You are always complaining about your sex life Sarah, but Joe must be doing something right."

I thought about trying to fantasize to get the juices going for me, but I couldn't think of anyone (Brad Pitt did not do it for me). It wasn't necessary to think of anyone the night we returned from Liz's party. My body continued to hum from having been near Rocky; my nerve endings were hypersensitive. When I moved on the couch there were tingles between my legs—as though fingers were inside my panties (and Joe was only playing with the remote). I started stroking his inner leg and he asked me again if I had been "smoking dope;" I told him no. That was the last of any conversation.

Joe took my dress off so fast it ripped (the material really was too light and sheer). He then pulled my panties off but didn't bother to remove his clothes—he just dropped his jeans and boxers. We did it on the couch, not bothering to turn the TV off. And even though the back of my neck was rammed into the arm of the couch every time he thrust into me—there was no pain. All my nerve endings were centered on what was happening between my legs. When we were done I watched him pull up his boxers and jeans and zip up his fly. I was sore and drained out like a rag doll with no motivation to pick up my dress and panties from the floor. Joe shut the television off and I remained lying on the couch with my legs splayed open. He then kissed his hand and placed it between my legs. It was a sexy move and my body responded with a delicious shiver. It was involuntary, I couldn't stir by my own volition and I purred to Joe, "I can't move."

"Then don't, honey." He picked me up, and I put my arms around his neck and rested my head on his shoulder. He carried me all the way up to our bedroom—like we were in an X-rated King Kong movie, leaving my clothes scattered on the living room floor behind us. I picked them up the next morning and threw the dress away.

CHAPTER 17

THE ROCKY ROAD TO MARITAL BLISS

should have sought therapy when I experienced lethargy all the time and I had to get stoned to have relations with Joe. I should have considered getting help again when I asked Anthony if he could get me some hash (I had heard it might be stronger than grass). Grass was starting to lose its effectiveness as a lovemaking-prep. Paulee never suggested I needed help for lethargy or dysfunctional sex. The only response from her was I needed to appreciate Joe and what I had more. When I told her I had the hots for Liz's husband—that's when she said I needed help (Paulee did not know me at all).

"You're a married woman, Sarah."

"I didn't say I was going to cheat on Joe, but it's nice to know my libido is healthy."

"That's what I'm afraid of."

There was no need for her to worry about me and my marriage. My introduction to Rocky did not start a scandalous affair; it actually enhanced my sexual relationship with Joe. After seeing Rocky, I used the residual sexual urges to strengthen our marriage, not weaken it. My strategy was to combine my residuals with surprise attacks on Joe. I was able to dramatically expand his enthusiasm to match my own. If I walked in on Joe when he was taking a shower or grabbed his balls when he least expected it—he would respond with the strength of a bear. Using the exponential function formula I discovered how to release the beast, but there was a negative dynamic. If there had been a meter gauging Joe's intensity level it might read—DANGER-PROCEED WITH CAUTION.

There was also another negative part of the equation—the bedroom was not a constant variable producing an element of surprise. Our couplings often looked more like attacks than lovemaking: up against the wall, the refrigerator, and on top of tables and counters throughout our house. The couch remained the most popular landing area, and I eventually bought a bigger one but not without first having a disagreement with Joe. He didn't want to spend the money and I even told him I'd pay with my own savings. He then told me money was not his foremost objection. He insisted his primary reason was that there was nothing wrong with the couch we had. That was understandable—coming from the person who was always on top, but I doubted his justification that it had less to do with finances. Even if he had been honestly unaware of his main concern, it was clear after he said, "I have a problem with you saying your own savings." Money had been on his mind, and he didn't stop there after I responded that it was my money; I had brought it to our marriage.

"Well, technically, in this state all assets between married couples are marital, you know." I was shocked by his statement (not the veracity of it but surprised he had said it). I honestly did not know if Joe was correct about my personal savings prior to marrying him. If mine equals ours was true, Pops had not been the only one who had needed a prenup over assets. That was not my immediate concern though—all I cared about was convincing Joe we needed a bigger couch. I was sure Joe would agree to it if I explained the problem clearly: "our couch is too small, Joe. My neck keeps hitting the arm, and my hip hurts from being forced to throw one leg over the back." He sympathized; he had not wanted me to be uncomfortable or hurt, but had another argument for why there was no need for a new couch. "Maybe we should be using the bed, Sarah."

It took longer than I wished but in the end after much debate Joe finally agreed. We bought a bigger couch, but he continued to complain about spending money. There were other expenses—replacing my torn clothing and panties. It sounds violent but I never worried about being bodily harmed. It was true I would often ask myself the day after a particularly energetic night: why does my elbow hurt, or where did this bruise come from? I eventually grasped the equation and considered suggesting a safe word during sex but shelved the idea. I was afraid the suggestion might result in a return to our former status quo. I preferred the occasional bruise from being banged on a shelf to being bored in bed. Joe wasn't trying to hurt me, nor had I suddenly acquired a taste for rough sex. Bruises and pain were just unavoidable sometimes when a 215 pound, six three man was ramming a 119 pound, five five woman against the wall or on top of a dining room table.

No safe word, but safety was on the forefront of our minds. When we made love in the shower and slipped we never used the shower again. Joe also vetoed the outside deck after I got splinters in my ass. He had a hard time removing them and it was quite painful; it pained him as much as me. He kept apologizing while I kept telling him to keep plucking. I needed him to stop expressing his empathetic pain; it was slowing down the process. When he finally finished and put alcohol on my sore little butt, he told me the deck was off-limits; he was afraid of more splinters. He had not liked being a paramedic.

"I would have to take you to the ER next time and explain why you have splinters stuck in your ass, and that's not happening."

Rocky was a blessing from Eros and helped save my marriage. Paulee had been really off the mark. For the first time since I married Joe I was pretty content and less inclined to think I needed therapy. The sex was far from perfect but it was energetic, and I had other things to focus on in my life. I thanked Liz in part for that; she helped shift my gaze to personal goals—along with the self-help books. *Self* is the operative word in the genre, and I took the fourth book's advice to heart, "You are responsible for your own happiness. You shouldn't expect a husband or anyone else to be responsible for making you happy. It's YOUR responsibility."

The book exemplified this major point unpacking the empty nest syndrome and succinctly put: parents who use their children exclusively to satisfy their need for self-realization are the ones who experience it. Perhaps I instinctively knew that all along. It was why even though I loved Rosie, motherhood had not completed me. I suffered, thinking I was an awful mother. The book eased my maternal doubts, and made me see I was right not to use Rosie or Joe to complete me. I had to do that for myself.

After applying for six jobs I landed a part-time teaching position at our community college. It was only two classes, but it was enough. I knew within a week I loved teaching at the college level. It had very little to do with the students; many of them were similar in temperament and maturity to the students I had taught, but there were welcomed differences. In college if students slept or did nothing in my class, I was not harassed by the administration to harass them. And there was no requirement to write anyone up for being tardy, or to ask for passes from unknown students walking in the halls.

I also didn't need to take a single phone call from a parent who was complaining it was my fault that their child (who did absolutely nothing) was failing. There were no more parent/teacher conferences where I sometimes had to suffer a parent's abuse. I can still hear an irate mother screaming, "I thought since the *No Child Left Behind Act,* no child is left behind, but I guess it's not true," This did not happen in college. I was not even allowed to discuss their child with them, unless the student gave me permission—I doubted that would ever happen.

But the best part about teaching at the college level was being able to focus more on my subject area; my professor from my education seminar class had been right. My lesson plans were better now and most of my students were more engaged. For those who were not, they were free to drop classes easily, unlike their counterparts from the past. They could just leave if they wanted, and I no longer had to send students to a principal's office every day for unruly behavior because they were bored or disliked my class.

Teaching at college was not without its negatives though. The top one—the pay sucked. That's why some say teaching is a calling and isn't for everyone (it's to compensate for the low wages). Even the salaries for full-time positions are lower than careers in other professions with comparable educational requirements.

It was one of the reasons Joe was not thrilled about my part-time job, but it was my passion just like Liz's to sing. He was not swayed by that. He asked me if it even made sense to keep the job.

"My sister makes more money being a waitress, Sarah." I couldn't argue with him. It was true and I held a masters degree, but I was not surprised it was hard for him to understand. He had absolutely no passion for his job; it was only about money and I told him so.

"That's right, Sarah. My passion is to keep food on the table for my family." It was possible to have both; to love your work fervently and get a fair compensation for doing it. I told Joe if I had my PhD and found a tenured full-time teaching position it would be a real income. He told me to get one and threw in, "because what you're doing makes no sense at all," for added emphasis.

He had no idea what it would cost. When I told him I feared he was going to have a stroke. Fortunately that had not happened, and after he recovered from his shock he continued to support me throughout the whole process, emotionally and financially. When I was accepted into a program he paid the bulk of the expenses. He would not even let me consider loans. He shut me down every time I broached the subject and always countered with, "it's crazy to take out loans with their high interest rates, Sarah." It was during this time that I learned something more about Joe's approach to spending money. He would dumpster surf to save it and was too cheap to fix his car's air conditioner, but if he believed something was worth it—he'd part with his money. He told me I was worth it, and he had managed to save a substantial amount being so frugal. With his money and mine (those personal savings I had brought to the marriage), I went to graduate school without taking out one student loan.

CHAPTER 18

SEX AND SUSPICIONS

was very busy for the next four years working on my PhD. My studies became the biggest part of my life. Discontent over my marriage had greatly diminished before going to grad school and what remained shrank even more. It was a new configuration of the parts in my whole life, and even though I was often over-whelmed by school work I liked the change of values.

When I looked at the sum of my life, sex had become miniscule, but I made time for it and I wanted Joe to make love to me—with prerequisites. I continued using surprise to pump up his intensity level, and because I was not naturally attracted to him I had to set the mood for myself. I watched a steamy movie, read trashy novels, or had a glass of wine. Paulee said everyone had to get in the mood like that after a while. I knew that was not true. I didn't have to do a damn thing to get in the mood after I saw Rocky; it just happened. Paulee got annoyed at me those days when I mentioned him.

"You know, Sarah, I don't know what you see in that jerk. He sounds like a predator if I am to believe all you say about this guy. Why do you like him?"

"I didn't say I liked him, Paulee. I said I get horny when I see him."

I did not go out of my way to see Rocky, but it was inevitable that I would run into him periodically. And when I did all those pesky erogenous zones would come to attention, like on the day he came home from work early. I had planned to stay longer visiting with Liz when he walked into the room, and I had just started to sip my wine. But I had to leave, and I surprised her when I jumped up and said, "Oh, I forgot; I have to go to the food store to pick something up." I left my unfinished wine and Liz with a flabbergasted expression on her face. Rocky was a strong aphrodisiac and Liz had already been talking about him for an hour. It was too much, I had to make a quick exit.

When I got home Rosie was out with my mother, and Joe was in his workroom. It was unfortunate timing; if he was fooling with a model airplane, even if his member was willing, he was less inclined to fool around with me. I ran to his workroom; I wanted to do a quickie right there on the floor. It wouldn't have taken long; he could have gone right back to working on his model airplane—he refused.

Had he realized what a gift this was? Most men would consider themselves lucky having a wife that extended such an invitation—but not Joe. I was a rare bird and very few of us exist. I was part of the eighteen percent of women who can climax solely by penetration (needing no additional stimulation). It has to do with anatomy—how a woman is built. When Paulee said, "Joe must be doing something right," it was only partly true. A man should never receive all the credit for making these tweeties sing. It was true, a man had to maintain an erection—one kudo. But a rare bird's satisfaction overall was due more to her clit being very close to her g-spot—not because a man was "doing something right." That was why I had orgasms with Joe so easily (even when I had not wanted to have sex with him, preferring masturbation).

My preference was Joe, not my vibrator, when I returned from Liz's house and asked him for a quickie—and what did he say? "I'm working on this plane right now, Sarah." He chose not to play with me; he preferred playing with tweezers and modeling glue. It pissed me off, and if I hadn't known him better, I might have thought he was hiding in the closet. I could have forgiven him for rejecting me if he was gay, but not to work on a model plane. I stormed down the stairs, went to our bedroom, locked the door and got out my brand new Georgio. A while later Joe knocked on the door.

"Come on, open the door, Sarah. You're acting like a child."

"Go away Joe," (but he would not stop knocking). "I'm not opening the door. I invited you and you refused to come in; you're too late now."

Joe had rejected my residual sexual excitement and it gave me no comfort to think I hadn't been the only one rebuffed. I knew Rocky experienced the same chemical reaction as I did by the way he stared at me, and his voice became throaty when he spoke (as though his testosterone level had suddenly risen). He was faced with the same dilemma. After having seen me he needed to channel his sexual excitement just as much as I had to. I could be magnanimous for Liz's benefit though, happy if she reaped benefits, even if I was left hot and bothered. Seeing Rocky was no guarantee of a positive outcome for me because Joe had to be factored into the equation. I doubted Liz would ever refuse Rocky to work on a model plane.

Paulee believed it was my problem alone, and *this chemistry thing* was one-sided: mine. His stare according to her was a result of me looking strangely at him, and his voice was my imagination. She accused me of threatening my marriage, and said I should stop sending signals to him. She was so harsh and so wrong. I never willingly sent signals to Rocky, but I acknowledged the chemistry between us was risky. That was why I had chosen to act responsibly and limited my exposure to him. He, on the other hand, hot and bothered and well aware of it, had chosen to act irresponsibly. I had tangible examples to prove it—beyond staring and hormone-induced voice modulation. Let's be real, the only reason he became friends with Joe had been to see me more.

I was always suspicious about their friendship; they were unlikely friends. The narrative was their shared interest in golf. "Why is it so strange?" Liz always asked me. I would counter with the significant difference in their personalities. Liz would then say, "opposites attract," or "they complement one another." I was unable to offer my explanation for obvious reasons. She was a good friend and I was partly responsible. Even if it was unintentional, I was throwing pheromones out to her husband. It was the only break I would extend to Rocky. I limited my exposure, while he orchestrated opportunities to be in position to catch as many as possible.

Rocky and Joe belonged to different golf clubs, but they golfed together taking turns playing at each other's club as a guest. When Rocky was the guest, he always came to our house before going to the club. The reason given was so they could go in one car; that was never necessary when it was Joe's turn—he went directly to Rocky's club. I asked Joe about it and he said it was only due to Rocky's work schedule, "what's so 'odd' about it, Sarah?" I never gave voice to reasons why I found it odd or asked any more questions. Rocky was his friend, why ruin the relationship for him? They were only my suspicions, but I could not stop my mind from questioning. And the paramount query—*why did Rocky always arrive at our house early?*

Two times stand out. The first was on a hot summer evening; they were planning to play an early round. Joe's club was only fifteen minutes away yet Rocky showed up an hour before. It was so muggy I had been surprised they even chose to golf, and Joe was complaining as usual about me running the air conditioner too much. I escaped his complaints and the heat by going out on the deck. I was enjoying myself:

smoking grass, drinking wine, and listening to music. There was a little breeze at times too, but it was still sultry. I was wearing my red bikini (the one Joe had always said looked like three postage stamps). It was not meant for public consumption; I only wore it on our deck, which had two privacy fences—one on each side. The deck faced the woods and someone might have seen me if they were walking up from them but it was never a concern. The deck chair was always close enough to the sliding door to go into the house if need be, and it was unlikely anyone would see much from a distance. I never expected someone to approach from the side. That's why I was startled by Rocky coming around the fence on the right.

'Hi, sorry to bother you, Sarah. I knocked on the door but no one answered." I had no idea why Joe had not answered the door, but Rocky was early. Joe was probably in his workroom with music on and didn't hear him. I became tongue-tied, frozen—with my hand suspended in the air holding my joint. I was very cognizant of the fact I was sitting on the lounge chair half-naked. I must have had a terrified look on my face because he said, "Relax, Sarah. I'm not going to arrest you for grass. Liz and I smoke, hasn't she told you? I plan to do it all the time when I retire. Can I have a hit?" It wasn't fear of him arresting me for smoking pot as I sat there in my teeny bikini; it was regret I had not brought a cover-up with me when I came out on the deck. I extended my arm holding the joint, stiffly like a mechanical toy, and after he took it my unease switched—from flesh to arrest. Joe's familiar chorus played in my head—"it's illegal, you seem to forget that, Sarah." How well did I really know this man? Was he trying to entrap me? My fear was short-lived. I saw his gaze traveling up and down my body—confirming my first impression. Arresting me was not what he had in mind.

The next time Rocky showed up too early will always be more memorable. It was on the day Joe went to the hobby store for glue. Once again, Rocky had not been expected for an hour and I was about to step into the shower when I heard the doorbell ring. Joe was always running out of the house leaving his keys and wallet on the table. I thought it was him and he was locked out so I ran to the door with only a towel wrapped around myself. When I flung the door open it wasn't Joe standing there.

"Oh, I guess I caught you at an inconvenient time. You know, you really shouldn't answer your door like that, you never know who it could be." That was certainly an understatement.

"I thought you were Joe." What business was it of his how I answered the damn door anyway? If I wanted to answer it butt naked I would. Was I breaking a law? I guess I sounded even more annoyed than I felt when I told him I thought he was Joe. He responded with an expression on his face which made him look like a chastised little boy.

"Sorry, I don't mean to lecture you. Hazard of the trade, I guess. Sometimes it's hard letting go of the job, you know." He was smiling with those dimples, and his eyes were twinkling. As usual he was undressing me with those eyes—it wouldn't take long that day. I was just as culpable as him though: I had a strong urge to invite him in—open the towel and wrap it around him like Dracula and press myself into his body. That's exactly what I was thinking when he said, "Why aren't you wet?" I was wet, but not in the way he meant. Then I got angry at myself. I couldn't control these hot urges, but I didn't have to entertain thoughts to fuel them. When Joe arrived, and came up to the door, all the irritation at myself got displaced on him.

"Where were you?" I screamed.

"Sarah, honey, I told you I was going to the hobby store and I'd be right back."

"Sorry, man, I guess I got here a little early." (You think?)

"No, problem. We can grab a beer before we leave."

Joe hadn't even seemed to notice (or if he did, to mind): I was standing naked with only a towel wrapped around myself in front of his golfing buddy. They were bantering back and forth, and I quickly left, leaving them at the door. When I reached the staircase, I called out to Joe. I told him I needed to talk to him for a minute. That was not the only thing I needed.

I was being a little dramatic when Joe walked into the bedroom. I opened the towel and let it drop at my feet looking like Aphrodite rising from the foamy sea.

"Joe, honey, do you think we can have a quickie before you leave? I'm randy as hell." Joe did not say a single word in response, and he had this blank look on his face. Less than five minutes ago Rocky was devouring me with his eyes and Joe's were void of emotion, asexual. I thought he was never going to speak, but he finally said, "Sarah, I think you need help." He left the bedroom without one more word to join his golfing buddy downstairs.

CHAPTER 19

THE THERAPY QUESTION

First Paulee, then Joe said I needed therapy. I didn't agree that I needed help because I wanted to have a quickie with him. It was the rage that overtook me when he said it, making me think: perhaps he had a point. He made me feel like an idiot standing there when he refused me. I bet if I had shouted down to Rocky he would have taken me up on the offer. I became so angry; I morphed into a harpy.

My rage scared me; I overreacted to Joe's rejection. Why? Pondering that question had kept me from throwing the nearest object at him, but Joe's hypocrisy had made me livid. How could he say I needed help, with all his sexual hang-ups and contradictions? He made uninhibited love on the dining room table but cringed if I got on top of him. He pushed me off as though I was repulsive. It was hurtful, and he never gave me an explanation for why it bothered him—which hurt even more. His dislike for oral sex (post-marriage) also damaged my self-esteem. I had to finally ask him, "Do I smell down there, Joe?" He replied without hesitation, "No, you always smell sweet, Sarah; it's just me, not you." I appreciated that (better than being told I smelled like a yeasty swamp), but we were still stuck in an emotional stalemate. We needed to clear the air around his damn hang-ups.

Sexually speaking the only thing Joe had been forthright about was why he disliked doggy style. He refused to do it, and disliked to hear or watch any suggestion of it. When we saw it depicted in movies he would say, "It doesn't look sexy to me. It looks more like an assault." I never agreed; it usually looked pretty hot but I kept my opinions to myself because he was always so stern. Knowing his distaste for doggy style I can only imagine how appalled he would have been if I had asked him to perform anal sex. There was no doubt in my mind that he would have been shocked and disgusted.

Anal sex was not a sexual preference for me anyway but not because I thought it was shocking or disgusting. It irritated my hemorrhoids which I developed in my early twenties. When I was diagnosed my mother said, "You're not eating enough fiber, Sarah." I did not think my fiber intake was the issue. I blamed my first vibrator, even though my doctor said it was unlikely it had caused my hemorrhoids. She might be right but I still believe it made me more susceptible.

Paulee asked me "why on earth" I had put a vibrator in my ass. She was confused and a touch grossed out. She is so naive; sex toys are not her thing and she would not put one in any orifice of her body. I have given up trying to convince her about their merits so I did not even approach the topic from that angle.

I simply told her I only tried it once: "I was young, curious, and still in the exploration stage to find out what worked for me sexually. Gay men do it, I figured it must feel good."

Men don't have the same equipment as women, but if anal sex didn't feel good—they would just keep blowing one another. I had the equipment, but when I was a teen I had a fear too—a fear of breaking my hymen. The sex toy I stole from Penny induced clitoral orgasms by stimulating your clit with no penetration. I had fun without fear of popping my cherry. When I bought the vibrator the following year, I had no intention of putting it anywhere but my ass.

I was not the only one concerned about popping cherries. Once we started menstruating my mother took Penny and me to see a gynecologist. Penny called them pussy patrols; our mother's way to check whether we were virgins. I agreed that was one reason, but reminded Penny she also had to admit our mother believed in every recommended preventative-care diagnostic that existed.

The irony was if a malady was found, she usually balked at traditional treatments. She was a nurse and part of her disdain was due to the adversary relationship which existed between many doctors and nurses during most of her career. She was not about to accept their word as gospel. She also genuinely did not like what she saw happening to many people taking prescription meds. I heard her say more than once, "the so-called cure is worse than the disease."

From my earliest memory our mother took us to an acupuncturist. It was not a pleasant experience. I laugh when I hear proponents insist: *the needles don't hurt, they're very small.* There must be different styles and different length needles. The acupuncturist we went to used very big needles and it was very painful. Penny could not wait until she was emancipated and found a doctor—"who uses pills," and a gynecologist of her own choosing.

Mom took us to her doctor for the yearly gynecological examinations, and no matter what her motivation was, I never wanted Dr. Bradley to say, "Mrs. Larssen, I am sorry to tell you, but it seems your daughter Sarah's hymen is not intact." Mom had suspicions about me because of the crowd I hung out with, and refused to waste time speculating. She frequently asked directly, "Are you having full-blown sex, Sarah?" Her choice of words was surprising, being a devotee of Dr. Ruth. That's why I answered, "If you mean intercourse Mom, no." I never lied to her so she believed me, but that did not dissuade her from leaving pamphlets about STDs around the house. She imagined I was doing something that warranted it, and if Dr. Bradley had made even the slightest suggestion that I was not a virgin, she would have grounded me until college. I disliked the yearly visits, like most females do no matter what their age, but when I was a teen I was not afraid of Dr. Bradley's scrutiny. As long as I continued to use only my fingers and the Magic Clit Puff my virginity would never be in question.

Once I knew Penny was a lesbian, I questioned why she had been more upset about the examinations than me. She certainly would have had less broken-hymen stress. I theorized it was because it was a male doctor, but it's still puzzling. Dr. Bradley had been very old, asexual and nonthreatening; a little dotty too. He always mixed up our names and wore very thick glasses—he was blind as a bat. I'm surprised he was able to find our pussies. He even wore a little light on his head which made him look like he was going into a coal mine—I found him amusing. It made the whole experience more bearable.

I was not unduly upset by the yearly visits like my sister, and I had a healthy appreciation of my sexuality as a teen. I only had one troubling experience—when I experimented with self-anal sex using the vibrator; I cut myself drawing a little blood. It scared me, and in retrospect I had overreacted. It was not a serious injury, but fear made me seek advice and comfort. I preferred not to go to my mother, favoring Penny with my concerns. That was the day she accused me of stealing her sex toy, and I hadn't even hurt myself with her Magic Clit Puff. But she wasn't very sympathetic or helpful. "That's what you get for putting things up your ass, Sarah," and she called me "a little pervert."

I reminded her recently what she called me and she denied it. She insisted that she had never called anyone a "pervert" in her life, and could not believe I would accuse a lesbian of talking that way. She recalled my injured bum but said "there is no way" she would use "such derogatory language." Nice to know she no longer thinks I'm one, but maybe she has a selective memory or some unresolved issues concerning LGBTQ lifestyles—and needs therapy. Which brings me back to the therapy question and Joe's hang-ups.

One evening we were watching a movie which depicted a scene where it wasn't clear whether the male lead was penetrating his lover's ass or entering her vagina from behind (Joe's detested doggy style). As usual Joe became agitated, and complained about it looking like an assault; I did not agree (it was rated R, not porn). The director wanted to show two consenting adults enjoying themselves—to titillate us, not disturb us (it was not the rape scene from *Irreversible*).

The complaint I have about watching these kinds of scenes is that they often make me lose track of the storyline. When the acting is too believable or graphic I often get horny and want to do it myself, or I start to ponder about the actors. Was it really them or body stand-ins, or were they having an affair in real life? Either way—horny or questioning—I stop paying attention to the movie. It was not clear what bothered Joe, but steamy sex scenes always distracted him. Making it too difficult for him to follow the arc of the story? Who knew, but he did at least lighten up a bit after the scene was finished that evening. It was still obvious he was thinking about doggy style though when he said, "Besides I like seeing your face."

I have no aversion to the position, it affords deep penetration, but I agreed with him on that point. I also prefer to see the person's face I'm having intercourse with, and thanks to my anatomy I don't need doggy style to achieve complete sexual satisfaction. I had needed Joe to open up more for my complete emotional satisfaction.

Joe being stingy with his feelings about sex was not a simple annoyance; it wasted time. When it came to our relationship I spent too much of it asking: *did Joe read something in our wedding vows that I overlooked?* His duplicity bothered me since we were married. I never realized how much until the afternoon I asked him for a quickie while Rocky waited in our foyer. The depth of my fury shocked me, but I learned something about myself. I often overreacted when I was angry with him over any little annoyance. I never had a clue why until I thought about it that day. When I screamed at Joe because he forgot to take the garbage to the trash—it was not about banana peels, it was about sex. I had repressed my anger; I had not completely shaken off the feeling of having been misled. I married a very different man than the one I had courted. I needed help, but I was not the only one. We both needed it.

When Joe returned from golfing I told him I thought therapy was a good idea—for both of us. He didn't agree.

"I'm fine, but if you want to talk to someone go ahead. I won't stop you. But I'm not gonna talk to some stranger about my life, Sarah. It just isn't me, okay? They're a bunch of quacks. Everyone knows those people are attracted to the field because they need help themselves."

If I hadn't read in the last self-help book, "you can't change someone else, you can only change your reaction to them," I might have continued trying to persuade him—but I had—so I didn't. I was really irritated by his dismissal though. Enough to review the tips on how to change my reactions when engaging with *pig-headed* people (my paraphrase).

Re-reading the chapter helped deal with the therapy irritation but did not lessen my annoyance over the forty-nine-dollar oral sex simulator rated triple A. It was advertised as having been tested by women across the country. Who were these women in their focus group? And whoever they were it was clear they never had a man go down on them—the oral sex simulator was a piece of junk. I planned to ask Joe to reimburse me if they refused to give me a refund, which was fair; if he had engaged in the practice I would never have been duped into purchasing it (just like I had been duped into the marriage, necessitating therapy).

It would have been better if Joe had agreed to seek counseling along with me. The problems in our relationship were shared, not mine alone. But that did not dissuade me from seeking it for myself, and I had not even been sure I was ready to openly explore some problems with Joe present. They concerned family planning and birth control.

I had wanted to have my tubes tied. I was tired of using my diaphragm and did not want more children, but Joe had wanted another baby. That was complicated enough but he said the ultimate choice of having another child was mine. That had made it worse. He was so damn nice about it, and I was so damn sneaky. I had been downright Machiavellian if I were completely honest. Joe thought all the sex we had throughout the house and on every piece of furniture we could light upon was unplanned. He was surprised I hadn't gotten pregnant, "I think you should lay off the dope, Sarah." I kept mum, and he had no idea that our relations were far from impulsive or carefree; they were calculated ambushes which I masterminded. I was culpable—my diaphragm was always securely in place without Joe's knowledge. I knew pot had nothing to do with my lack of fertility, but I was never honest and simply said, "I don't want another kid, Joe." I feared my admission would damper Joe's enthusiasm which I worked so hard to stoke. I had not been ready to fess that up in couple therapy.

My deception was shameful, and it was not the only guilt trip I was riding or refused to get off by the time we had reached this destination. The other had nothing to do with procreation but concerned our sexual practices and it was an expensive ticket price to ride. When I justified my actions to Paulee—"I only do it to enhance our lovemaking," it was hard to convince myself let alone her. It's not surprising, I was not putting much love in the mix. I used sex-deprivation to arouse the beast in Joe.

I would feign a stomach ache or another malady for at least five days. After I *recovered*, Joe was enthusiastic and energetic, and there was no measurable difference in his performance compared to surprise ambushes. But there was an unexpected and unwanted effect. After I had used stomach aches too often, Joe was concerned for my health: "Don't you think you should go see a doctor or do something?" Deprivation had made our sex life better but at what price—if one measured my negative accountability?

Using deprivation as an arousal technique was awful enough, but when I remembered how I used it for thirteen months I felt even worse. I had been too wrapped up with pregnancy and my own sexual frustration to appreciate what I was doing to Joe. It must have driven him mad; I now saw how he suffered after only five days. But he never became angry with me for refusing to have sex. My errant behavior kept piling up like cow dung when I thought about his pain, but I continued to inflict it—even if only for short periods of time.

There was a clear and simple reason why I never stopped—it worked; and it was not only about releasing the beast in Joe. Sometimes I yearned to make love on a bed instead of a table or against the wall; surprise ambushes were never effective in our bedroom. It's also important to note that there was a mitigating factor: it took only five days for Joe—*to be ripe for the picking*; the sentiment boys in high school thought drooling over me. They were never allowed to pick, but

I had no restrictions. I would snuggle up to Joe and whisper in his ear, "I don't have a stomach ache anymore." How about that for erotic talk in the bedroom? It may not sound erotic but Joe would immediately rise to the occasion. Most men can get hard if a soft breeze touches them.

It's the way men are wired, according to my mother. Even baby boys have erections when you change their diapers. I was thirteen and horrified when I was first made aware of that while babysitting for Mrs. Anderson's baby. Had I done something wrong? Or was there something wrong with Timmy? He was years away from puberty. My mother assured me it was perfectly normal and she should know, she worked in the pediatric wing of a hospital for years. Joe was no baby, but he was usually just as easy to arouse—unless I was competing with a model plane or golf. Arousal is only the first step in the process and Joe ignored a hard-on if he made a deliberate choice to do so. It was more difficult of course after a long time doing without— shining light again on the part I played in his distress. But I refused to stop refusing sex when it worked to my advantage, or admit my culpability to Joe.

When I considered all of these dynamics, I decided finding my own therapist was preferable to couple counseling, even if Paulee said it was "self-serving" where the martial issues were concerned. I suppose that was true, but it wasn't like I hadn't told Joe he needed therapy. There was also another reason I needed personal help exclusive of Joe—my creative block.

I had finished all my coursework for my PhD program, but now I was stuck. I could not find topics for my dissertations. I only had two more years before my time would be up. If I were unable to finish I'd be a candidate forever. Would they even call me a PhD candidate if I never completed my dissertations? I didn't know. The only thing I knew was all my enterprise and our money was wasted if I had nothing to show for it. I had to break out of this block. I was stymied and reduced to writing stupid jokes, like challenging Euclid's fourth axiom—parts that intersect with one another are equal. My punchline was: *Joe and I have been intersecting for years and our parts aren't equal.*

I could not come up with serious topics; and the more I couldn't formulate ideas the more I was annoyed and frightened until my creative juices were completely blocked. I was chain-smoking cigarettes now in addition to increasing my pot use and Joe complained about the house smelling like a dirty ashtray. Former smokers complain the most; he told me he quit cold turkey and never had a relapse. His resolve was stronger than mine—I couldn't stop.

I needed professional help and more specific than what I found in self-help books. I didn't regret having spent the money on them; they were useful and held many truths. I had found practical information that I applied to my life but books were no longer a viable remedy. Besides, I had finally finished reading all of them, although it took me five years to do it. When you are in graduate school and have a family it's hard to find time to read anything, other than a textbook or *Harold and the Purple Crayon*.

Even though I needed more personal streamlined advice, I remained a proponent of self-help books; I continue today to recommend the baby book I read when Rosie was an infant—it was right on the mark. It was a shame Joe had resisted and we hadn't applied its useful information, which brings me to Rosie at age seven; she was another reason why I sought professional counseling. She should have been a shared problem and not one I had to address alone, but Joe was in denial. He would not listen when she was a baby and refused to listen when she was seven. She was a spoiled brat, and I blamed him for it. I needed outside objective intervention dealing with my daughter because I received no help from her father.

Once I decided to seek help (and not because Paulee or Joe had told me I needed it) I began my search for a counselor or therapist. I did not want a local practitioner due to confidentiality concerns. Counselors and doctors always say they won't share your information, but they're human (just like educators). I recalled teachers at the high school where I had worked who shared sensitive information about their students—when the policy forbade it. I had been culpable of it myself when I occasionally told Joe something that should have remained only between parents, administrators and myself. Joe had probably paid no attention, but that was not the point. I imagined choosing a therapist blindly, ignorant of the fact that he or she was the spouse of one of Joe's buddies at his flight club. Was it really a far reach to dismiss a casual conversation between my therapist and their spouse: "Janak, I have a client with that surname. Is he married? What's his wife's name?"

I wanted a counselor outside of my area, which made me think of Liz. She lived in Belmar but continued to travel to doctors in Lawrenceville, New Jersey, where she grew up. Lawrenceville and its surrounding areas would work for me. It was far enough away from Jackson and people who knew me. I estimated the miles from my house to the therapist I chose, and based on my calculations dismissed my concerns about confidentiality. I forgot Joe's flying club was in Robbinsville (the club was only twenty minutes from the therapist's office). My error was an overlooked bad omen in retrospect, but I didn't have any premonitions.

CHAPTER 20

CAROL ANNE CLARKSON, LSW

had no idea what a therapy session was like, only those depicted in films or books. Would she have me lie down on a couch? Probably not, after all she wasn't a psychiatrist, she was a social worker. Social workers don't do that. But I was not sure, for all I knew psychiatrists did not ask you to lie on a couch either (except those fictional ones in films and books). Whatever her style might be, it was not a good idea if she asked me to lie down. After my long drive I was sleepy, not to suggest I was relaxed about this appointment. I was nervous to be perfectly frank. The idea of talking to a stranger about my problems made me apprehensive. Face-to-face was more challenging than reading books where there was a separation. One only had to identify with the text and consider the advice—I had been in control. Perhaps that's the reason the self-help sections in bookstores are so big.

I had no trouble finding where her practice was located. My GPS led me right there with no re-routing or unanticipated surprises. I wasn't surprised until she ushered me into her office. I had expected a room with a wall of books, and perhaps a plant or two for decoration. I hadn't anticipated walking into a mini atrium. It looked more like a room I'd find in a home rather than in an office complex. The shelves and desk were covered with numerous plants, pictures and little mementos but there wasn't a single book. She did have a couch though, but it looked a little too small to lie down on. The second big surprise was a rocking chair next to the couch. While it was one of the most eye-catching features of the room, I also noticed a chair and a small table with a box of tissues strategically set on top—within easy reach no matter where one sat. When I saw it I thought: do people often break down and cry? Dissatisfaction and frustration had driven me to see a therapist, and I doubted that I would ever need to wipe tears from my eyes. I also found her office to be comforting.

As soon as I walked in she made a sweeping gesture towards the couch and rocking chair, and told me to sit anywhere I'd like. She told me I could call her Carol Anne or Mrs. Clarkson, whichever one I preferred. I loved rocking chairs so that's where I chose to sit, and I was no longer feeling nervous when I said, "Thanks, Carol Anne." She projected a very welcoming persona, one that made me feel less anxious. Being able to put your clients at ease is a necessary asset for anyone in this profession, as much as experience and training. I had no idea how old she was when I talked to her on the phone, but I was happy to see she was an older woman.

I would have been uncomfortable with someone my age or younger; it was a little complicated but I was cognizant of my reasons for it. If she had been a younger woman I would have kept asking myself—why is she able to get it together at her age and I can't? I did not want a competitive thread creeping into my sessions. I was already upset with myself enough for not having completed my PhD. I had not wanted a constant reminder of it by working with someone my age who had theirs.

Carol Anne looked older than my mother, who was in her early-sixties. Was it because she had salt and pepper hair? I wasn't sure, but she also had a stern look in repose that lent a more matronly look to her countenance. If I had not known she was a therapist, I would have presumed she was a grammar school principal. A fair and kind one, but her demeanor suggested she would not tolerate nonsense. It had not been off-putting; I was no kid.

She asked me to tell her a little about myself. I had done a bit of this over the phone when I initially made the appointment, but I was happy to tell her again: "I've been married for eight years and have one daughter, who just turned seven." My PhD candidacy in mathematics was new information, and it really grabbed her attention. She started asking me questions: had it been hard to get accepted into the program? Was it a four-or six-year program? How did my state school compare to private universities? Etc., etc.? Therapists need to know their clients but twenty minutes into our session we had only discussed graduate programs for mathematics. Carol Anne had not gathered any more information about me. I wasn't going to complain yet, but for a fee of one hundred and sixty-five dollars out of network, I hoped she would soon move to the objective of the session.

Finally she asked why I was seeking counseling. I told her: I had some issues with my husband I wanted to work on, concerns about my daughter being a spoiled brat, and was experiencing a creative block writing my dissertations. If it had been left up to her to pick what we would work on first, without a doubt—it would have been my creative block. She surprised me when she asked, "What would you like to talk about today?" She let me choose.

Rosie was first to come to mind due to an incident that occurred a couple of hours prior. She had been pestering me for another popsicle, which was annoying in itself, but more so than usual because I wanted to give her an early supper before I left; Joe and I were eating after I returned. I refused to change my plan and chose to ignore her whining. I was only upstairs a short time after our ice pop tussle, and when I came downstairs Joe and Rosie were watching the Cinderella DVD—Rosie was multitasking. I yelled her name; she quickly turned with no hesitancy and gave me a big grin. Her face was stained blue all around her lips, like a clown—but she failed to make me laugh.

"Rosie, I told you no more popsicles before dinner."

"Daddy gave it to me."

"Joe, why did you give her one?"

"I thought we were eating at eight."

"We are eating at eight, she is eating right now."

"Well, no harm done. It's just a little one. She's having her dessert first, okay, and they're fruit, right?" Had Joe seriously believed any fruit would produce that royal blue color? Or that it was—*okay*? I began to elaborate my position on this and Carol Anne interrupted me.

"Well, I see by the clock we have to stop for today. We can continue this conversation at our next session. Would you like to make an appointment for next week?"

My answer was yes, without heartfelt enthusiasm, I had not been sure I wanted another appointment. I did not feel better after the first one. I had felt worse, all worked up after relaying my story about Rosie. The nice comfortable feeling rocking in my chair at the start had been lost.

I was no longer optimistic about the value of talk therapy. After one session, I not only had marital problems, concerns about Rosie, and a creative block—I now worried about wasting money; graduate school had cost us a load. I could have told Paulee or Liz what I shared with Carol Anne and saved one hundred and sixty-five dollars. So why did I make a second appointment? I took a serious look at my options: it was true I was able to talk about Rosie with them, but it was also true talking with Liz and Paulee had limitations—especially when it concerned my sex life.

I never talked specifics about that with Liz for obvious reasons—her husband indirectly played a very active role in mine. I was a little uncomfortable when she talked about hers with me too. It was too titillating; imagining what she described made me more hot and bothered about Rocky.

Even sharing my intimacies in general, not sexually related, was problematic. I needed to watch out what I said to her on any topic because Rocky and Joe were buddies. Their friendship was not only bizarre and suspect, it created an unwanted dynamic in my relationship with Liz. I learned that when Joe found out about my involvement with Las Vegas. It did not always stay there.

Liz's boys and my Rosie were around eleven months when she started going to Las Vegas to sing in a club to cover for a singer on vacation. It was only for a week but it took some maneuvering. She told Rocky she was visiting her parents in Florida because she believed he would not have been supportive. She asked me to pick her up at her house and would tell Rocky I was driving her to the airport. I was actually taking her to pick up a rental car. The first year she drove with her twins all the way to Las Vegas, and I thought she was taking a real risk. I told her she needed to keep checking in with me during her drive or otherwise I would contact Rocky. I was concerned about her safety and nervous about helping her, but I got a vicarious thrill (same as when Dee shoplifted).

Liz drove to Vegas with her twins only for the first year. After that she drove to her parents, left her kids with them in Florida, and from there took a plane to

Vegas. I could never imagine driving those distances with two toddlers, or lying to my husband about doing it. She was a bigger risk taker than me and I continued to worry about her, but after a couple of years I became desensitized, convinced she would be fine. The vicarious thrill was gone. It was just a yearly routine, and no longer momentous—until Joe questioned me one evening.

"When did you take Liz to the airport?"

"What are you talking about?"

"Rocky told me you drove Liz to the airport. When did you do that?"

His questions made me realize this was no vicarious joy ride, I was actively involved. I always made the analogy that doing this for Liz was like looking at Dee's pilfered items when I was a teen. I was experiencing a thrill watching them behave in outlandish ways. I was not doing anything wrong myself. I had drawn the wrong analogy; a more accurate picture was me driving a getaway car for Dee—I was helping Liz drive away. When Joe questioned me I could not entrench myself more by lying to him, even if Liz was my friend. But I tried to mitigate the situation.

"Please promise me you won't tell this to Rocky."

"I'm not promising anything until I know what's going on." Why did he always have to have such a high moral compass? It would not have been to my advantage to ask that question, and I chose to tell him the entire story. He was surprised I had allowed myself to get entangled in "this deception," and he refused to lie to Rocky.

"I don't want any part of this, Sarah."

It was hopeless; once Joe set his mind on something he was an immovable rock, but I was able to at least persuade him to not volunteer information. If Rocky asked him again, he would tell him everything, but he agreed not to initiate the topic. He "hoped in return I would stop helping Liz deceive her husband."

He only said "hoped in return." It wasn't like his silence had been contingent upon my not helping Liz again in her ruse. I reminded myself of that every time Liz and I were naughty girls that I had to help her, especially when I considered Rocky. She told me he never wanted her to sing in clubs because guys would hit on her. Apparently it was alright for him to hit on women. I had no proof Rocky had ever cheated on her. But I am pretty sure if I encouraged him even in the slightest way, he would have an affair with me—without a second's thought for her or his buddy Joe.

I also have so much respect for Liz's passion to sing. It's so strong, and she had only wanted to sing for one lousy week each year. She had been willing to take risks, lie to her husband and drive for hours alone on the interstate to do it. I complained when I had to drive over 30 minutes for my passion to teach.

I don't know if Joe and Rocky ever discussed the rides I gave Liz *to the airport* again. If Joe had asked I would have told the truth, but I never volunteered information. Liz eventually stopped lying to Rocky about her yearly gig but the cautionary reminder remained moving forward. I had to think very carefully about what I did and shared with Liz since our husbands talked to one another. I could not be as open with her like I was with Paulee.

Even though I can share more with Paulee she was not someone I could rely on entirely either. There were also limitations to what I could speak about due to another problematic factor—Paulee's friendship with Joe. We talked about our sex lives frequently, but I couldn't complain about him—she is not objective; she always defends him. And she will always stay friends with him even if I were completely removed from the equation; unlike his so-called friends who left when he and his girlfriend Maureen split up. That would never happen with Paulee. While there is no doubt in my mind she will always be Joe's friend, sometimes I wonder if she feels as strongly about our friendship. But I had needed more than a girlfriend when I was considering options. I needed someone objective with no allegiances to Joe or me.

Driving to my second appointment I had not been confident Carol Anne was that someone. The only thing I was sure of—she was not friends with Joe, and I assumed she was not close to anyone who was; still ignorant of the distance between Ewing and Joe's flying club. If I had been cognizant of it, I would not have been sure about anything. Ignorance really is bliss, so I was willing to give her one more go—hoping for the best.

At our second session we continued our conversation about Rosie. I use the word *conversation* because Carol Anne would interrupt me at times for clarification or interject her ideas—she was listening and participating—my hopes expanded. Talking to Carol Anne might be more beneficial than venting to friends (even friends with less limitations than Liz and Paulee). I had Carol Anne's full attention when I told her I found myself screaming at Rosie all the time; so much that I was not enjoying my own daughter's childhood. I was *the bad cop*.

There wasn't a true bad cop/good cop framework to describe Joe and me—he had refused to assume a role. He undermined me constantly though, leaning good, and it often appeared like he had deliberately chosen not to work with me. If I told Rosie she couldn't have another treat, or the toy she saw in the store, or to finish her homework before going outside, Joe disregarded my wishes. He gave her the treat, bought the toy and let her go out to play, and he always had the same defense: "I didn't know you already said no, Sarah." I never doubted his sincerity, but also knew he gave her what she wanted most of the time; it was no surprise she was spoiled. When I told him that, his other favorite response was "She's a good kid." He has been oblivious to most of Rosie's negative behavior for her entire life, and he had never seen his "good kid" when she heard *no* because the word never crossed his lips.

I told Carol Anne Joe was never present when I had said no, amassing screams, cries, and sometimes even more menacing behavior. Once trying to remove her from the car she tried to bite me; she was not successful. I guess I had been lucky if it was true that human bites are more serious than dog bites. Joe had infuriated me when he responded, "Maybe, you're exaggerating a little?"

I had no bite marks or bruises for evidence—only tales to tell. When I gave him a very detailed description of an altercation in a supermarket where Rosie kicked over a display stand, his response had been as irritating as Rosie's tantrum. He said she was probably tired or not feeling well. "When I take her out to golf with me she's an angel the entire time. I don't know what to say, Sarah."

I knew what to say but I stopped trying, and I had Rosie's MO. She kept herself in check when he was present because there was no need to act out. Daddy was there—he always made sure she got what she wanted. And that's why I wasn't surprised by his tale of her being an "angel" when they golfed.

We introduced Rosie to golf as a family outing at Ship Ahoy miniature golf course when she was three. When she turned five Joe wanted to teach her for real at his club. I was surprised they sold golf clubs for a five-year-old, but Joe said he could have bought them for a three-year-old. He had been able to control his enthusiasm. She received her set as a present from Daddy on her fifth birthday. I watched her first lesson but opted out on subsequent golf trips. I figured it would be a good bonding experience for them without me, not that they needed more glue.

They've had a strong connection since her infancy. Rosie loved her daddy, but I was never convinced that she loved golf. Every time they played Joe would buy her ice cream and pizza and a toy at the clubhouse store. That was the reason why she had been "an angel the entire time." I was honest with Joe, and had no qualms at all admitting golf bored me to distraction. But if he had promised dinner at a fancy restaurant or bought me expensive jewelry to play—I would be an angel on the fairway too.

I thought my examples for Carol Anne had been clear, but I wasn't sure. After hearing me she said it sounded more like a parental problem rather than one stemming directly from Rosie. I understood how Joe was a factor, but a *parental problem*? I was the cop, not the spoiler. She had to explain more fully: "Rosie's behavior is a result of the parental relationship opposed to some innate flaw in the child, and she appears to be a smart little girl." The latter was not a revelation, I was cognizant of that. Rosie knew if she asked her father she'd get what she wanted, even if I had already said no. The ideas that were new: I was only frustrating myself by getting angry for no purpose blaming a seven-year-old for this behavior. We had trained her to act this way.

"She's only doing what a seven-year-old will do who has not been given any boundaries." She told me Joe and I had to sit down together and negotiate the terms of those boundaries before I could hope for any change in Rosie's behavior. I was willing to try but I wasn't so sure about Joe.

He surprised me, but he could be unpredictable just like his sex-preference shift post-marriage. That surprise had been unwelcome but his willingness to listen about Rosie was a positive change. Especially since he continued to insist she was "a good little angel," and accused me of exaggerating. It's not that he didn't believe my tales about her, he just thought I had embellished them for dramatic effect. And I had been willing to accept his *drama queen* label because he agreed to try some strategies suggested by Carol Anne.

New rule: if the little angel asked Joe for something, before he bestowed it, he would first ask his little cherub, "What did Mommy say?" He agreed to follow my lead and it was heavenly—Rosie's behavior improved. The shine on her halo was short lasting—she started lying to him. The usual punishment when we caught her was to send her to her room. Joe would not fight me on it but he could be more annoying than she was. Every five minutes he would ask, "Don't you think she's been up there long enough?"

"No Joe, we should wait at least until she stops crying." He agreed but still continued to question the length of time out. His nagging bothered me more than her crying until I reminded myself: at least we were communicating and if we continued to negotiate as partners on how to raise Rosie my annoyance was a small consequence to suffer. And Joe hasn't changed, to this day he cannot handle hearing her cry.

It was a challenge; Rosie was seven and she had not been spoiled overnight—the layers ran deep. That intelligence of hers also made it more complicated. When lying no longer worked she figured out a simple solution—she asked her father before me. After she adopted a direct route I became nonessential; if I was by-passed it was not necessary to lie. Joe failed to see how this new tactic worked for her but not for us.

"What happened to 'what did Mommy say,' Joe?"

"She asked me, Sarah. Why does she have to ask you too as long as she asks one of us?" Had he really been serious?

Rosie's new game-change: she got what she wanted and orchestrated a power play between her parents. Her new strategy had a weakness though because Joe worked full time. I was the principal wish-granter by default due to my proximity. He still managed to give her more things than did her any good, beyond whatever she might request from me. I could not keep count of how many Barbies lived on our living room floor. I had been so exasperated one morning after stepping on a little high heel shoe with my bare foot that I screamed at him: "Stop trying to buy your daughter's love, Joe."

I hurt him when I said it. Rosie loved him and it had nothing to do with toys or treats. I shouldn't have said it but my foot hurt and sometimes I just lost it. I walked it back when my emotions were more tempered. I rephrased my intention more constructively.

"She has to learn she can't get everything she wants, Joe. If she grows up thinking she can, she's going to be a very unhappy adult when reality sets in." Joe is a realist, he knew what I said was true, and he tried to restrain himself but bad habits are hard to admit to or break. He denied that he gave her everything she wanted—"I don't buy her a toy every time we play golf, Sarah." It might have been true, but he probably doubled up on the ice cream and pizza.

It took several appointments to work on the *Rosie concern*, and continues to be a work in progress. But the advice and suggestions Carol Anne made when Rosie was seven were helpful, especially after understanding that it was a parental problem; Joe and I had to work together. I screamed less at my daughter after Carol Anne's help, and redirected my drive to negotiating with Joe. Rosie behaved as she did because of us, and the onus was not totally on Joe alone as I had always thought. It wasn't totally my fault either—I hadn't given birth to the devil's spawn as I had secretly feared.

Carol Anne had been very helpful with Rosie over-all, with one exception—*the interloper problem*. She didn't ask me to elaborate or offer a single piece of advice concerning Rosie disturbing Joe and me when we made love. Rosie had interrupted us consistently when we were in our bedroom; admittedly we seldom made love there but it annoyed me when we did. It's important to add a salient point—we never made loud noises to wake her. It also seemed to be calculated on her part: she never fell asleep, and waited for the oppor-tune moment. Joe scoffed at me when I gave him my take; he insisted we were making noise and disturbed her. Suggesting we needed to be quieter had been nuts.

Joe was always quiet, out of or in bed. I was the noisy lover during our courtship but grew quiet after we married. I practiced silent climaxing. I developed the skill in the early years of my marriage, and I became quite adept at it. I didn't want to express bodily sensations audibly, it ran counter to the wishes of my head. It was a curious reversal from that of women who faked orgasms—I tried to hide I was having one. I did not want to give Joe the satisfaction because I was angry about his weird sex rules. He seemed to always know when I came in spite of my efforts but that did not stop me from doing it, and after Rosie was born it was a useful skill to maintain. There was no way I had awakened her. I had perfected my technique to stifle any lovemaking sounds.

My mouth opened but I pushed my scream or moan right down to my belly button. I made no noise at all, but it was like Rosie had a sixth sense. She knew exactly when I was about to climax. Only seconds away—I was thrown from the precipice by a little voice at the door:

"Daddy, can you get me a glass of water?"

I doubt that Joe would have been able to stop if he had been at the same point as me in the ascending excitement. It's a presumption; I can't be positive, not having a man's body. I don't know how it feels for a man building to a climax—is there a point of no return? The only thing I know empirically is that Joe always stopped. I felt him deflate right inside me—like a balloon with its air being let out. I became so angry at him for stopping one night that I took my fists and beat him on his shoulders as hard as I could.

"Why are you stopping, damn it?"

"She might be sick or something, Sarah."

"She wants a damn glass of water, Joe."

I told Carol Anne l was an awful mother when I did that. What kind of a mother doesn't want to run to her child in need? Carol Anne made no comment.

It wasn't like it was an emergency, right? Rosie hadn't been sick or scared. Had I truly been a bad mother because I wanted Joe to keep making love to me? No comment again.

I could not let go; I yearned for feedback. I posed a final question—was this a nascent dynamic, symptomatic of some kind of mother/daughter rivalry between Rosie and me? The only reply was silence, and this time it had felt like an assault to my senses.

It was disturbing how Carol Anne refused to utter a word. I left her office feeling like a narcissist. When I returned home I asked Joe if he thought I was a good mother.

"You're a great mother, Sarah, why do you ask?"

"Oh, just something that happened with Carol Anne today was making me feel maybe I wasn't."

"Well, if she said that she's nuts. I told you they were quacks."

Joe expressed positive feelings about my mothering skills, but I made sure to spend more time with Rosie just in case I was a little weak in some areas. I played with her more, and read her two stories every night after that face-to-face with Carol Anne. Reading stories to Rosie had been my domain, not Joe's. I was the more proactive parent when it came to reading children's books. I tried to be a good mother.

I would ponder over that session for a long time until it crossed my mind—perhaps Carol Anne had not said anything because it was another parental problem. She went over that already; I needed to apply new strategies from previously learned knowledge.

Number one: I suggested to Joe we leave Rosie's ducky cup in her room at night; if she wanted water she'd have it. It would help her learn to be more self-sufficient. She could keep it right on her night table next to her *Cow Jumps Over the Moon* table lamp.

Number two: we should find a greeting card with a heart on it, and let Rosie cut it out. I'd hang it outside our bedroom door when we were making love. We would tell Rosie not to disturb Mommy and Daddy when she saw it on the door—unless it was a real emergency. It was a possible solution for the bedroom, but a different one was needed for when we were doing it on the dining room table or against the kitchen wall. But maybe that wasn't necessary or even relevant. She only interrupted us when we were in the bedroom.

Joe agreed to both of my suggestions but not without irritation as usual. He had a problem with the heart. He said I was being "sexually suggestive" and Rosie was old enough to understand what it implied. "Why not let her pick her own picture?" I had an urge to ask my own question: Are you from another planet? I replied instead, "Joe, it's a heart, you act like I'm suggesting a picture of animals fucking."

In retrospect the question about his origins would have been preferable; I shouldn't have been vulgar. Joe hated it when I was but he could be so weird sometimes. It didn't matter what picture was hung on the door as long as it sent the same message—"Do Not Disturb." And now he had annoyed me by saying I was "sexually suggestive" using a heart cut-out. Debating with him was a turn off—it made me seriously question if I even wanted to have sex with him.

Rosie had not been privy to our domestic drama over cut-outs; she picked a giraffe—a single one, without a mate in sight to copulate with. There was nothing suggestive about her choice but a giraffe will always be an erotic symbol for me.

After the problem was resolved with *coitus interruptus a la Rosie* in the bedroom, I don't know why I couldn't shake off the residue of Carol Anne's behavior. Why had she acted like that? Or more precisely—not acted? Was it really because it was a parental problem she was not wanting to expound upon again? I spent some time thinking about it before I formed a new insight. This was not an isolated behavior. Every time I had made any reference to sex Carol Anne seemed uneasy and clammed up. When she had done it before I assumed she thought

I was going off on a tangent (which I admit I have a tendency to do sometimes), and it was her way to keep me on task. I was taught a similar technique: to simply not speak and stand gazing at an unruly class to grab their attention. But once they were quiet, I did speak—that's where I and Carol Anne had changed course. What was the issue with Carol Anne? I formed a number of theories, and I knew musing over Carol Anne was a clever way to procrastinate; I was avoiding my dissertation work—but I could not stop. She was almost as addictive as cigarettes. I had to re-read her webpage.

I read it closely, more than when I first considered contacting her. I ultimately came to the conclusion that my theory about sex was wrong; it was not a topic I needed to avoid, if germane to our discussion. Digressing and my over-active imagination were the problems. She wasn't a sex therapist per se, but she should not be uncomfortable discussing sexual topics. She worked with couples; those kinds of problems had to come up with her clients on occasion. Don't couples fight the most over money and sex?

When I had first read Carol Anne's webpage I thought she was a perfect fit for me because her practice was for singles, families, and couples. She had experience dealing with all my concerns: singles-with career problems (like me and my dissertation block); families (I needed help with my spoiled brat); and couples (for my problems with Joe). After re-reading the webpage I was convinced even more she was the right therapist for me which enabled me to form a conclusion. When Carol Anne clammed up she was not having a good day; she had no will to respond. It wasn't very professional—especially for a therapist, but she was only human. There were days I checked out when teaching too; nobody is perfect.

I was confident that working on my dysfunctional marriage would not be a challenge for her. My discontent with Joe had not even been paramount on my agenda at that point in time—problems with him could wait. My dissertations and creative block were on the forefront of my mind.

Carol Anne asked me to describe my actions when I worked on my dissertations, starting with where I was physically and what time of day. I told her I set a regular time after Rosie went to school on Tuesdays and Thursdays (the two days I didn't teach), and I began immediately after cleaning up the breakfast dishes. I had a little desk in my bedroom where I worked. Or to be more precise, where I sat staring at a blank piece of paper or my computer screen. I simply could not come up with any good ideas, which in turn stressed me out necessitating the need to smoke a joint. Pot worked to calm me but it also made me sleepy. I needed to drink a cup of coffee and smoke a cigarette for a boost of energy, and before I knew it—the morning was gone. I had laundry and housework to do, papers to correct, and decisions to make about dinner before Rosie and Joe came home. I had no more time to work on my dissertations—I had wasted another day. Carol Anne did not waste time commiserating with me and got right to the point.

"Why do you work in your bedroom?" Following her lead I was succinct.

"That's where I keep my pot." When I said that her face became stern. She looked like that grammar school principal again—the same expression I picked up on when I first met her, but more annoyed. I have experienced similar negative reactions from other people in the past. Joe is always warning me to stop talking about smoking pot to people "all the time." I never receive any sympathy from him, only admonishments: "You're breaking the law, Sarah." He has a point, but he is wrong about me talking to people "all the time." I am very selective to whom I share the information but one can never be sure about reactions, even with close friends. But I don't share with random people, and Carol Anne was not random. She was my therapist. Shouldn't one be open with their therapist? How can a therapist help if we are not truthful about what we do and think? I knew that from reading the last chapter in one of my self-help books: "Tips to get the Most Out of Your Counseling Sessions." But I did not have to worry for long about misspeaking that day, Carol Anne quickly interrupted my thoughts: "You did one thing right."

I was impressed with myself that I had done at least one thing right since I had zero results so far for my efforts. She told me setting aside a regular time was good. Patting myself on the back was short-lived; she followed with the many things I needed to change. First, I had to find a special place reserved only for working on my dissertations, and avoid areas that are normally intended for other activities. Her reasoning was that this can help to keep distracting thoughts from intruding, and one can stay more focused on their task. She gave one example: if a person chose the kitchen they might be distracted by food thoughts creeping into their mind. She was right; the bedroom made me think of sex or pot. She also said I needed a good night's rest the night before my work days, and before I started to work I should try to relax. Before I could even counter with a word about pot she said, "You should avoid marijuana, however."

For the rest of our conversation I noticed an interesting behavioral difference between Carol Anne and me. I always said *pot* or *grass*, but when she referred to it she always said *marijuana*. If grass was going to even metaphorically touch her lips she refused to sound like someone who smoked it, and it definitely was not her choice for relaxation. She told me I "should try meditation instead of marijuana." I didn't know much about meditation, other than people repeating a phrase.

"Yes, that would be your mantra." I then expected her to go over the steps leading me how to do it. Instead she gave me the titles of two books. I was paying one hundred and sixty-five dollars out of network for this session, and she was sending me back to the bookstore?

She told me after meditation I would be ready to start brainstorming for ideas for my dissertations. She explained how the approach I had been using wasn't productive because I was skipping the brainstorming step and leaping into evaluation. Before evaluating, I should simply write everything that comes to mind—to release the creative juices—that's what brainstorming means. "After you do that then you can decide if something is good or not; remember, you don't evaluate while you're brainstorming—it blocks creativity."

I followed her suggestions and changed my routine, starting with meditation. I came up with a mantra keeping her in mind:

Relax, No Pot, Don't Judge
Relax, No Pot, Don't Judge
Relax, No Pot, Don't Judge

Thanks to Carol Anne, my creativity was released. When that happened I realized my *joke* was not one after all. I used it as the basis from which I came up with my research questions that culminated into my dissertations. Based on Euclid's 4th axiom—things that intersect with one another are equal with each other—I proposed to find out whether it was more efficacious to study mathematics and science as discrete subjects, or as one unit of study that intersects. My hypothesis was that students who study them as an intersecting unit will have a greater understanding of both, opposed to those students taught mathematics and science as discrete disciplines. My research project was approved by my advisor.

It took two years to complete: finding subjects to participate; doing a quantitative study—collecting data; interpreting the results qualitatively; and preparing written and oral dissertations on my findings—which I defended on completion. It would have never happened without Carol Anne because I had been gripped with fear of not meeting my program deadline. She had energized me, filling me with hope and the belief I would be successful. She had been worth every penny of her one hundred and sixty-five dollars out of network fee for releasing my creative block. But that's not the whole story.

Once I started my research I had been very busy so I no longer saw Carol Anne weekly. It had been several weeks since our last session when I saw her again to resume therapy for my dysfunctional marriage. I missed her, which should have been a warning. It had also been indicative of a flaw in that self-help book's last chapter—"Tips to Get the Most Out of Your Counseling Sessions." Its author overlooked an important concept: *don't get lulled into thinking your therapist is your friend, or even likes you.*

Carol Anne was nothing like any friend I ever had, but even I got caught off guard in behaving as though she were. I expressed it through my language to the detriment of our therapeutic relationship, and I don't even use off-color language that often. There have been times when Joe was annoyed if Rosie was nearby and overheard me on the speaker phone with Paulee. He would ask me to finish my call in another room. He once said, "you two sound worse than truck drivers." It was not like Rosie hadn't heard this kind of language before at her grandparents' house, but this was Joe's domain. When we were at my in-laws' Joe removed her from hearing-distance of his father's foul mouth. Joe was able to tell me to move, but Mac was not a man who could be told what to do or say, especially if it was coming from his son.

Joe seldom cursed and never used crude language; having grown up with a father like Mac he made a concerted effort not to sound like him. The most he might say was an occasional *damn*. Was that even still considered a curse? Not to me certainly; that was tame compared to what I heard dealing with teens on a daily basis. I was desensitized to cursing (another example of incompatibility between Joe and me). But my language was never a problem for him; I'm not Mac—a man who can make truck drivers blush. I only got raunchy sometimes when I talked about sex.

It was a combination of the topic and feeling very relaxed (as though I were talking to Paulee) that made me slip up with Carol Anne. She was sipping her tea, and I told her the main reason I was having problems with Joe was I hadn't known him well enough before our marriage. She asked me why I had then decided to marry him. "What was the overwhelming reason?"

"Do you know how women say men often think with their cocks? I was just thinking with my clit too much—he was a great fuck."

As soon as I said it, Carol Anne started coughing and spilled her tea all over her desk. I was to blame for setting the wrong tone. I made Carol Anne uncomfortable—rendering her useless for the rest of the session. She clammed up on me. I had wasted my money that day but I thought she would recover. I was wrong.

Things did not improve. In the following two sessions I would talk and she would only listen (or at least I thought she was listening—she didn't say a word). I rationalized, maybe this was a new technique she was employing. Let the client release their toxic energy in order to heal, similar to primal scream. If so, it was ineffective; I had no release or improvement. Driving to my third appointment I made the decision: if she continued to offer no advice or even utter a single word—I would have to be straight with her. *Your technique is not working.*

I was not at all hesitant broaching the subject of my sexual problems. Immediately after her usual opening—"What would you like to talk about today?" I replied, "my sex life," and hoped she would roll with it—say something, anything. When she said "Okay," I was encouraged. I noticed a little nerve twitch by her eye but I assured myself it was incidental and not an indicator of any importance. And then it was my turn to clam up for a second, overwhelmed by relief and elation. I could finally share my tales of erring, and anger—in its many variations.

It's not only unique to me that anger is usually the easiest emotion to access, and that day was no different. That's why I began lamenting about my frustrations with Joe and Paulee. It did not deter Carol Anne, and at one point she told me to elaborate more. She was actively involved with what I was saying, and I believed my therapy was now on the right track.

I was in my zone, not even paying attention to Carol Anne anymore. It was my drama re-told over and over in my mind now bursting forth for her ears. My frustrations and grievances with Joe and Paulee over their narrow views of erotic satisfaction and their complete ignorance about the impact of sexual style on a person's desire. They never gave any consideration to how it affected me when Joe's behavior changed abruptly after marriage. Paulee always disregarded that, and I stopped discussing it with Joe long ago. He did not see a problem and Paulee agreed with him; my feelings were dismissed.

"It's not what truly gives me angst though or drove me to seek help—I was played when I married my husband and I only realized recently how angry I still am about it. I have too much bitterness in me. Even my friendship with my best friend Paulee is being affected by it now."

I told Carol Anne I might strangle Paulee if I heard her say one more time—*you have nothing to complain about, Sarah, you are so lucky to always have an orgasm.* Of course it was emotional hyperbole but I was angry and hurt. I started to describe how much, but I was unable to unpack it because I heard someone else's pain.

It sounded like crying. My first thought was it might be coming from another office; the building was used by several therapists. A patient was crying so loud I heard them through the wall. I was chastised; my pain now seemed sorely disproportionate to that of someone else's; this person was really having a tougher time than me. I was about to say that, but when I looked up it was Carol Anne who was crying. What was wrong with her? I asked her if she was okay, but I only made her tears flow more freely. After several awkward moments she finally answered me, but her voice kept getting caught by little convulsive gasps. She told me she never had an orgasm in her entire life, and she had been married for thirty years. She feared she would go to her grave and never know what it was like. I moved the rocking chair I was sitting on a little closer to her chair and handed her a tissue. She wiped her nose and thanked me. What was wrong with this picture? If anyone had been watching it, I looked like the therapist and she was the client but I wasn't doing an effective job. She continued to cry so I asked her if she had ever tried masturbation to figure out how to come, and then she could tell her husband.

"Oh, Henry won't listen to me." I presumed Henry was her husband, and I was about to tell her she really didn't need Henry anyway—but this was getting too bizarre. Who was paying for this session, her or me? I told Carol Anne I was going to leave a little early if it was okay with her. It shocked her back into her senses. She abruptly sat up straight in her chair, and with a tear-free, gasp-free voice said, "You have fifteen minutes remaining."

"I know, but I don't feel well." She was not the only one shaken by a sex topic this time. She asked me if I wanted to make another appointment; I hesitated but finally said, "I have to check my schedule. I'll call you." The only thing on my mind was leaving.

I kept my word, I called her back. But I never scheduled another session, and when I told her I was going to stop therapy for a while she wasn't pleasant. Understandable, no one wants to lose a client. It was her response, "Well, I'm not surprised," delivered in a haughty tone that puzzled me. Why was she scolding me as though I had done something wrong? She was the one who had broken professional boundaries. She owed me an apology but instead I thanked her for all her help with my dissertations and Rosie. I meant it too, and I had also hoped heartfelt thanks would soften her up. They had no positive effect—it was an uncomfortable break.

I told Joe I was stopping my therapy to devote more time to finishing my graduate work. I never told him what happened, but he had been right about therapists if Carol Anne is typical. She definitely needed to find help herself, but I wish her no ill will. I also sincerely hope she experiences an orgasm before she dies.

CHAPTER 21

THE CELEBRATION

When I got my PhD, Paulee and Anthony joined Joe and me for a celebration at a fancy restaurant. Joe never stopped calling Anthony a *loudmouth* and Anthony still thought Joe was a *cheapskate*, but they agreed to a truce for the night. Anthony had also finally come to terms with me being with *the beast*. I knew it the day he casually remarked, "I guess you're lucky, Sarah. He must be good in the sack, well-hung, right? There's gotta be something." I wasn't about to discuss my sex life or the size of Joe's genitals with Anthony. I was about to protest when Paulee told him to shut up and mind his own business, and they were at each other again—their usual turn. Recalls like that made me cross my fingers: I hoped we could all get along at the celebration without any incidents.

I begged Joe not to be stingy about the tip for one evening and Paulee asked Anthony to tone down his language. Joe was more generous than usual that night, but there was no apparent difference in how Anthony spoke. In fairness to Anthony, I had never done a quantitative study on how many F-bombs he dropped on an average evening to compare. While it was conclusive and an observational fact that Joe gave a bigger tip than in the past, it was hard to determine whether Anthony reduced his expletives. I would have to do a study with Anthony as my subject, just for fun. When I said that to Paulee her response was, "That's fun, Sarah?" She was not the only person who might have asked that; there were better leisure activities to pursue than a study on Anthony. Saying it was only indicative of how my mind was wired those days. Studies, subjects, data and comparisons dominated my thoughts—I was stalled in research mode celebration night. It was the centerpiece of my focus for two years, and much of my success achieving my goals had been based on effective research, but that had not been the only thing. There were other variables—Joe had been one. Any honors I received should have been deservedly shared with him.

Joe had picked up the slack again, doing most of the housework and caring for Rosie. This time it had not been due to my lethargy; I had enough energy but it had all been directed towards obtaining my degree. If Joe hadn't helped me I would not have been able to earn it—and retain my home and family. It would have been an either-or dilemma without his help. I found it surprising myself why I was not giving him more gratitude for what he had done (it wasn't only Paulee who was puzzled about it). Irritations and repressed resentments should have melted away but they were analogous to hidden icebergs. Once my research was concluded and I had my diploma in hand they began to slowly rise to the surface.

They were small enough at the celebratory dinner that I overlooked them, ignoring the crisis warning ahead. We were having a great time. Anthony and Joe were amicable with one another, the food was good, and the wine flowed. It was a nice celebration with only one negative, I had not invited Liz. She would have asked—"Can Rocky come?" She was aware of the celebration and knew Anthony was invited. It would have been understandable if she hinted about invitations. Especially since Rocky was Joe's buddy and Joe did not even like Anthony. But she never pursued the subject (Liz is not a pushy person like Paulee), and I was lucky the guest list never crossed Joe's mind. He had probably been too consumed with thoughts about tipping and he never asked about Liz and Rocky. Seeing Rocky might have upped my lovemaking a few notches, but I had not thought it was worth being uncomfortable all evening having him ogling me.

I had made the right choice. I wore my new black dress for the celebration which showed an ample amount of cleavage, along with my tat. And my boobs and tat did garner attention as I had figured they would, but at least I had been spared Rocky's unwelcomed leers.

There had been no need to use Rocky as an aphrodisiac celebration night. When Joe and I left the restaurant I was almost giddy; not from the wine, but from happiness. It triggered our courtship again, returning to Joe's townhouse after a double date with

Anthony and Paulee—only I had a PhD. And we had the house to ourselves, thanks to my mother. She had been invited to join us for the celebration but chose to give us a free evening instead by caring for Rosie. We made the most of it—making love on the couch with a DVD running that we never bothered to pause. Courtship days, but something was different.

My neck wasn't getting rammed into the arm of the couch each time Joe thrust into me. We were making love on our big, new couch. The one I picked out and fought for because Joe did not want to spend money— we were married; my courtship fantasy busted. There was no deviation from our usual sexual practices. Why was Joe always in the dominant position? It irritated me a little no matter how sexually satiated I might be. A dull irritation was always present like an itch on my back I couldn't fully reach. You scratch my back, I'll scratch yours was not practiced in our marriage—my itch was growing stronger with a need to scratch with every thrust.

I have never stopped being happy or proud about getting my degree, but the high of being Dr. Sarah Janak wore off quickly. The satisfaction over my achievement exponentially decreased as the icebergs rose more prominently to grab my attention. It was time to find another therapist.

If I had answered Anthony's two questions: first— was I lucky? It was too complicated to say, hence my need for professional help. Second—it was a resounding yes. Joe was—but I have a question for you, Anthony; why do men always think size is so important? And I had also learned at this point that sex was not the sum of me. My life had many factors with different values. And some factors were missing, like a puzzle I was unable to complete. The dilemma I found myself in then was not being sure what was missing or what I valued. I had needed to do a research project on that, not Anthony.

CHAPTER 22

DR. BARNABY CLAPP, EdD.
ASSECT

My stress was diversified, as it had been with Carol Anne. For one I was filled with anxiety over finding a full-time tenured position now that I had the credentials. What if I was not successful? I had made it sound so easy to Joe that securing the degree would enhance my career goals. Had I deluded myself? That was the frame of mind I found myself in when I decided to look for counsel. I had no idea what the best steps were to take next in my search for a position. I needed direction, but I am not saying my career was taking precedence over sexual issues, the second layer of diversification. My discontent with Joe was a thorn in my side which needed to be plucked out, and when my resentments resurfaced the pain made me lash out at him for every minor irritation.

How to find a job was more of a mystery than my exaggerated reactions to Joe. I knew my reactions stemmed from repressed anger, but I had no clue how to rid myself of these feelings any better now than when I sought help with Carol Anne. I needed to continue therapy and it was a priority to pick up from where I had stopped with her. My sexual relations had grown in importance since graduating from school. They were now as big a block as my creative one had been. I had to address it if I hoped to move forward in a career or my marriage. It was messing with my head too much, making me overuse pot and smoke cigarettes again. Productive work searches and my marriage were being threatened, but returning to Carol Anne was out of the question. I needed a new therapist. A generalist, who was also certified as a sex counselor—and preferably a man.

That's not to suggest there aren't women sex therapists. I had grown up with the knowledge of women sex therapists from childhood. I had listened to Dr. Ruth's radio program since I was a little girl (younger than Rosie), and watched her TV show with my mother and Penny every night. The show came on after our bedtime so Mom would record it, like she had taped the radio broadcasts when they had aired, and played it for us at a more reasonable time. Some people were shocked when I told them my sister and I watched Dr. Ruth each night. I always stressed that the shows had been pre-recorded and my mother was not letting us stay up late. Paulee looked at me like I was nuts when I said that; "Forget about the time, why was your mother letting you watch the show?" She thought it was inappropriate viewing material for children, and most people whom I told agreed with her.

It did me no harm, except for trouble one day in the third grade. We were having a spelling game and I not only spelled *vulva* but eagerly defined it for my bewildered classmates. Mrs. Yang was very upset and called my mother. She did not share Mrs. Yang's sentiments and was quite impressed by my recall. I was not punished or chastised but she reminded me once again not to share highlights from Dr. Ruth's show with my friends or at school. I was not cognizant of the consensus that it was a taboo subject in certain contexts. It was confusing because Dr. Ruth looked like my best friend's grandmother, only shorter, and my mother would never answer my "why not?" She would simply say, "because I told you not to talk about the show with anyone."

Paulee thought my mother had been way too progressive. Others, like Pops' sisters, blamed her for Penny being a lesbian (too much penis talk every night at a young age, I guess). I loved my great aunts, but they were idiots—Dr. Ruth and my mother did not turn Penny into a lesbian.

Dr. Ruth was influential though and shaped me from a young age. Thanks to her I am well-informed about sex and very comfortable talking about it. If that was negative for some peoples' tastes—I'm sorry, but I only see positive results from years of hearing and watching those programs. I was a virgin until I was twenty-three and always practiced safe sex (and I did not have hang-ups like Joe). I also credit my mother's refusal to explain why I could not share my knowledge about Dr. Ruth for developing my inquisitive mind—a necessity for anyone considering graduate work of any kind.

Even though there are female therapists, I wanted a male because men are more comfortable than women with their sexuality. What's not clear is if it's natural or due to different cultural norms for men and women, but it didn't matter. Whether the difference is innate or acquired, it's still a simple fact—men and women view their sexualities differently. Even women who have no *Carol Anne hang-ups* surprise me sometimes with their views about masturbation. I've known women who are sexually active and even promiscuous like Dee who are turned off to masturbating. For some it is a genuine dislike; to them I say, "You must be doing it wrong." Others simply don't get it if they have a man in their life and ask, "Why bother?" Paulee fell into that camp.

"Why do you need to masturbate and use sex toys, Sarah? You're married."

I tried to explain to her that I masturbated in addition to having sex with Joe, it was not a substitute for him. I admitted there was a time when I preferred it over him, but that was past history. And when I was a virgin I used it as a substitute for a man, but once I started having sex with men I continued to play with my sex toys. Fingers and shower heads have limitations, but a good toy always worked, in addition to being fun. Paulee did not give them the credit they were due.

"You focus too much on the first word and not enough on the second, Paulee. Adults need toys and play as much as children." I was not able to change her mind, and if I gave her a sex toy as a present she'd only laugh—like it was a joke, and never try it.

Men value masturbating, unless they were shamed when they were young. Even Joe with all of his sexual hang-ups had no problem about pleasuring himself. I accidently walked in on him one day and there was not a hint of embarrassment, only a little annoyance. I disturbed his rhythm, and I apologized for interrupting his focus. I was about to leave and he stopped me; that's when the sexual dictator side of his personality surfaced. It wasn't as irritating as his sex rules when we made love though. It might have even been a turn on if I had taken a more active role. He told me to strip, lay down in the bed, and turn into him. He wanted to feel my body while he masturbated.

When I reflect on that memory I understand why Paulee said masturbation is a substitute for having sex with a partner. I was right there, why had he needed to do it? But if I asked that question I was thinking like her. Still, I wonder why he did it when I was lying there—naked right next to him. It was a question for a sex therapist, but not why I had sought help; it was off-point. Men's attitudes about masturbation only serve as an example of how men are more comfortable than women about sex, and why I preferred a male practitioner.

My concern over a therapist's comfort level wasn't the only reason I had preferred not to have a woman. I was not the one having the problem—it was Joe, and he refused to seek help. Men understand other men better than women do. I believed a man's insight would help me to better understand Joe and lessen my resentment towards him. I was faced with a challenge though because the field was dominated by women, and I speculated about it. Were there more women with problems than men who wanted a woman therapist? Or more women who were willing to seek help preferring a female practitioner? Based on my experience with Joe, I chose the latter explanation.

Even though it wasn't easy finding a male therapist I refused to give up, and after an exhaustive search I found one—but only one. I was not able to make any comparisons, but I crossed my fingers and hoped for the best. I also reminded myself once again that after Carol Anne the bar was very low. It was initially one positive point in his favor. Another plus was his practice was not local. I continued to have concerns over privacy and to be selective with whom I wanted to share my personal information. I sometimes even regretted talking to people I chose to be open with, like Paulee. She was grossed out when she heard I was considering a man.

"How can you talk about your sex life with a man?" It was a stupid question because I knew most of Paulee's doctors were men.

"Just as easily as you do Paulee."

"I don't talk about my sex life, Sarah, because there isn't much to talk about." She was exaggerating but I got her point that for her it would have been uncomfortable. I had to admit I was a little nervous, but not because he was a man—I questioned his credentials. He had a doctorate in education with certification in AASECT—The American Association of Sexuality Educators, Counselors and Therapists. I can talk about sex with anyone but was this "man" qualified, would he be able to help me? I assured myself and Paulee if he did not work out I would find someone else—she should lighten up. She finally did after I told her his name—Dr. Barnaby Clapp.

"Barnaby Clapp, Sarah? For real? He sounds like a type of gonorrhea. But I guess if you're a sex therapist the name fits."

Joe knew I planned to start therapy again with a new person, but I never told him Barnaby Clapp was a sex therapist. If I had there might have been questions. I wasn't opening up that can of worms with him (hence my need for professional help), and since Joe was not aware of Dr. Clapp's specialty all he said was, "I hope he isn't a quack."

Dr. Barnaby Clapp, like Carol Anne, was about an hour drive from Jackson. He was south rather than north though, and far from Robbinsville (a good omen). There were more similarities besides miles when I compared them. Dr. Clapp's office complex also housed a group of therapists and the reception room of his office suite was a carbon-copy of Carol Anne's. Where I saw marked differences was when I stepped into Dr. Clapp's personal office space. He had a wall of books, a couch big enough to lie down on, and only two plants (they looked like an afterthought and artificial). Another glaring difference, there was no rocking chair. I had loved Carol Anne's rocking chair, but there were other choices to sit my bum down. In addition to the couch there were two straight-back chairs with cushions; and centered between the couch and one chair was a small table with a box of tissues. Tissues on a table must be standard fare in therapists' offices, but the only person who had used them last time was Carol Anne.

He told me to call him Dr. Barney and to take a seat. I chose the couch, but not to lie down, I sat very upright in the middle. If I appeared uptight to someone, they were wrong. I was comfortable immediately with him—he was old, short, and reminded me of a male version of Dr. Ruth.

He asked me what was going on—why I wanted to see a sex therapist. I gave him enough details from which he could form a template; and after I finished he asked if there was a possibility of my husband coming to therapy with me. I told him there was absolutely no possibility. He said that made things more challenging, but he would try his best to help me. I did not correct him to say the sex issue was not really about me. I figured that would become apparent quickly, and I was eager to start my solo flight sessions—into Joe's psyche.

"I can't ask your husband why he doesn't like to perform oral sex, or dislikes you on top, or is disgusted by doggy style position, so let's start by me asking you—why do you like doggy style?" I told him I had no strong feelings for or against it. It wasn't clear why my opinion on the matter was helpful or germane about Joe's feelings. I hoped this man knew what he was doing.

"I don't have a concern about doggy style position, Dr. Barney. I only mentioned it to illustrate how Joe is a real prude."

"It's too early to determine what is or is not useful information or to form judgments about anything. Let's just try to explore for the time being, okay? What are your most foremost concerns? My apologies, you start." I told him how Joe not only refused to perform oral sex, he would not let me go down on him which was truly weird. I apologized for being judgmental again, but it was hard not to feel that way. "Dr. Barney, he had no aversion to oral sex when we were dating, and he didn't protest if I was on top during inter-course." I sought this man's empathy who I had just met twenty minutes prior.

"So, before you were married to him, you did all of these things? Oral sex, and a variety of sexual positions, like doggy style?"

I almost wanted to simply say *yes* to everything in order to move on. We were focusing too much on

Joe's least favorite sexual position. It was insignificant, we never did it—ever. It was only a problem when we were watching movies. Then I recalculated, Dr. Barney did say it was too early to determine what was relevant or not. He was the therapist, but I began to ask myself—is this guy competent? I hoped my therapy with him was not literally and figuratively *going to the dogs* again. I could not get Carol Anne to speak about sex with me at all and this guy would not stop talking about doggy style. I had reservations, but I decided to give a detailed response to his question, overriding my concern over his competency. I did not have much to lose at this point, other than time and gas money; I had not invested an undue amount of enterprise or trust in this man, and I could always find another therapist.

"We never did doggy style position, but oral sex was a part of our sex life and making love with me on top had never been a problem. He changed after we got married. I feel like I was a victim of false advertising."

"But you tell me you still always have an orgasm, is that correct?"

Oh, here we go again. So much for empathy. I was glad we weren't going to continue discussing rear entry penetration, but this question of my having orgasms did not sound encouraging either. Was I about to add Dr. Barney to the list of people who always say, "What's your complaint, lady"? I hesitantly told him *yes*, but was relieved when I did not hear that familiar refrain. Dr. Barney was interested in my orgasms though, which made me silently utter my own familiar refrain: *it's Joe's problem, not mine.*

He asked how long it took for me to climax. I knew the answer immediately because I'm a clock checker by nature (stemming from my childhood love of numbers on the face of a clock), but I'm never overly focused on time. If I am engaged in the pleasurable activity of sex I don't care how long it takes. Just like I don't care how long it takes to eat a delicious hot fudge sundae. The length of time appeared to be a salient point for Dr. Barney however, and I realized its significance for the first time myself after our discussion.

Time plays a huge part in the dynamics of a quickie. Even taking into consideration that Joe and I only remove the necessary garments and I don't need foreplay—it takes fifteen to twenty minutes for me to climax. No wonder Joe says no when he is preoccupied with something or anxious to leave the house—it isn't so quick. I didn't have much time to ponder this new revelation before Dr. Barney asked his next question.

"Does your husband have problems with ejaculating?"

"No."

"So how long would you say it takes for him when you're having intercourse?"

"Well, he usually comes really quick after me."

"That's interesting. It seems like he wants to make sure he's satisfied you first. Since on average, it will take a man five to seven minutes to climax."

Really? Dr. Ruth must have said it but I had forgotten. In truth, as a young girl I was often bored by her show. I would have preferred to watch cartoons, but I did recall two memories after Dr. Barney told me how long it takes for a man to climax. The first was when Joe said he waited for me to come, and when I said don't wait, he laughed. I had failed to see the humor, but if Dr. Barney was correct—I was the joke. The second memory was Paulee, who told me when she first started sleeping with Anthony he would take his time. He made sure she was satisfied, but now he's on and off—one, two, three. That's a more accurate description of a quickie, compared to Joe and me. I would have liked to discuss this more with Dr. Barney but he changed topics quickly; now triggering memories from ancient history.

"Let's talk about oral sex. Why do you like performing it? You know most women, even those who do it, would choose not to. They do it in the hope their partners will reciprocate. Or more often they simply want to please their sex partner. But again, I come across very few who say they really enjoy doing it."

I did enjoy doing it, and reciprocity was not my motivation. Even if it was true that stoking Joe's fire made our overall sexual experience better for me too, I was not being dishonest. I had been sincere when I told Dr. Barney my primary motivation was a desire to give Joe pleasure—and he wouldn't let me. Dr. Barney then asked, "Is that all you want, to give pleasure? His pleasure, and heightening the overall sexual experience, is that all you get out of it?" I didn't know what Dr. Barney was trying to root out. It took some time talking with him before I came to a full realization of what he was suggesting—I liked the power it gave me over men when I did it? It was true, I could make them whimper and moan, but my God, Dr. Barney was making me sound like some sort of dominatrix bitch. I might like giving a blow-job or being on top when I have intercourse but that did not mean I was a control freak. Yet Dr. Barney refused to stop; he continued to move his theory forward as though I were one.

"Perhaps your husband doesn't like to feel he is being controlled or powerless. I might add if that is true, he must have really fallen hard for you to let you take control during the courtship considering how it might have made him feel."

This was too much to take in, and I wanted to talk about it more because Dr. Barney was missing a very important part of the picture. Joe certainly had not acted like he wasn't enjoying himself when we were dating. He did not act like he thought I was controlling him. We needed to examine this more but Dr. Barney said we had to stop. We couldn't discuss it any further because my time was up, but he had one more question.

"Did your husband ever speak of being molested as a child? The aversion to the position of doggy style and oral sex suggest that he might have been a victim of molestation."

"No."

I said it quietly but inside I was screaming—*what?* It was an absurd idea, but Dr. Barney's question made me remember when Joe was sleeping like a beached whale and I went down on him. I had only wanted to turn him on and I was a little annoyed at his response. Oh, he came alright, but what did he say? He was dreaming someone was raping him.

CHAPTER 23

THE RECKONING

Driving home it was hard to concentrate on the road. Dr. Barney had introduced new ideas that were spinning around in my head, colliding with entrenched truths and feelings that the years had rooted deep inside my brain synapses. There was a virtual vertigo revolving inside of me, and when my brain did stop it was most often on Dr. Barney's idea that Joe might have been molested as a child. It was too unbelievable to think that was true. As absurd as Dr. Barney suggesting Joe might be an extraterrestrial alien (both ideas were out of my world of comprehension).

It took the entirety of the drive home to finally accept the possibility of the idea, leaving the next step to speculate when, where and who. Joe's father came to mind because he was a verbally abusive man, and Joe was his favorite target. Mac was always making cracks about Joe being a *fruit*, a *dumb ass*, and a *wimp*. How Mac could call a man of Joe's size a "wimp" was beyond me. Joe told me Mac was worse when he was a kid but Jean was able to curb him. According to Joe, his mother was the "real ruler of the house." And after Joe grew, his size worked as a buffer. But imagining a younger Joe, it was not a stretch to think that Mac had sexually molested him along with the berating and insults.

I met Joe's parents for the first time at our wedding, but I didn't really know them well until after we were married. It only took a few visits to their house for me to ask Joe, "What's up with your father?" He told me Mac never stopped being angry with him for not shooting a deer. Mac had taken him hunting when he was ten for a father/son bonding experience, but it produced a longstanding riff between them instead. Joe was not a hunter, and he wasn't interested in anything Mac thought a son of his ought to be interested in. Mac was an avid football and hockey fan and encouraged Joe to try out for both, but Joe preferred solo activities to team sports. He was a fat awkward kid and always the last to be picked on a team. He was still fat when he got to high school but he was also big and Mac continued to pressure him to go out for football; Joe refused. Mac continues to hold onto that resentment and his disappointment about Joe not shooting the deer. Every time I was in Mac's living room he pointed to an empty space on the wall and says-*that's where we would have hung that 10-point buck with those beautiful fucking antlers. But I have a fucking pansy for a son.* His words differed slightly each time but the message was always the same—Mac was angry with Joe. Which was ridiculous for incidents that happened years ago. It was not even justified which also made it unforgivable, yet Mac refused to let go of his displeasure.

At every gathering with family and friends Mac derided Joe for not liking hunting or sports. Joe loves golf, but it is not manly enough to be considered a real sport by Mac. Joe took it and archery in high school. His parents readily dismissed the golf but were pleased with his archery choice; their good feelings had not lasted even as long as one hunting season. Jean and Mac went to the Pine Barrens for bow-hunting every year; they put up a deer stand and waited for hours each day to ambush Bambi's parents. They thought it was great sport but their only son refused to join them. Joe gave the excuse that only two people would fit in the stand. It was true, but not the real reason why he didn't want to go. While Joe genuinely enjoyed archery and aiming at targets, he had no desire to hunt; he did not think killing animals was fun. He agreed with his father that people who ate meat and criticized hunters were hypocrites. He would even back his father up on that point, but continued to decline invitations to hunt with him.

Mac has never stopped disparaging Joe about his refusal to hunt. But sometimes he tried persuasive arguments opposed to insults. He was memorable at one family gathering when he bombastically made the proclamation, "At least the animals we hunt have a sporting chance to get away, not like the poor suckers in slaughterhouses." Joe agreed, but added he wouldn't want a job in a slaughterhouse either if he could avoid it. His comment had not sat well with Mac that day as usual and it opened up a barrage of negative remarks.

There is a very thin line between emotional abusers and molesters. Mac had been the best candidate but I had to also consider Joe's mother.

Jean was not like Mac, but she treated him like he was nine years old. It was surprising she didn't cut his meat for him. She was inappropriately over-protective: "You look like you're gaining weight; it's not good for your health " or "You look pale, are you eating enough?" Her behavior could be viewed as emotionally abusive—too critical. One positive was I never seemed to be on her radar. I had no mother-in-law issues with Jean. She was too focused on "Joey." I was even spared when she had a grievance that dealt with Rosie. When Rosie was young, she had wanted to babysit for us but we chose my mother. She would complain to Joe, "I'm her grandmother too, you know." Her frequent lament was always aimed just at him, as though he were a single dad and I had played no part in preferring my mother. Jean knew no boundaries with an adult child, but I had not seriously thought she was a candidate. If anything she often seemed too protective with adult Joe. Which returned me to Mac, and even though he has a nasty streak, I believed Joe when he said, "at heart Mac is a coward." I rejected the idea that he had molested Joe, especially with Jean in the house.

While I dismissed his parents as molesters, I knew they had been central players in shaping him. They were control freaks, who continue to try to exert control over Joe as an adult. I don't understand how Joe tolerates them. When I asked him how he did it he said, "I don't even hear them most of the time." He taught himself how to tune them out years ago. Yet I clearly saw how Joe might have developed feelings of powerlessness growing up with them (even if there had been no molestation), and his upbringing affected his tolerance of power plays with other people. He was able to ignore Mac and Jean but refused to ignore anyone else. He never even tried—he always resisted or reacted. Joe would not let people control him at work or anywhere else. He never raised his voice or became physically aggressive but he did not let people bully or cheat him. His sheer size was enough to guarantee that from happening without having to use force; Mac being the only exception. In other contexts Joe held a dominant position in his quiet way, like in our relationship. He had orchestrated our sex life to his liking since our marriage, and I did not buy Dr. Barney's theories. I wasn't convinced Joe had been molested or viewed my sexual needs as restraints, but I had been willing to keep an open mind. I continued my therapy with Dr. Barney, and also continued to favor the notion that Joe needed help—not me, and he was a selfish prude.

It took several sessions with Dr. Barney to accept the idea that Joe might not be the only one with control issues, and that I might be contributing to the sexual problems in our marriage. Joe did not want to feel victimized by a controller and Dr. Barney theorized my need to be one. I resisted his premise entirely at first because I've always maintained I only wanted to control myself. It was only after Dr. Barney made me look at myself more deeply that I began to understand and consider the suggestions he was introducing: *I had a desire for power—specifically over men, and it began at the very start of my sexual awakenings.* I had to admit I wanted to tease and torture those little nerd boys and took pleasure in what I could evoke in them. It had been a real turn-on when they had looked at me, with their eyes popping out of their heads. I gave them hard-ons and it was pleasurable, but I only allowed them to look—not touch, ha ha.

I was aware of what I was doing when I was a teen, but never saw a similar pattern after I matured until Dr. Barney pointed it out. It was a challenging idea, and also uncomfortable to be scrutinized by Dr. Barney—especially when he examined my wardrobe. He said I might be a grown woman but I might consider the premise that I behaved like my teen-self when I chose my clothes. I was speechless and he kept talking.

"Perhaps your dresses and tops—showing your cleavage—are not only fashion statements and what looks good on you. Your choices may also express your desire to make men look at you, which is a form of control." I squirmed a little when he said it, afraid my neckline was too low. I am a natural flirt, but I was not trying to flirt with Dr. Barney.

I also resisted his suggestion that my wardrobe expressed a personality flaw. Lots of women flirt, and flirting was harmless play. And after I was married I never tempted anyone to come nearer than a look—they couldn't touch. That thought made me pause; it was familiar behavior, but I had never seen a pattern. Dr. Barney was right—I had been playing the look-don't-touch game as an adult just like I had as a teen, but there was a big difference. In high school I was being mean, as a mature woman I was engaging in innocent flirting. My clothes were not a problem; it was a little extreme to point at them as a form of manipulation.

I was evolved, secure in the knowledge I was no longer immature and self-absorbed—until I thought about sex deprivation. That's when I had to admit—as an adult, my behavior sometimes had gone beyond innocent flirting and playing with Joe. I would even agree it could be seen as manipulative and downright cruel when I denied him sex and flaunted my body in his face. Paulee had been right, it was the behavior of a *cock tease*. Love and mutual sexual satisfaction were not the only goals I wanted in my relationship with Joe; I wanted power. If I was unable to get it I was not above using destructive tools to exert my own rules.

I chose a sex therapist because of Joe's sexual problems only to discover I had problems of my own. My acceptance of this realization about myself was a valuable step forward for my growth as a person, but it did not lessen my irritation about Joe's hang-ups or the feeling of having been deceived by him. The power struggle in the bedroom would have never surfaced if Joe hadn't changed after our marriage.

I made it clear to Dr. Barney that if I had known that I wasn't sexually compatible prior to marrying, I would have never married Joe but I hadn't been prescient. Dr. Barney's suggestions that Joe might have problems with control and I might be assuming a controller position had been helpful information, but it did little to eradicate all of my negative feelings. Why had his sexual hang-ups been latent, only to surface after we took our vows? Molestation was a mitigating factor that would soften my heart, but Joe being molested was only a theory. I had to find evidence, and I wasn't looking forward to searching for it. How does one simply ask, "By the way, were you ever molested as a child?"

I didn't know how to approach it, and it was the paramount question, no less the answer if Dr. Barney's hunch was correct. It could be life-changing, dispelling resentments and discontent. Dr. Barney had shaped a new view of Joe and our marriage with his counsel and ideas. I liked his Joe who had emerged before my eyes by the power of his suggestions. It was a positive perspective and I longed to confirm it, but I was able to procrastinate; it was multifaceted. I did not have to start with the molestation question. I could begin with a topic I was more comfortable with, thanks to Dr. Ruth. *How long did it take for Joe to reach climax?*

"If you were not waiting for me, how long would it take you to come?"

"Four or five minutes."

"Well, why do you wait, Joe?"

"You're not serious are you, Sarah?"

"Yes I'm serious, why do you wait?"

"Because I love you, Sarah."

Love—why hadn't I thought of that? But why would I? I had no experience in ethnographic research. Examining Joe was the closest I had ever been as a researcher in that type of study. It's no wonder his answer and its ramifications took me by surprise. All these years I thought it was only coincidental that we had nearly simultaneous orgasms. If Dr. Barney was correct, is that even possible in most relationships—without the man making a concerted effort? I understood now why Joe balked sometimes when I had asked him for a quickie. How surprised I really would have been if he had done a—one, two, three, like Anthony—and left me on the floor unsatisfied. Joe never wanted to be rushed when he made love to me. He made the concerted effort every time to wait because he loved me. This realization jump started very tender feelings towards him, and that night sex was different—it felt like lovemaking.

We were in our bed, not ramming against a wall or on top of a table. Less explosive and energetic, yet still exciting in its sweet slowness. It connected me to Joe more and I used my mind more than my body for the first time in our marriage. That not only fostered sexual satisfaction, it was a catalyst. An incipient intimacy was created; one I had wished for many years ago. I was also able to push other frustrations aside briefly. They did not go away entirely, but they weren't taking center stage. I needed to continue asking my questions to confirm Dr. Barney's theories so I could push them out of my sightlines. I had to be able to understand Joe more fully if I hoped to eradicate all of the resentment I held towards him. I had been holding on to it for so long that one intimate satisfying night was not going to erase it.

I continued with my questions and my efforts were not wasted. I was finally introduced to Joe. I learned more about him during this time than in our eleven years together. He had never even told me about his first sexual experience in spite of me sharing mine with him. Now he opened up: the first woman he had sex with was a prostitute. I had not expected him to say that.

He was eighteen working on a fishing boat in Alaska after graduating from high school. The crew would be out at sea for ninety days, and when the job was done they'd return to port with paychecks and appetites for booze and women. Not Joe though, not the first summer. He had never been with a woman, and was the youngest member in the crew. He said the guys were a tough bunch but he liked them, and unlike his own father they looked out for him. They taught him how to do the job over the four summers he worked and also helped him *find his manhood*. They introduced him to Sadie's House.

"Really, Joe, 'Sadie's House'." You wanted to name Rosie after the madam of a whorehouse?"

"I have fond memories." I was so glad I had vetoed the name. After Joe told me, every time I looked at our dog Sadie I envisioned a whorehouse in Anchorage, Alaska. Joe told me his only experience with women for years was with the prostitutes at Sadie's House. They made their money by how many patrons they could service, like McDonald's. He was very fast, so he was one of their favorites. When he began to have relationships with women who weren't "pros" he had to work on how to hold back. He was ashamed to say he hadn't always worked very hard—until he met me.

By his accounts his time on the commercial fishing boats had been life-changing in many ways, and at the age of eighteen the best experience of his life. His parents had not wanted him to take the job, but Mac refused to pay for college—Joe needed to find work. He saw the wanted ad looking for people to work on a fishing boat in Alaska in the back of one of Mac's hunting magazines. He never regretted taking the job: it was strenuous work (eighteen hours a day) but he earned enough money for school and grew up over the four years; his baby fat melted away, replaced with muscle. He said the main objective of taking the job had been money but the life experiences were more valuable than what he earned. My own opinion was it gave him a newfound confidence. It helped him to endure living with Jean and Mac.

"Is that where you learned how to navigate using the moon?"

"What are you talking about?"

"You said you knew moon navigation." He laughed at me, he had forgotten that, and working on the boats was exactly where he had picked it up from someone, but it was not used for navigation. It was silly of me to think that since it was the twenty-first century and Joe told me he learned it just for fun during breaks.

"You know I'm not much for reading, and the breaks were too short to settle down with a book even if I wanted to."

He wasn't much for talking either. It took all these years before he told me he had worked as a commercial fisherman like Pops. Joe opening up so much was a rarity, it was the perfect opportunity to ask *the question* since he was in a talkative mood.

"I'm curious, has anyone ever been molested in your family?" He didn't say anything for a while; I thought he was simply going to ignore me. I knew he heard me but he had a blank look on his face, staring right at me with big saucer eyes.

"What makes you ask that question?" Now what was I going to say? But I had to come up with something.

"I just… (what? I did not know what to say but I had to say something). I have been made aware recently of how it is pretty prevalent in families. More than one would think. I asked my mother the same question." This was going to be as difficult as I had feared.

Again there was a long pause. Long enough to make me start to feel uncomfortable, but was it more uncomfortable for him? It took him a full-minute to answer me.

"Well, let's just say there was a reason I stopped going to church, okay? And I don't want to talk about it anymore."

I don't know what I expected Joe to say, and I had posed the question. Why was I surprised by what he said? I guess there was always a part of me that held to the belief that Dr. Barney's theory couldn't be true. I was wrong and left speechless after Joe spoke. He was cryptic at best but I got enough detail, and I was glad he didn't want to talk more about it. The message was clear with few words—Joe wasn't a prude. No wonder he had never talked about his first sexual experience with me; it had not been a story about Sadie's House. There was an explanation for his sexual hang-ups, and there was nothing quirky about it. Dr. Barney had been correct about his speculation. Had he also been right about Joe's drive to win me over during our courtship? He suggested it was stronger than his aversions, forcing me to reflect on how uncomfortable it must have been for him. Instead of enjoying sex Joe was blocking out painful memories. After the marriage when his behavior changed, I had angrily chalked it up to the stereotype: men always change after the hunt is finished (I should have remembered that Joe wasn't a hunter).

Joe was still a typical guy changing his behavior, but his reason was atypical, and he never stopped trying to please me, with the one obvious exception which had brought me to Dr. Barney initially. But examining the other parts of our marriage, he never grew complacent or uncaring. The flowers, the massages, the little gifts that started during our courtship had continued throughout our marriage. And the most significant thing I could never overlook was how he had made it possible for me to get my doctorate degree.

I finally understood Joe, but that hadn't changed the reality—he needed help. I refused to pressure him to seek it, it would have been futile. But I wasn't hesitant about peppering the entire house with Dr. Barney's business cards. I had been outright obvious when I left one propped against the wing of the model plane he was working on.

Finding out that Joe had been molested when he was ten made it easy for me to let go of my annoyance over his hang-ups. I was still bothered by him being dishonest, lecturing me on our honeymoon about appropriate marital sex. He never once mentioned what had happened to him. Maybe it shaped his attitudes about sexual behavior and what is appropriate after marriage. I could see the connection even if it was warped, but the biggest problem had been his lack of transparency. If he had been completely open I might have been spared heartache. Joe wasn't the only victim, but I could no longer be angry with him. And once I let go of my rancor I experienced a tangible sensation. I now understood what the cliche meant—*lifting the burden off your shoulders*; and it was multifaceted. When it lifted I was filled with a desire to nurture him in a similar way I had done before. I wanted to put my arms around him, to protect him from backstabbing co-workers.

I continued to see Dr. Barney for me, not Joe. I wanted to understand myself more. Did I really need to exert power over men? I did not want to dominate or control Joe, and I was wallowing in feelings of remorse about my past behaviors. That's when Dr. Barney began his dissertation on the anatomy of control. His central point: *control is not intrinsically negative or positive. One's motivation had to be examined to determine that.* He made an analogy with driving a car.

"You are in control when you safely drive a car with a passenger to a destination; it is a mutually satisfying experience for both of you. You are also in control if you speed, drive recklessly scaring your passenger who wants to get out of the car. What is the motivation when you drive? Are you doing it to help, or was it even sought by another asking you to take over? Or are you using it to dominate someone, to make them do something they don't wish to do? That's what you have to ask yourself."

Dr. Barney said my desire "to be in the driver's seat" was understandable in part. It was a natural response when one looked at norms in our culture and the political and social institutions. Women are not equal to men in so many areas: "There is a need to balance the scales. Especially for a woman with a background like yours." I wasn't sure what he meant until he explained his conclusions, based on my upbringing and childhood.

"In you I see a woman who has been raised by a single mother who was strong and self-reliant. It's not hard to understand why you want to emulate her." I never thought of my mother as particularly strong, but it was true she did raise two little girls by herself. She had some help from her parents, but shouldered the majority of the responsibility herself caring for my sister and me. I suppose I've always taken her for granted. It was my unique experience; I never thought it was unusual that she did all the minor house repairs—running around with her power drill. I thought all mothers did that, and I could not wait until I was bigger and had my own power drill. When I was old enough, the desire faded; I did not elect shop in high school, but retained an interest in battery-operated devices, which was germane to another theory of Dr. Barney's.

He thought I had been an unusual fourteen-year-old girl, sexually speaking. Barely out of puberty, not only was I completely comfortable with my sexuality, I was my own master. It was not surprising that I would want to continue to be in control of my own sexual pleasure, but I agreed with him, I wasn't driving the car alone now. I did not want to manage Joe. Dr. Barney said ultimately we both needed to learn how to share the driver's seat, but since he only had me the focus would be on my part. He told me I had to invite Joe to be a passenger if I wanted to drive. He suggested that I ask Joe if there was any context where he would be comfortable with me in control—but it had to be a mutually satisfying ride.

Keeping Dr. Barney's dissertation in mind, I voiced my concerns. I was reluctant to approach Joe until I was absolutely sure my motivation was pure, free of any desire to dominate or force my will. That's when Dr. Barney replied, "power and control are artificial constructs in this context. You are not physically strong enough to overpower Joe, but he is not strong emotionally. My prediction is he will resist you, and it needs to be a safe ride for both of you." I feared that I might have created a negative image of Joe when Dr. Barney spoke of resistance—Joe was a teddy bear. I had to make it clear to him that Joe would never react in a physical way. But he would never do anything he didn't choose to do either so I followed Dr. Barney's advice. I approached Joe with the question he had suggested and instead of dismissing me Joe responded, "When I'm tired I wouldn't mind you doing all the work." Why was it so easy? It made me wonder if our sex life would have been different if I had framed my question this way years ago. Joe added a caveat though: if I was the one on top, I was going to have to keep pulling back in that position if I expected him to last. It was okay with me; we were making progress.

I did not broach the subject of oral sex until weeks later. I snuggled up to him one night and spoke to him in a straight-forward manner, no attempt at coquettishness. "I don't want to hurt you, I love you. I only want us to make each other feel good." We did it. He told me I tasted sweet, I told him he was salty—a perfect combination.

My sex life was healthier than it had ever been in my marriage. I also had a better understanding of myself but my work with Dr. Barney was not finished. I finally needed to either pay up or get off the guilt trip. The first step was to face my culpability about not wanting a second child, and as usual, Dr. Barney began his examinations with a question.

"Why didn't you want another child?"

"I was too mixed up about my marriage, and I wanted to work on my degree. Also, Rosie was enough to handle, and still is."

"Those are all good reasons not to have another child. Nothing to feel remorse about. Sometimes a child will make a marriage and family unit stronger, but usually it only adds more stress. And if the marriage is already shaky, it may crumble."

Dr. Barney helped me see that I shouldn't feel sadness or shame because I hadn't wanted another baby. It was clear when I listed all my reasons I had made the right decision at the time. It was more complicated than that though because Joe never knew I was using birth control and he had wanted another child. I always accused him of not being open but therapy helped me see how I had acted the same. I wanted to manage it all by myself—one machination after another.

The other deed weighing on my conscience had been more difficult to broach with Dr. Barney. It was difficult to admit how I denied Joe sex for over a year when we were first married. Even worse, I had continued to do it later, as a strategy to bring more excitement to our sex life. I was filled with remorse.

"You are not alone. As human beings none of us are perfect; we often do things out of acrimony or for selfish reasons that we later regret having done."

He told me I needed to learn how to forgive if I wanted to move forward. Not only to forgive Joe for his offenses, I needed to forgive myself. Forgiving myself was taking more time than it did to forgive Joe. Dr. Barney encouraged me to share the things I had done that I regretted with him. He believed it might help me to move forward—it sounded too risky. I never did that, but I finally succeeded in forgiving myself (even if it did take longer than necessary).

It took two years of therapy before my life moved in pleasant predictable ways—until there were changes. Life is always filled with changes; and even with all the work I had done with Dr. Barney, I wasn't always able to keep myself from tripping along the way—but I had a propitious outlook. Hang-ups, anger, machinations and self-approach were no longer stumbling blocks.

I even had enough confidence to continue my life's journey without professional counseling. Joe told me it was a good move, but that was to be expected. He still thinks all therapists are "a bunch of quacks."

PART TWO

THANATOS LOOMS

CHAPTER 24

CHANGES

When Rosie turned twelve, we lost Pops. He was only two years shy of his one hundredth birthday. I was sad he didn't reach that marker, but more for simply losing him. It was not comforting when people said, "Well, he almost made one hundred, you should be happy he had such a long life, right?" It failed to make me feel better, which in turn made me feel selfish. The universe had given us much more time with Pops than others are often granted with loved ones. He had been blessed with a long life, but it was still difficult to accept his death even at his age. It seemed sudden because it was hard to think of him as old. Only a few months before he died he was very active, and he did not look his age. He even looked years younger than his wife, who was twenty years his junior.

In the thirteen years Pops had been married to Marie she had gained weight and had been afflicted with a number of health problems. Time had not treated her kindly, but she was probably one of the reasons Pops had maintained his enthusiasm for life and youthful looks. My mother appreciated the loving care Marie had given him, especially in those final months.

She had reappraised her long before Pops' decline, but it took years for her to be convinced Marie was not a gold digger. And she never regretted pushing for the prenup; Pops' house stayed in our family after his death. Marie was allowed to live in it for as long as she wanted, and Mom had no problem with that, nor did she ask her to pay the property taxes. She planned to do all the minor house repairs to offset expenses—she still had her power drill.

Rosie had loved her great-grand daddy. He taught her Norwegian songs and told her stories about his life in Norway where he grew up. He always liked to tease her too. She was only seven when he asked, "So, are you married yet?" She would laugh, answering, "No, Grandpop, I'm seven." It was the same running joke when she answered "twelve," but it would not have been surprising if some had failed to see the humor the last time he posed the question. She did not look twelve years old; she could have passed as a bride, excluding those countries or cultures where young girls are made brides at her age. Rosie did not resemble a little girl in any culture or country, and it was a big change from the year before. Had Pops even noticed? If so, he overlooked it and made no attempt to change his long-standing question. If the humor continued to work, why change it?

Our house was quieter the year Pops died because we lost our dog Sadie too. The vet told us larger dogs did not generally live as long as the smaller ones; Sadie's age at her death was typical for her breed. A few months later at Christmas Joe bought me a Maltese puppy and we named her Holly to note the holiday. It was supposed to be my dog but that was short-lived. Joe carried her around all the time as though she were a baby; he was also the principal feeder and treat giver. He gave her far more treats than recommended and was not consistent with training. The dog books said you can spoil a dog. As usual he wouldn't listen to me, but I refused to get into a bad cop/good cop routine with him over a dog.

It only took a short time for my dog to bond completely with Joe, and she changed his mind about small dogs being snappy. Holly wouldn't hurt anyone; her only purpose was to love and be loved. She had only two flaws: she seldom listened to our commands and was always having accidents in the house. Joe didn't seem to mind, "She's a tiny dog, the mess is really easy to clean up, Sarah," and he cleaned up after her himself. He walked the talk and the dog so I had no complaints. He also tried to continue to housetrain her; he was a proactive dog-daddy. I wished he could be more proactive when it came to his daughter.

Rosie was always hard to handle. All those sessions with Carol Anne could attest to that, but she got much worse when she turned twelve. Joe said it was due to her mourning Pops and Sadie. I agreed those losses were factors contributing to her behavior, but she was also going through puberty. That made her precociousness along with her willfulness magnify tenfold.

I recalled as early as three Rosie had refused to wear the clothes I picked out for her. "Come on Rosie, let's put the pretty yellow dress on. You like yellow. Yellow like the sun, or like the daisies you helped Mommy plant." Neither idea appealed to her that day. She made her opinions loud and clear—she did not want to look like the sun or a daisy. I was exasperated with her, but I had to laugh when she referred to herself in the third person and couldn't pronounce yellow.

"Rosie doesn't want 'wellow' dress." Her sentence structure was impressive even though she eliminated an article. I was sure Paulee would be impressed when I told her; she frequently complained about her seniors in high school who couldn't construct a good sentence; Rosie was pretty good for her age.

Her grammar had dramatically improved when she expressed her strong opinions about her hair style one year later. Besides being impressed by how smart my kid was, I was a little flattered when I caught her cutting her curls off in my bedroom; she told me she wanted hair like mine. There was no way she could have been that manipulative at age four. I took her at her word—she wanted to look like her mommy—me. That helped temper my immediate reaction and I also saw the irony in the situation.

When I was young I wished I had curly hair like hers. It wasn't my mother I wanted to emulate though. I wanted hair like my fourth-grade classmate's, Donna Decker. I wanted her buck teeth too. I kept pushing my teeth out and biting my lower lip to encourage them to protrude. My mother kept scolding me, "Why are you doing that, Sarah? Stop biting your lip." When I told her I wanted buck teeth, she told me it would not make me pretty; and she wanted her girls to look pretty. Donna was one of the most popular girls in our fourth-grade and I thought she was beautiful. My mother didn't know what she was talking about, and was obviously not in sync with grammar school standards of beauty. Rosie held strong opinions and was unyielding concerning her looks from a young age, like me. I identified with her, and appreciated her spunky nature. But my first reaction was horror when I saw her beautiful curls on the floor.

After she told me she wanted hair like mine, I made the concerted effort to calm myself and was about to tell her she had her daddy's curly hair—but I stopped abruptly. It would have been confusing and counterproductive. He kept his hair so short his curls were nowhere to be seen. I hadn't even known he had curly hair myself until Jean showed me a picture of two-year old Joey. If I told Rosie she had curls like her daddy the only thing that she would have seen was they were missing. How could that be explained? The obvious conclusion would be he had cut them all off—like she did (sheared would be more applicable in Joe's case). I chose to tell her instead how I loved her curls, and when I was her age I wished I had them but, "I was lucky; I got a little girl with curly hair."

One who now also had a bald patch on her head; she had cut right down to her scalp, just like dad. Hair grew back I reminded myself; I used bows to cover the offensive area until it did, and I didn't punish her for cutting her curls. She was put in time-out for being in our room by herself without permission and using my scissors. I made a note to hide them in a more secure place. I knew I'd find her alone in our bedroom again even if I told her it was off limits. She not only had curls like her daddy, she was also tenacious like him.

She never found the new hiding place for the scissors but I often caught her in our bedroom. No surprise there, but what she was doing at age five made me do a double-take. I found her looking in the mirror applying cornstarch to her face. I store my diaphragm in a little case which looks similar to a compact for face powder. My gynecologist told me to put cornstarch in the case to keep it dry. Rosie thinking it was face powder was not that far-fetched. It's not clear what she thought the little rubber cup was for, or why her face would look better with paper white cornstarch accents. When I asked her what she was doing she said she was putting powder on her face like me. I sincerely hoped when I applied makeup she didn't think I looked like her. I preferred not to question her on that subject and dealt instead with an important life's lesson. "You shouldn't touch things that don't belong to you, Rosie. The powder belongs to Mommy."

It had also been an opportunity for another life's lesson. I could have talked about the birds and bees with Rosie, but I had not wanted to venture into the topic of birth control with a child. I would have been forced to explain the little cup. How would I have deconstructed that—it keeps little babies safely up in heaven? Or at least that was what I hoped it would continue to do. The only thing I was absolutely sure about was not wanting to use this incident as a lesson about procreation or birth control. Rosie had only been five years old; I wanted to enjoy her naivety for as long as I could. I chose to lock the diaphragm in the fireproof cash box where I kept my pot so she couldn't try any more makeovers with cornstarch, and made a mental apology to Dr. Ruth for shirking my responsibility to teach Rosie about sex.

Rosie's strong opinions about her wardrobe continued into her pre-teens—no change from her younger years. I was the one who changed. I no longer found her cute or was impressed by her grammar. The days of yellow dress debates were long gone; when she hit twelve we argued over midriff tops and low hanging skin tight jeans. She wanted to wear them to school to show off her fake belly button ring. Or at least I hoped it was fake since I told her she could not have her belly button pierced. She believed she had "the right" to pierce her body because I had a tattoo. It was an artificial distraction but I continued the debate countering "it was not the same." I also pointed out that, "I was seventeen when I got a tattoo." She finally stopped fighting with me about body piercing when I compromised; she could get a tattoo when she turned seventeen. Unfortunately this did nothing to stop our tussles over clothes and makeup. It was also around this time I began noticing my underwear mysteriously disappearing.

Rosie got her period shortly after her twelfth birthday, and it took less than a year for her breasts to be the same size as mine. People were shocked when I told them her age, and after she blossomed, not only did I find her in my room stealing my makeup (she was not using cornstarch anymore), she also stole my bras. X-rated ones I might add—not meant for day wear, and she also stole several of my crotchless panties. When I wore these bras and panties I knew why. Where, with whom and why had she been wearing them? I prayed to Aphrodite: *please give me a sign that she is only prancing around by herself in front of a mirror in her bedroom.*

I never received a sign so I was forced to question Rosie about my underwear, even though I knew after doing research for my degree that she would be a flawed participant. She always insisted she hadn't taken anything. It's a known fact that participants lie in studies; response bias if suspected must be factored in when determining your results. It was verifiable in this case; I found the bras and panties in her bedroom. Why had she even bothered to deny taking them? I guess it was such an ingrained habit at that juncture it had become an automatic reflex. She had been lying since she was seven; nothing had changed except now she lied about crotchless panties instead of popsicles.

Her strong opinions about her hair did not change either, but when she hit puberty she liked her curls. She refused to have her hair trimmed and had a mass of blonde curlicues all puffed out around her head. She looked like a lioness with a mane. There was even a fight getting her to pull it back when it was simply inappropriate to wear unrestrained. I tried to explain to Joe that her hair could get caught on something when she was playing sports. He laughed at me until her lacrosse coach contacted us.

Rosie those days reminded me of Penny in the magazine layout where she was posed like a sexy wild cat with a massive head of curls. Penny's natural hair was straight like mine though and her curls were only styled for the shoot. That had not mattered to Rosie, and it was Rosie's dream as soon as she turned twelve to be a model like her aunt. She mimicked her whenever possible. And it was Penny's hairstyle that especially drew her to the cat ad. I told her Penny had washed her wild curls away with cream rinse after the shoot had finished. "Aunt Penny doesn't walk around on the street looking like that." It landed on unresponsive ears.

It's not that I no longer loved Rosie's curls. It's only when they became as uncontrollable as her behavior I wished she got my hair instead of Joe's. And Penny's wild cat ad created more hassles beyond hair skirmishes. What's appropriate in a magazine layout for an adult woman model is not appropriate for a girl in eighth-grade. My sister was half-naked in that ad. It fueled Rosie's penchant for skimpy tops and low-slung jeans. When I reminded Rosie she was not an adult model in a magazine she scowled, which prompted me to ask myself: *are her lips puffier than they were before?* I hoped she hadn't done something to make them fuller, and I regretted saving those magazines for her to find.

Clothes, makeup and hairstyles were not my only worries. At twelve my little cherub had discovered the power of her body and she was boy crazy. These were more alarming transformations than a sudden preference for puffy hair or lips. I feared more than her hair getting caught in a lacrosse stick. Boy crazy: throw a few hormones into the mix and you have a recipe for STDs and unwanted pregnancies. Some people, like my sister, would say I had been the same as Rosie when I was her age. Penny hadn't known me any better than I had known her. I was never boy crazy, nor was I so overindulged by a father that I believed nothing bad would ever happen to me.

Rosie had cost me a number of sleepless nights, and Joe was simply no help at all. Or he hadn't wanted to see she was no longer his little girl. She would always be his daughter, but she wasn't a child any more and he treated her like one. I told him that the day I saw her sitting on his lap, begging him to drive her to the mall.

"You shouldn't let her sit in your lap like that, she's too old now."

In that very calm, measured voice he used when he was pissed off, he asked me, "What are you suggesting?"

"Well, I don't mean that your thoughts or intentions are in any way inappropriate; but there is a time when a brother and sister should no longer take baths together, and there is also a time when a young woman should not be sitting on her father's lap. She isn't a little girl, Joe."

Why could I see that and he couldn't? Other people saw it. Paulee obviously did when she said, "Your Rosie looks like a young woman these days. I would kill for her body, and I can't believe she is only twelve." Paulee was on the mark with her observation. Rosie was a few weeks away from her thirteenth birthday and she had a grown woman's body. Rosie and I were body doubles. Paulee confirmed my perception, and she also triggered the memory of my prom fittings. I could hear my mother clearly, but I forgave her for being a neckline Nazi. Her worries about my behavior were needless, but I now understood I was not the only one she worried about when I was a teen (or at the fitting for my wedding gown for that matter). A mother needed to worry about other people when they had a daughter who looked like Rosie and me.

Paulee was complimentary and envious when she talked about Rosie's blossoming attributes, but never offensive. I wasn't bothered by what she had said. My concern was about others who womuld view Rosie only as a sexual object and not as a beautiful, maturing young woman. She unfortunately encouraged negative gaze with her behavior and choice of clothes. I had similar inclinations with clothing at her age, but I was in control of my actions. I wasn't convinced Rosie could control her sexual impulses and there was nothing I could do about it.

Tantamount to that worry, I had no ability to control the actions of others. Joe had an awakening of sorts about that when we went to a Labor Day picnic at his parents' house a week before Rosie's birthday. He was made aware of how others saw her differently than he did. It did not change his perceptions but he had to at least admit that my perception of Rosie was not isolated. I was not being *overly dramatic*.

Joe and I called it a family picnic, but ever since Trump began his political career all of Mac's gatherings were more like political rallies instead of parties. Jean and Mac loved Trump, and so did all their friends who were frequent guests. I didn't care who anybody voted for; I only wanted to be left in peace to eat my hot dog, but the atmosphere was filled with an air making it challenging that day. Mac was more pugnacious than usual and he upset Joe when he spoke about Rosie. I am not one of Mac's fans and I don't often find his talk or jokes appealing, but I was glad he said what he did about her. It's not that I commended his actions, but I thought his words would help Joe see what had been right in front of his nose.

We were running a little late leaving the house when Rosie came down the stairs wearing skin tight sports shorts that barely covered her ass. She was also wearing a tight white top, cropped at her midriff with a low neckline (it looked more like a band than a top). Rosie has nipples like mine—they're a little erect even in neutral. Joe tells me I look like I'm always, "ready to go." It's a cute little eroticism when your husband says this but I didn't want people to say it about Rosie. If I could clearly see her nipples through her top, others certainly could. But I don't know why I was focused on that one aspect. Did it really matter, when her boobs were bursting out of the little strip of cloth masquerading as a top? I told her the clothes were inappropriate, especially for her grandparents' picnic.

"Why? I'm not wearing the stupid sundress you bought, Mom. It makes me look like a nerd."

"You don't have to wear the sundress, but I don't want you going to your grandparents' with what you are wearing, okay?"

"There's nothing wrong with what I'm wearing and I'm not changing."

Unbelievable. I would have never talked to my mother like that; I also had the decency to hide the clothes I knew she would object to and put them on when I was out of her sight. I was ready to fight when Joe came lumbering down the stairs.

"What's going on? Come on, we're late."

"I don't think what Rosie is wearing is appropriate to go to your parents' house."

"She's fine. It's a picnic, and it's hot outside." He was totally blind, and did not back me. The strategies I had learned in Carol Anne's sessions to deal with Rosie's behavior were often ignored by Joe. Rosie gave me a little smirk as she sashayed out of the house after her father. I hoped they were not planning to have water fights with the garden hoses. The weather was also a concern. If there had been unexpected showers it was unlikely her top would have given her sufficient cover.

When we got to the picnic the family was outnumbered by my in-laws' MAGA hat friends as expected. They were all talking about how great a president Trump would be if he were elected. After they finished extolling Trump's virtues, they began their attacks on the left-wing people who were ruining our country. One of their favorite groups of people to demonize were college and university professors; they thought we were all commies or socialists. It is true that the basis of all the social sciences is socialism, but I taught mathematics. I hoped they were aware of that and would cut me a break. I wished Mac, in particular, would make the distinction between the hard and soft sciences and refrain from this sort of talk (if only out of respect for me). Respectful isn't really an adjective to describe Mac, and it didn't really matter what your discipline was; having a college degree in general was very problematic for him. He frequently made a point of how it was a waste of money to get these "dumb ass" degrees, and this day was no exception.

"Sarah, I'm right, aren't I? That degree of yours cost a shit load of money, right? I never asked, did Joe give you his approval to waste all that fuckin' money?"

"Yeah, Dad, I totally gave my approval."

"Well, you are even a dumber ass than I thought." Mac said it in front of all his friends and the family; Joe did not say one word in response. I really disliked Mac; I wanted to throw my hot dog in his face, but before I finished pondering all the reasons not to, Jean added a little damage control to the mix to reduce Mac's testosterone level. She knew he often became more combative when Joe refused to stand up for himself, especially if there was an audience (how dare his wimpy son embarrass him in front of people).

"Mac, leave the boy alone. This is a party, we're supposed to be having fun. Don't mind your father, Joey, you know how he is."

Yes, we knew Mac; but her implication that we needed to overlook him was annoying, and she added to it when she called Joe, "Joey," which drove me crazy. I asked him if he wanted to leave.

"Nope. That's just what he'd like to see. Then he'd know he got to me."

Mac enraged me, if only I had the nerve to really throw my hot dog at him—but I was a wimp. And I was irritated with Joe because I knew he wasn't— I wished he would fight back. Reflecting on that, I wonder if the universe was listening to me in part— Mac finally *got to* Joe—and he reacted.

Jean had just brought out the pies and asked if anyone wanted ice cream when Mac said, "Hey, where's Rosie? I don't want my little piece of tail to miss dessert." He then immediately turned to his friend Sam and asked him if he had seen the "rack" on her. Her breast size was apparently a subject of pride for Mac. His son was a disappointment but his granddaughter, who was only twelve, had "a great pair of knockers." Sam had the decency to look uncomfortable when Mac was talking about Rosie. I was happy to see it; another person besides me thought there were lines that Mac should not cross. He was saying these things about his own young grand-daughter, not a stripper in a club. Joe heard him too and he wasn't blocking Mac out this time; he stood up and took a step towards his father. Joe could look intimidat-ing but it was never more apparent than that day. There was tension in the air, and Mac's face paled. He was afraid of his wimpy son and did not say a word. Nobody did until Joe turned to me and said, "We're leaving."

Joe made his apologies to his mother telling her we had to go home—*we needed to let the dog out.* Joe doesn't lie. It's probably a blessing he isn't much of a talker. He's one of those nerdy people who wouldn't even tell a white lie to spare someone's feelings. He was flustered and probably had forgotten Paulee was taking care of Holly for us. I wasn't about to correct him, lie or not, I wanted to leave. I only wished Joe would have it out with his father before we left. Not a physical fight; I did not want Joe to hurt him, but punch him with words. Why spare Mac's feelings? He never cared about anyone else's and he was always offensive, but Joe did not give me the satisfaction. There were no punches or tongue lashes. Joe had still been able to shake Mac up by the looks of it, but had he really learned a lesson? Probably not, but it was

Joe I was concerned about, not Mac. Mac's remarks about Rosie had not been arbitrary or simply crude, and I crossed my fingers hoping they had taught Joe something. The whole miserable picnic would have been worth it if Joe understood the subtext of Mac's words—and that subtext had been running around all afternoon half-naked in her grandparents' backyard.

When we returned home Joe said very calmly that he was never visiting his father again. I knew he was angry. He did not have to shout or raise his volume to make that clear. He assumed that irritating measured tone—it was always a dead give-away. I was also able to measure his feelings by what he said, opposed to how he said it. I determined whether he was drunk the same way. He never staggered or took his clothes off in the middle of a public road. Liz told me a drunk Rocky had done that on their honeymoon—a pretty good indicator of having had too much to drink. Joe was more subtle. I knew he had one beer too many when he said he wanted to take me on a cruise to Hawaii. He refused to go to Cape May, New Jersey for a day. He had to be drunk to say something like that. And his exact words: "I'm never going to my parents' home again," was a good indicator of Joe's state of mind—he was really pissed. It was an unrealistic statement, but I didn't change the thread. I played along with the conversation.

"Well, how is that going to work, Joe? You are never wanting to see your mother again?"

"She can come to our house to visit." Jean never came to our house, and she never went anywhere without Mac. It was as though they were surgically attached. Joe was very aware of that so it was a waste of time to point it out. I had needed to take a different tact to make an argument, but there was a problem. How to put it delicately so he wouldn't become angry with me.

What I had wanted to say: "Well, maybe if Rosie's boobs and ass weren't hanging all out your father wouldn't have talked about her like that." But if I had been completely frank I would have provoked Joe so I was forced to say: "I told you Rosie wasn't dressed appropriately. It was okay for playing volleyball on the beach, but not for going to your parents' party."

"That sounds a little like victim shaming to me, Sarah." I suppose it was, and I apologized for saying it. Besides, Mac's words had not brought about the effect I had hoped for; all they had done was reaffirm once again that he was a pig. His words, just like mine, had failed to change Joe's view of Rosie. Joe refused to see reality: Rosie was no longer his little baby girl, and she had matured into a sexual being. I had to find a new strategy to open his eyes before an unwanted pregnancy did—words were useless.

CHAPTER 25

HAPPY THIRTEENTH BIRTHDAY ROSIE

Rosie wanted to go to the movies for her birthday with her two friends, Patty and Doreen. Paulee and I took them to the mall for lunch and a movie afterwards. The movies, along with a pair of small stud earrings, were gifts from Paulee. It was very generous of her and the sapphires in the earrings were tiny but looked real. Paulee told me they weren't pure and it was "obvious by their color." It was not obvious to me but Paulee knew jewelry. Anthony might be deficient in some areas but he was not stingy when he gave her gifts. Pure or not they were very pretty and it seemed ungrateful to wish Paulee hadn't bought them, but it was problematic if jewelry required piercing of any body part. Rosie had been too fixated on mutilating herself. Ears are benign, unlike belly buttons or nipples, but I had been firm—she had to wait until she was sixteen to have her ears pierced. Where nipples and belly buttons were concerned she had to wait until she was emancipated—she would never have my approval. The thought of piercing my nipples was cringe-worthy. I know some women get sexual pleasure using breast clamps but that is not a sex toy I would enjoy.

When Rosie opened up the little box at lunch she was ecstatic, thanking Paulee enthusiastically. She wanted to run immediately to the jewelry kiosk after we finished lunch. Were those kiosks even sanitary and safe? I thought of my mother and how she had worried about me contracting hepatitis when I got my tattoo. As a parent I was now able to identify with her as Rosie grew more challenging. I never fully realized how difficult it was to parent until I had to do it myself, and all hell broke loose when I told Rosie she could not pierce her ears that day.

Rosie did not like to wait ten minutes for anything—three years probably seemed like a lifetime to her. So I wasn't surprised by her reaction when I said, "You're going to have to wait until you're at least sixteen to get your ears pierced, Rosie," and she replied: "You have got to be shitting me." I told her if she didn't watch her mouth we'd leave after lunch—no movie, and I didn't care if it was her birthday.

Hindsight tells me I should have waited for lunch to be finished to make my proclamation about ear piercing. If I had pulled her aside it wouldn't have been as disruptive. She took after her grandfather, she was always worse in front of friends. Now Paulee was dragged into it too, and she regretted having bought the earrings; she had thought Rosie's ears were already pierced. She told Rosie she'd return them and get her a necklace with her birthstone. To me she said, "Some cultures pierce their baby girls' ears when they're infants. All of Anthony's nieces have their ears pierced." Gratefully only I heard that—and I did not have a problem with pierced ears. Paulee did not have to convince me, my fear had been there would be a snowball effect with Rosie. But what she said to Rosie was appreciated; it cut her tantrum short. Rosie did not want Paulee to exchange the earrings for a necklace; she promised to wait until she got older to have her ears pierced.

I don't know why I did not ask Rosie to give the earrings to me. I knew she wasn't happy about waiting three years to have her ears pierced, and another name for her promises were lies, but I was distracted by her outburst. I was also worried about Joe forgetting to pick up her birthday cake at the bakery before it closed. It was no excuse, I should have grabbed them when I had the chance; it was no surprise she disobeyed me. Rosie had her ears pierced before Paulee's earrings gathered one speck of dust in her jewelry box.

Three weeks to the day of her birthday Rosie went to the jewelry kiosk with Doreen. Rosie could pass for eighteen easily which was frightening, but they probably never even asked her for an ID. The girls working at the kiosks looked like young teens themselves. Rosie's defiance and appearing older than her age were more troubling than what she had done. It was only her ears; what kept me up at night was worrying about her other body parts. Doreen's mother was more distraught about it than I was. She had taken the girls shopping at the mall, and she assured me they had only separated for an hour. She wanted to give them a little space to shop where they wanted, and they were to meet up afterwards at the food court.

"I'm so sorry, Sarah. I had no idea they were planning on doing this. I feel just awful."

I told her not to blame herself too much. Rosie would have done it sooner or later—it was only a matter of time. I had often let Rosie go off with her friends with a designated meet up time too. What was really disturbing about this stunt was Rosie had pulled it with someone other than me. I feared if she wasn't careful some mothers might declare her off limits, and she would lose girlfriends. My mother did that with a few of my wild friends (luckily Dee had only been placed on restriction for a couple of weeks). I warned Rosie but it made no impression; her behavior did not change.

Rosie was always defiant, and her negative behavior was on-going. Her ear-piercing caper was *the birthday sequel,* and I haven't even finished with all the other memories from her birthday. Her unwanted behavior was not confined to a tussle over ear-piercing. She caused a big brouhaha over movie choices when we went to the theater after lunch. I would only let her and her friends see a movie rated PG-13, and there were two choices—*Greater,* or *Me Before You;* Rosie threw a fit. Her friends kept their mouths shut during our entire exchange. Why had they been such angels? With Rosie it had always been one emotional blowup after another; it was hard to focus. It took ten minutes of histrionics in the theater lobby before she finally agreed to *Me Before You*, but I had not trusted her. I told her she had to give me every detail of the plot. The way these theaters were designed it was too easy to walk out of one screening room into another after the movie started.

It was a welcomed relief when she and her friends finally walked through the turnstile; and while they were at the movies Paulee and I went shopping. When we returned the girls were laughing and talking. They had liked the movie, including Rosie, and gave us enough details that I was fairly confident they had seen it. Teenagers, you had to love them, if they didn't kill you first. Reflecting on all the drama, it could have been worse. She could have chosen to sneak out of the theater to pierce her ears that day; she at least waited three weeks to use her gift. That was my gift from the gods; I could not have handled any more defiance on her birthday.

After the movie I dropped Rosie's girlfriends off at their homes, and Paulee went to her place to feed her cats. She and my mother were coming over later for the family birthday dinner. Rosie's behavior that afternoon had been unpleasant, but I pushed it aside. I chose to muse on what my mother would have done in my situation instead, even though it was impossible to emulate her. There was nothing to mimic because my sister and I never acted like Rosie. Rosie's behavior had to be genetic from Joe's side of the family, and Joe was another reason I ignored Rosie's theatrics. There was no point in telling him about it because he would not have backed me up. If I had suggested a punishment, he would have said, "It's her birthday, Sarah. Are you sure you're not overreacting?"

Joe was kept in blissful ignorance and grilled steaks, hot dogs and hamburgers for the brat's birthday celebration. I had made potato salad and a large tossed salad in the morning before our trip to the mall and Joe remembered to pick up the birthday cake. We managed to get through the meal and sang *Happy Birthday* with no emotional incidents, except for Paulee who was overly contrite. She was really sorry but she had to go home after we served the cake—she had a splitting headache. She was not even staying to watch Rosie open her presents. I hoped Rosie and I weren't the ones who had given her a pain in the head—Paulee loved it when people opened presents at a party. I promised to give her the rundown the following day.

Mom gave Rosie a watch with little sapphire stones in its face and some money. Joe and I gave her a pink saucer chair, a Crayola jewelry making kit, and some lip gloss. I was pleased when she had asked for these gifts and not something age-inappropriate like a bikini thong. She was really happy when she opened our presents too, and for the first time that day I felt celebratory—my little girl had turned thirteen. I asked my mother if she wanted another glass of wine to toast Rosie's birthday but she had to leave. She was covering for someone the next day and had to get up early.

That's why my mother and Paulee were not there when I gave Rosie my gifts. Perhaps reactions would have been different if they had been present. I'm pretty sure my mother would have sided with me, but it wouldn't have mattered; Paulee and my mother canceled each other out. Paulee was clearly on Joe's team when I told her about my presents.

It started in a positive way when I handed the gift box to Rosie. I told her it was something she could use in her saucer chair. She was all smiles while she tore off the gift wrap, opened the box and moved the pink tissue paper aside—until she saw my gifts. Her smiles vanished, replaced by an expression that looked like I had given her a box of dead kittens.

"Oh, gross. That's disgusting, Mom"

Joe took the box from her and looked inside. His face assumed a similar expression as his daughter's—more dead kittens.

"Sarah, can I talk to you privately?" I followed him up to our bedroom, feeling like a chastised little girl.

"Why are you giving Rosie a book on masturbation and that thing? She's only thirteen. Why are you encouraging her to be sexual?"

"I'm not encouraging her 'to be sexual' Joe, puberty is already doing that. I'm only trying to direct her to ways she can express it safely. You're acting like I gave her birth control pills, or made an appointment for her to be fitted for a diaphragm."

According to him a book on masturbation and a sex toy were equivalent to giving her birth control.

"No, they aren't Joe. One is showing her how she can pleasure herself, and refrain from having sex too early; the other is encouraging her to go out and do it."

"But what if she hurts herself, Sarah?"

"That's why I gave her the book. And I gave her a little clitoris stimulator so she can have clitoral orgasms. She doesn't have to insert it like some sex toys. She won't break her hymen."

Joe looked appalled after I said that—those kittens were not only dead they had released a foul odor which permeated all through the house. He was angry. His voice as usual was not loud or threatening, but when he finally responded—sarcasm dripped off his words splashing me in the face.

"Well, I'm really happy you're such an expert, Sarah, but I'd be happier if you hadn't given a sex toy to our thirteen-year-old daughter. And she's our daughter, not yours alone. I think you forgot that."

Now I got angry.

"What would you prefer Joe, her masturbating, or blowing some pimply ninth-grade boy? Or getting an STD? Or maybe getting pregnant? You wanted another baby. You can be a grandfather."

I don't know which scenario worked the most effectively to get Joe over to my side. If I had to choose one, I'd say it was the pimply ninth-grader. I cannot make a definite decision about that, but I was sure about something. Words alone are not always effective, but if combined with action, they are more likely to yield results. It did not matter which words moved

Joe—he retreated, and I was glad I had acted by giving Rosie my gifts.

Joe grudgingly agreed that Rosie could keep my presents. He stopped fighting with me but did not drop the subject. He told me if he had been given a choice, he would have preferred that I gave her my gifts when he wasn't there; or at least a heads up about what I was planning. I was split on those points: I agreed I was wrong not to have told him. We could have discussed it and might have avoided an argument. It also made me pause—maybe I needed to review Dr. Barney's notes on motivation and toxic control, but I disagreed about giving the gifts to Rosie without him. It was never a consideration; Joe needed to see them as much as Rosie needed them. He had to be shown she was no longer a little girl. And Rosie's sensibilities had to be considered above all. I had not wanted to encourage a negative vibe—her sexuality was not something to be ashamed of. Why shouldn't her father be present when I gave her a book on masturbation and a sex toy?

When Joe and I returned to the living room Rosie was gone and so was the gift box with my goodies. I heard music coming from Rosie's bedroom and I went to check on her.

"You okay, Rosie?"

"Yes, Mother."

"Okay, Daughter, happy birthday."

After I was secure in the knowledge I had not emotionally scarred my daughter, Joe and I started to clean up; the party had been small but had still generated plenty of mess. When we were done we watched TV until turning in and we never discussed that evening. Nor do I know if Rosie read the book or tried the toy. I never asked her because I knew she would have protested: *none of your business.* She was not enlightened or force-fed Dr. Ruth since she was five like me (whichever way one wants to look at it). But sometimes I thought I heard a humming coming from her room; it was probably my imagination. The toy I bought for her was very small and quiet. It was one of the reasons I chose it. Some of them are loud, and I hadn't wanted her to feel self-conscious thinking we heard what she was doing. She often took Holly in her room too—it had been another consideration. One time when Holly was on my bed she started to growl and bark at my loud toy. Not great for focus. The cats had never minded, maybe they thought I was purring.

CHAPTER 26

TOP AND BOTTOM AND IN-BETWEEN

Rosie was changing from a little girl to a woman. Sometimes a fraught time, but an exciting and welcomed part of one's life. I was changing in ways I was not happy about. My eyes were the first. I've always had 20/20 vision—the only glasses I had ever worn were sunglasses so I was a bit negligent on having regular eye exams. If I had been regular, maybe I wouldn't have been taken by surprise walking across campus one afternoon and my eyes started to water profusely—no pain, but they wouldn't stop tearing. I made a long overdue appointment for a complete eye exam. The doctor told me I had dry eyes. How could that be true when I could fill buckets with my tears? He said my tear ducts were working overtime trying to keep my eyes moistened. He gave me several eye drop samples for dry eyes and I squinted all the way home with dilated pupils.

A year later I was eating my breakfast when I noticed I couldn't see the food clearly if I looked down at my plate. I was scared. I told Joe I might be having a stroke or at the very least—my retinas were detaching. Joe laughed. "How many degrees do you have, Sarah?" Whenever Anthony thought Paulee was insulting him he would say, "I think that's a crack." That's what I wanted to say to Joe.

It was funny, I had acted foolishly—my retinas hadn't detached and I wasn't having a stroke. And I knew that people my age will eventually need reading glasses, but I thought it was gradual—not suddenly as it happened to me. That's what made me overreact, and I readily admit to not being a naturally calm person. Perhaps compared to Paulee I am, but not when measured against anyone else.

That's why I often asked myself—why does Liz always say, "You're so laid-back, nothing bothers you." Perhaps it was due to my years teaching math to teenagers, when you wanted to ring their scrawny little necks but you suppressed it. I developed a knack for feigning a cool, calm exterior. You cannot lose your cool, even if you're stressed to the breaking point when you work with teenagers.

I was glad Liz had never noticed how flustered I was when Rocky unexpectedly came home. I never wanted her to be aware of my reaction because she worried about him cheating on her (I didn't want her to think he was doing it with me). She's never said specifically that he cheated but her stories suggested her state of mind. She told me how women were always hanging all over him. He would tell her they were friends of his buddies, he only knew them casually, and he never introduced her to them. It was also upsetting to her that he refused to wear a wedding ring. I told her Joe hadn't worn one for a year. That had not made her feel better, but she would have felt worse if I had told her Joe had been upset when he lost it. He was the one who wanted to replace it, and I was the one who said, "What's the point, it won't be the same ring I gave you on our wedding day."

"It's a symbol, Sarah." He made me feel like an unromantic clod so I gave him a replacement band for a Christmas gift. I wanted to have—*Don't Lose This One*—engraved inside, but that would have really made me an unromantic clod.

I might not show my emotions with my students or when I was near Rocky, but I always express them with Joe. Exemplified by the day I lost it over reading glasses.

"What do you mean you're having a stroke?"

"I can't see my scrambled eggs clearly on the plate, Joe." Panic pushed my octave up a little bit higher on each word.

"Well, can you see when you're looking up?"

"Yes."

"I think you need reading glasses, Sarah. You're not having a stroke." He tried not to laugh, but he couldn't help himself and I could not get angry with him for laughing. I had really overreacted. The more I thought about it I realized that my emotions had been especially erratic for no good reason lately—like I had PMS all the time. I needed to have my bottom checked out along with my top.

Non-stop PMS wasn't the only reason I wanted to see my gynecologist; my eyes were not the only things out of focus and dry—so was my poor pussy. Intercourse was becoming painful and I thought this happened only after menopause. The doctor told me I was experiencing perimenopause. There were two? She said it could last a few months or as long as eight years until I reached full blown menopause. I didn't appreciate the distinction between the two since perimenopause could also dry out your pussy, make your breasts tender, lower your sex drive, and give you hot flashes. She also added fatigue, weight gain, and acne. Would she say the root cause of my feet getting flatter was due to perimenopause too? Maybe she did; she was still listing symptoms when I stopped listening. I got it—and I didn't want it. It was overwhelming, and there wasn't even an advantage to perimenopause. I needed to keep using birth control—I could experience pregnancy along with the other undesirable symptoms.

I was a little upset but was assured that not everyone experiences all these negatives, and she was right. I never had hot flashes or a diminished sex drive, but the latter resulted in another problem. My libido was at war with my pussy and my pussy was losing; intercourse was hurting like hell more each day. I was tempted to use my clitoral stimulators exclusively, shutting Joe out—literally and figuratively. I did not want to do that, so perimenopause forced our lovemaking to change.

We now set aside more time for foreplay. It was foreplay in a non-traditional sense. It wasn't a prep for intercourse. I came and Joe cummed before we even attempted to have intercourse. It was a sex play in two acts, but unlike a traditional play, each act had a climax with an intermission between. Joe needed to regain his manhood to start after the first act, and while he recovered I lubed up in the wings. The second go-around was solely for him—his act to take center stage; I was a supporting player, with one line: "Think Sadie's House, baby, make it quick." It was a joke with an element of truth. He knew it was not necessary to hold back anymore (lubricants are not as great as advertised).

I had to face it, I was only in my early forties and I was aging, but Joe was impressive. He had two orgasms in our sex play and not many men his age could. I'm pretty sure Dr. Ruth might have said that in a radio broadcast, but it was years ago. I was only a kid when I listened to those programs; I didn't remember if she had ever mentioned male menopause. If there is one it hadn't hit Joe yet, and he was three years my senior.

Our sex life changed: less thrusting and more licking, sucking, touching and fondling. I was satisfied, and sent thanks to Aphrodite that I never had a dry pussy in the early years of our marriage. It would not have survived if I had experienced early perimenopause at thirty. I hoped Joe was satisfied too and I believed he was, if playing more with my boobs was any indicator. That was fortunate for both of us—and I'm not only referring to a man's erotic fascination with boobs or my own tactile pleasure. He was the one who found the lump under the lower part of my left breast. At my annual well-check appointments my gynecologist always asked: "Do you perform breast self-exams?"

I always lied and said "yes." I'm not sure why I lied, and one would think someone who played with her pussy so much like me would also do breast self-exams—but I never did.

CHAPTER 27

TO HAVE OR HAVE NOT

When you have a cancer scare one of the worst things to endure is the pain of waiting. After finding the worrisome symptom you first wait to get a doctor's appointment. If it is a cancer concern they are often quicker than usual, but in my case they didn't say, "Come right in." I had to wait three days. Next, they scheduled a biopsy, another delay; and finally getting my results took over a week. Added up it was a total of many hours of marking time, cooling heels and twiddling thumbs—and my emotions were changeable. One day I would wish the phone would ring, other days I hoped it never did. When I knew the results were positive I stopped caring about how long I had waited for appointments and results. The focus now was on my fear.

The first oncologist told me the tumor was very small and a single mastectomy would be the best plan based on my family history of breast cancer. My mother always says to get at least three estimates if you need to hire someone to make a major repair on your house. I was going to follow her advice; I wanted three evaluations for the major repair on my body, and I did not like the first doctor's plan of treatment one iota. The second oncologist's plan was even more undesirable. He not only advised removing the breast with the tumor, he also suggested a double mastectomy as a preventative measure. Three was the magic number, and the third oncologist proposed a lumpectomy and removing a few lymph nodes from under my arm. It would be a three day stay in the hospital if I chose to go with him.

It was a no-brainer, I chose to have a lumpectomy and both Paulee and my mother did not agree with my decision, but were split on protocol. Paulee thought I should have the single mastectomy and my mother thought the double was more advisable, which shocked me. My mother was a woman who touted noninvasive procedures and alternative medicine her whole life; I was shocked that she wanted me to get a double mastectomy. She had even encouraged me to use pot to ease my morning sickness when I was pregnant, which surprised me since she always complained about me smoking. When I had asked her "why the change of heart," she replied, "I never said I was against it for medicinal purposes, Sarah." I did not expect her to give me herbs or to send me to her acupuncturist for breast cancer, but I couldn't understand her pressuring me to get a double mastectomy. Or why she was not comfortable with the oncologist I chose. He was a well-respected, licensed, legitimate doctor, and he proposed the least radical procedure. I would think she'd agree he was the best choice, with her penchant for non-invasive medicine. Instead she called us both fools (him for proposing a lumpectomy and me for choosing it).

"Did you tell him your grandmother died from breast cancer?" I assured her that he was aware of our family history. That's exactly when she called us fools and became more aggressive. My doctor was spared face-to-face contact with my mother, but I was not so fortunate. To emphasize just how unwise and shallow I was she said, "They are only breasts, Sarah. This is your life we are talking about. More important than your boobs."

Paulee never insulted me, or pressured directly for a double mastectomy. She chose a more subtle way to express her opinion about the latter. She kept reminding me about Angelina Jolie (who got a preventative double mastectomy and then implants). Why couldn't I do that?

Joe was the only one who cared about my breasts as much as me, and he was the only one who supported my decision—so I attacked him. I took my mother's words, throwing them in his face, telling him he cared more about my breasts than my life.

"I hope you don't really think that, Sarah." I didn't; I was angry and scared. I apologized for saying it. He said, "Not a problem," and held me that night until I stopped crying. He whispered in my ear he'd support me in any decision I made—he only cared about me.

Paulee thought a single mastectomy was better than a lumpectomy, if I was not choosing the Angelina

Jolie route, but she continued to be supportive. She helped Joe and me by caring for Holly. He took off from work and was practically staying at the hospital non-stop. Rosie had also been another problem to consider and Paulee offered to care for our incorrigible daughter. She could not be left alone, and it would have been a problem with Joe not being home most of the time. Paulee did not think Rosie was *incorrigible*, but I knew she would not have been able to control her. My mother had been a better choice than Paulee; her house had the advantage of not being walking distance from Rosie's friends or any teen hang-outs. Joe had to call my mother to see if Rosie could stay with her for the three days I was in the hospital. She refused to speak to me after I chose to have a lumpectomy. She never came to visit me at the hospital either.

When I woke up from the operation my hand went to my left breast. Joe gently took my hand saying, "It's still there, baby." This wasn't some irrational fear on my part. My doctor had told me the plan was to remove the tumor and the lymph nodes under my arm but also warned, "once we get in there we might find something unexpected." Mammograms were not perfect; if warranted my breast would have been removed and I had agreed to it.

I was relieved and happy I still had two breasts, until Joe scared me. I knew he was only trying to make me feel better, but it was unsettling when he said: "Even if they removed both and I had to wheel you around in a wheelchair, I'd love you." It made me question my prognosis. Had they told him something he wasn't telling me? I was not completely comfortable about my future until Joe brought Rosie to the hospital to visit me.

"Hi, Mom, how do you feel?" She then spent the rest of the time looking at her phone, ignoring me completely. That's when I knew I was okay.

After the immediate relief of being alive and in one piece, I noticed the room was filled with flowers.

"Where did all these flowers come from, Joe?"

"I guess you have a lot of well-wishers, Sarah."

When he went to the cafeteria a nurse came in and I asked her the same question. She said she thought most were from my husband. That turned out to be true, but there were tulips from Liz and a plant from Paulee. I was surprised to also see my sister Penny had sent flowers, but there was nothing from my mother.

I was sore from the operation, but once I healed, the only evidence of having had one was a little pucker on the underside of my left breast. It was hardly noticeable. If someone looked at my breast their eyes would have been drawn to my tattoo—not the little imperfection.

The surgery was only the first part of my protocol. I had six weeks of radiation treatments after the operation. My breast swelled a bit and I had some redness. It looked like I had fallen asleep on the beach and the left side of my bathing suit had fallen off—exposing my breast to the sun. I had similar burns in my life before from sunbathing topless. It wasn't a new sensory experience, and the treatments had no other adverse side effects. The real discomfort was being back in the waiting game—now waiting to see if I'd reach five years of remission. Waiting seems to be a core activity throughout one's experience with cancer.

CHAPTER 28

ROSIE POKED THE BEAR

In 2019 Rosie finally poked the bear. I did not know it at the time but it was also the year before the bear went into hibernation. Rosie poking him would pale in emotional significance compared to that. I never knew sleeping bears could be as threatening to your well-being as ones who were awake; but let me start at the beginning.

At the start of 2019 Joe began to work more than he had ever done before. He often traveled out of state and made long daily commutes when he worked locally. He left at 6 am in the mornings and returned at 7:30 or later in the evenings. When he got home he ate dinner, flopped in front of the television and zoned out. Sexual overtures were not well received—he was simply too pooped; and talk, which was always an issue with us, was reduced even more. It was hard to fault him though, he was exhausted.

There was no time for his hobbies during the week either, but if the weather permitted he would golf on the weekends or go to his flying club. I started to accompany him to the flying club in order to spend more time with him. It was kind of fun watching the model airplanes being flown but there was not much opportunity for discussions while we were there. We could talk while driving to and from at least—it was better than nothing.

Less talk was not that bothersome because it did not deviate far from our norm, but less sex was new and problematic. We only made love once a week which was troubling, until I reassured myself. After seventeen years of marriage we were still statistically more active than many couples. I also had my toys to play with and started to use them more frequently than making love with Joe. It was different from when we were first married though. I wanted Joe to make love to me now. I was not trying to avoid him, but opportunities were few.

I did not complain; how could I? I was the reason he was working so much. It had been ten years since I got my PhD, and I still could not find a full-time teaching position. The investment made had not reaped dividends. It had only left a big hole in our savings which Joe was trying to fill. Since getting my degree I had only been able to find work as an adjunct professor. When Joe began his grueling schedule I taught at three community colleges and one four-year university. Joe's sister Lynne continued to make more money than I did working as a server in a restaurant.

After a few years looking for work I determined that many schools preferred to hire younger applicants who had recently graduated from five-year programs. Naturally, it was not a formal finding but it was the buzz in my circle of academia. It was not all unsubstantiated complaining; the buzz had some merit. Full-time positions were often offered to recent graduates in their twenties. Their only teaching background was their assistantship while they worked on their PhD's. I am not suggesting these are not valid teaching experiences, but why were they viewed as equivalent to my many years working as an adjunct?

Another problem: there was a glut of people holding upper-level degrees, which is often the case when the economy was weak and jobs were scarce. There is an exponential increase of people returning to school. The reasons why I hadn't been successful were valid, and Joe never suggested I had been complacent or not trying to find full-time work; in the end it did not matter. I still had not been able to help him fill the financial hole we were in and he was frantically trying to fill it by himself.

I tried not to bother Joe as much as possible. When the sliding door would not lock going out to our deck and the mirror in the hallway fell off the wall (after Rosie slammed the front door), I dealt with them myself; or I asked my mother to come over with her power drill. She was overly helpful those days; she was remorseful about the way she treated me when I had my lumpectomy. I had forgiven her, but her actions continued to be a painful memory, and I had no problem asking her for help. I should have, knowing her busy schedule, but I didn't. I was letting her correct a wrong—we were doing each other a favor the way I saw it, and I couldn't ask Joe.

I tried especially not to burden him with Rosie problems. He had been involved when Rosie started to ignore curfews but for the most part I handled her myself. I was confident that I could with years of experience dealing with teenagers as a teacher. I was deluding myself. My one child was far more difficult to handle than scores of students. I could not cope with her even when it concerned education. Rosie had C's in most of her subjects, and the personal insult—she was failing geometry. She took it sophomore year, summer school and again junior year. A count of three times and she was in summer school again to repeat geometry. It almost seemed like she was doing it on purpose to torment me—her mother, who held two degrees on the graduate level in mathematics.

The second week of summer session I received a note from Mrs. Aronson, Rosie's geometry teacher. She needed to speak with me about Rosie and wanted to meet me. I always went to parent/teacher conferences and this would be no exception. Joe was working but he would not have attended. I was the pro-active parent when it came to speaking with her teachers, and that was what Joe preferred.

Mrs. Aronson and I started our discussion with the usual amenities and then she began with, "I know mathematics is not an easy subject for many students," to introduce the topic of Rosie not completing even one assignment in the first week. I replied by telling her that Rosie had good grades in math until high school, and I would have thought she would have a genetic predisposition to do well in the subject with my background in mathematics. "I teach it at the college level." I took her by surprise, and she acted uncomfortably standoffish after I said it. My intent had not been to brag about myself or belittle her. The only reason I told her was to accentuate my disbelief—how was it possible my own kid was repeating geometry for the fourth time? I was of course deluding myself again. There was a strong probability of continued failure based on her history. All of Rosie's teachers, except for Mrs. Aronson—who clammed up, had repeatedly told me she did not work to her fullest potential. Once she hit seventh grade, every teacher would say in some fashion—*she's very smart but she does not apply herself and has many missing assignments.* Their feedback was always so similar it sounded memorized from a teacher's manual, but it was true and no surprise. Once Rosie hit puberty, she only cared about her hair, her clothes, her nails, talking on the phone with her girlfriends—and boys.

Rosie's grades were not my only concern in the summer of 2019, I worried about her general safety and chastity. It is not an exaggeration to say she was often dressed like a prostitute when she left for school, but I can't even describe it as dressed. A more accurate description was *undressed,* and I had been unable to physically restrain her from walking out the door when she was hell-bent on doing it. I tried to stop her by screaming until I accepted the fact that I was destroying my vocal cords for no purpose. No matter how many times I bellowed out, "You can't leave the house dressed like that"—it failed to keep her from leaving, slamming the door behind her. And she never forgot to punctuate her departures with colorful language.

She had a foul mouth and it was no surprise; she learned it from an early age at her grandfather's house and often used some of Mac's favorite expletives. She called me a "bitch" and "cunt" frequently and threw F-bombs daily. She would never have talked or dressed the way she had if Joe was around. The problem: Joe was rarely home anymore that summer—Rosie dressed and talked how she pleased.

I often blamed Joe the most for her bad behavior because he spoiled her, but he was not a player when it came to her foul mouth. It was also unfair to entirely blame Mac for Rosie's expletives. I was also partly responsible for the way she talked. It was my choice to never tell Joe what she called me; he would have put a stop to it, and Rosie knew it. That's why she refrained from using that verbiage in front of him.

My explanation for not telling Joe about Rosie's hand-picked lexicon, meant only for me, had nothing to do with his being gone or not wanting to bother him. His work schedule was new but Rosie's gutter mouth wasn't. She was an early bloomer—she had been cursing since she was twelve. I never mentioned it before because I was more focused on her behavior—not her knee-jerk responses to my admonishments. I have a developed filter enabling me to focus on behavior over language from years of teaching.

I had heard inappropriate words, and had been called harsh names many times before Rosie uttered her first expletive. I simply do not get that upset about name-calling or F-bombs. In high school my reaction to the verbal abuse had been to calmly say with a smile, "Alice, Marjorie, and Carol, I've called the office and they are waiting for your prompt arrival." The girls were always worse than the boys, but I never lost my cool no matter who was expressing their angst, and I was not feigning calmness. When it came to abusive language, I sometimes even found it amusing. I might have been truly annoyed about their talking in class, or refusing to put their phones away, or whatever had ticked me off in the first place—but their expletives were not a big deal. It was the same with Rosie when she called me a "whore."

"Is your father a 'whore' too, Rosie? The payoff is mutual since we each give and satisfy one another, right?"

"Oh, gross; seriously, Mom? I don't want to hear about your sex life." Funny girl.

Her language was not what I was really worried about nor her clothes. As offensive as her language and slut wardrobe were, they only irritated me. I knew she would grow out of all these behaviors on her own eventually. Teens rebel and adopt crazy clothes and hairstyle fads. What I worried about were her poor grades ruining her chances of getting into college; she had to start applying herself in school. I tried to handle things myself as long as I could, but I needed help from Joe. I did not anticipate it being too taxing on him after a long day of work and I had no plan to pounce on him the minute he walked in the door. I waited until he had eaten and watched a show on television before I broached the subject with him.

I was confident we would come up with a strategy. We had worked together in the spring when she had acted out. Joe and I grounded her after she came home at midnight. He had been quite upset with her, and even though he hadn't reacted as strongly about the school issue, he did not undermine me when I punished her for skipping three days after Christmas. Apparently Rosie had gotten used to having no school and wanted to add more days to the holiday break. Flunking math had nothing to do with her aptitude. It was another act of defiance, and I was sure Joe would agree with me.

"I'm concerned about Rosie, Joe. She's in summer school for the second time, and I'm afraid she's going to fail geometry again. I don't know how she is going to get into a college if she doesn't start applying herself."

"Well, not everyone is a scholar, Sarah. And it didn't get you very far. Does she even need college? It was probably a waste of time for me considering what I ended up doing."

It was implicit, but clear, and the first time he ever made a suggestion about me not finding a job or the futility of my degree. His comment was not filled with detail, all the same—it was a direct punch to the gut. I was more hurt and surprised than angry, but

I needed to defend myself; I never said she must go to college. Then again that was probably not true, I might have said it. What could she do if she didn't go to college? I wasn't being disingenuous though when I said it would be okay with me if she wanted to work in a nail salon or be a masseuse. I only wanted her to seriously consider her future, and work towards some goal. "Whatever she chooses to do, Joe, shouldn't she try to do her best in her profession?" When I asked him that I pointed out how he was one of the highest earners at his job.

"Well, maybe she is a late bloomer like me, Sarah. I wasn't so good in high school either."

That's what happened. He dismissed it without helping out at all. So much for the help I had anticipated. He made me livid.

"Maybe we can get her a job working on a fishing boat in Alaska when she graduates, or better yet she can work at Sadie's House, it's a better fit."

Joe did not say a single word in response; he simply turned away from me and went to the kitchen and took a beer from the fridge. He then went up to his workroom without a glance towards me, as though I was not even in the room. I once read the worst thing you can do to a person is ignore them. It's worse than arguing, or calling them a *bitch*, *cunt* or *whore*. I was invisible to him. It would have been better if he had lashed out at me; I shouldn't have said that about Rosie. I wanted to call out to him to apologize but his name stuck in my mouth, strangled by a feeling of panic and abandonment; I asked myself—where are these emotions coming from? A sudden memory came to me like an answer to my question:

I'm very young and I'm waking up in the middle of the night crying, but I'm not in the bedroom I remember growing up in. It's a different bedroom and I am calling for my daddy. My mother comes into the room to comfort me. She tells me my daddy would be with me if he could, but he was looking down at me all the time.

I always thought I had no memory of my father. I was wrong, I did have one but it had been buried deep inside of me. Joe triggered this emotional recall about abandonment and anger towards my father because he had made me feel the same way that night. It was irrational thinking in both contexts. My father had not willingly left me. He never came home again because he was killed in a car crash on a bridge connecting St. Paul and Minneapolis; and Joe had not left me—he had only been angry. But enough that he never came up to bed. I waited for him; I was unable to fall asleep. I found him slumbering peacefully on the couch the next morning. One of us had a good night's rest.

We never resumed our discussion about Rosie's grades. Joe continued his grueling schedule, and our time together to discuss anything remained limited like it had been for months. That night stayed on my mind though, even if it was irrational to believe a little altercation was serious. I was foolish to question Joe's love, but it was the first time since we were a couple that it had seemed like he didn't love or respect me. The feeling of being unloved was too short-lived to measure, but the feeling of abandonment persisted. It was measurable.

Joe loved and craved me, but he no longer believed in me. He always used to say, "I love your brains," but it had not sounded like that anymore the way he had spoken. It was a form of abandonment. He no longer thought I would find a meaningful position—the higher degree in mathematics had been a futility. What was even sadder—I agreed with him. And what good were brains anyway if I didn't use them? It was time to get realistic. I had to re-evaluate what I was doing—perhaps look for a different career, but our lack of time together was more of an immediate concern. It took precedence over old news. I had been looking for a job for ten years; I froze that pursuit, especially since I had no clue what career to pursue if I left teaching.

I chose to focus on us, to find spaces where we could spend more time together; it yielded results, I convinced Joe to take a few days off (just the two of us alone—without flying buddies or Rosie). When Rosie went off to summer school on his first free day, we spent a relaxing quality-time day together. It was rejuvenating for us both, and I was definitely not invisible.

Rosie had not known Joe took time off or was home the first day of his mini vacation. During the week he always left before she got up. Usually when she left for school he was long gone but that day he was in bed, an ironic reversal. When she returned from school, he was out on the deck. She retreated to her room as soon as she came home, continuing to believe it was only me in the house with her.

It was only a short time later when she came out of her room ready to do—who knew what—all decked out in her usual garb. She was wearing a tiny little top showing off her breasts with a very short skirt which hung low below her belly button. It always seemed like she especially wanted to show off her navel judging by the style of clothes she consistently wore. I didn't approve of her clothes but had to admit she did have a cute innie—my aesthetic preference. I wasn't thinking about that when she walked into the room looking like a prostitute though; her skirt was so short and tight I wondered how she managed to sit down. Her hair and makeup were also cringe-worthy but they completed the look. I silently applauded her but vocally repri-manded: "Where do you think you are going dressed like that, Rosie?"

"Out with Dorrie, bye."

"You are not going out like that, and I also want you to do your homework before you go anywhere."

She said, "Fuck you" the very moment Joe walked into the room. What followed immediately was a fixed frame. They both looked like they had suddenly been zapped into frozen statues caught staring at one another—eyes wide and mouths slightly opened. Joe was the first to speak and I never dreamed I'd hear those words come out of his mouth.

"Rosie, listen to your mother, go up and change your clothes."

Had her reaction been due to her hearing the words "listen to your mother"? Or was it because she didn't realize who she was talking to when she replied? Joe was a quiet calm man, but he was a difficult presence to simply overlook with his linebacker stature. My guess is she was not only very aware of him, she also believed she could lead him around by the nose. Why not continue to do so? I was not sure what enabled her, the only thing that was clear and loud was when she screamed: "Oh, fuck you too, you fat nerd."

Calling him "fat" was uncalled for. It was true he had put on a little weight around his middle. He ate too much fast food once he started his frenzied work schedule but he didn't look fat. Her perception might have been different from mine, but it was still disrespectful to say that to your father. It was also disrespectful to call him a "nerd," although I totally agreed with that particular name-call. It was true without a doubt—he is one. I had been uncertain about him when we first met, but knew it for sure after we married. Nerdiness is not only about being a math whiz. It also can be applied to socially awkward people who have an excellent recall for obscure information; Joe would be a commendable contestant on a quiz show if he ever were so inclined. Marrying Joe was the universe once again getting back at me; this time for torturing those nerdy little boys in high school. Years later a grown-up nerd was allowed to do more than look at my boobs and drool; he was able to fondle and suck them—and screw me. It was the ultimate revenge.

Joe being a nerd was not the point however. Rosie should have never said it, but it was not as insulting as what she called me. "Nerd" is not an expletive or equivalent to her names for me. The "fuck you" that continued to vibrate in the air after she slammed the door was different—problematic in practice and theory. I failed to come up with a good rationalization for her throwing an F-bomb at Joe and am ashamed to admit—I was not very upset about that. The scales had finally been balanced in the family. I was no longer the only one she lobbed them at. I would have pondered more on her choice of epithets and my reaction to them but there was not much time. My daughter moved really fast after she screamed at Joe. She was out of the house in a flash and left us standing in the dust staring at the slammed door.

I don't think what Rosie had said moved Joe at all. My guess? Looking like one of Sadie's girls had done it. His voice was calm and not rushed when he asked—*where is she going,* but he moved faster than I had ever seen him move; father like daughter and very impressive. Just like a bear. They look like they're slow when you see films of them lumbering along—until they are provoked into speedy action. Joe had been provoked, and he was in pursuit of Rosie after I told him she was headed for Doreen's. I asked him if he wanted company and he replied, "Not necessary." He seemed to have a plan when he took one of my jackets from the hook by the door, grabbed his keys, and walked out. I kept my fingers crossed Rosie did not give him too much trouble.

Doreen lived in our complex in the next court. I don't know why it took Joe almost two hours to return and I had started to fear Rosie had caused him to have a heart attack. It was with a sigh of relief when they finally returned and Joe appeared to be fine. It was Rosie who looked a little disheveled. She was wearing my mid-thigh jacket which did not fit her properly and her makeup was smeared all over her face. It was obvious she had been crying. Perhaps I should have been more worried about her safety than Joe's. Nerd boys who have suffered from social rejection often have repressed animosity; sometimes they are the ones to fear the most. It was an unrealistic speculation of course. Rosie's appearance was dramatic but I could not form a logical connection between it and Joe. Rosie was Daddy's little girl. Joe had never raised a hand or even his voice with her.

Rosie would not make eye contact with me but in a muffled voice said, "Sorry I cursed at you, Mom," and went up to her room. Her apology sounded like she had been coerced but I was still impressed and asked Joe what had happened. "I don't want to talk about it."

He forced me to pressure him for information the way he had obviously pressured Rosie to apologize; I tried my best but failed. Joe refused to talk, favoring his taciturn nature over me. I had to turn to Rosie for answers and when I asked her what happened she replied, "Ask him." That had not yielded any results initially; it was analogous to reading a novel with missing pages. There was a huge part of the story unknown to me, and to this day it's frustrating as hell not knowing what happened. I only know what I witnessed firsthand to piece together a picture.

The next day Rosie asked me for garbage bags, and when I asked her what she wanted them for she said, "Ask your husband." I don't know why she switched from pronoun to noun. I knew *him* referred to her father when she said it the day before. Saying both— *him* and your *husband,* was just her way of telegraphing to me she was pissed at Joe. This wasn't the kind of detail I was searching for; Joe at least gave me a little more information when I posed the same question to him.

"She's gathering clothes she no longer needs, and we're going to take them to some charity to donate." I read between the lines, but doubted that the clientele looking for those styles frequented thrift shops. Her clothes would have been good Halloween costumes though, if you wanted to be a sexy maid or hooker.

In addition to making her donate her slutty clothes, Joe laid down some rules. The one she complained about the most: Joe drove and picked her up 24/7. The mall, parties, and friends' houses were all contingent on Joe's work schedule, or mine with his okay. Simply put, she was restricted from going anywhere unless he was able to exert his control. It made choosing clothes, friends and activities more problematic for her. When she gave me an earful about his decree, I told her to complain to her father, not me. It usually shut her up.

Joe's rules resulted in some obvious changes in behavior, but she did not transform into a respectful, sweet and ever obedient child after poking the bear. I had not been greedy though, I was satisfied with any measure of positive change. She no longer wore clothes that looked like she should be standing on the street corner flagging men down in cars, or cursed loud enough at me to be absolutely sure she had. She continued to give me a hard time about cleaning her room and doing her homework but with a welcome change—she would eventually do both. She finally passed geometry that summer too, and her grades improved overall in the fall quarter. It was a major achievement, but paled in significance to her shift in attitude towards Joe, changing the dynamic in our family.

Rosie learned a lesson—she couldn't lead her father by the nose. It was a revelation for me, but I don't know why I had ever thought she could based on my own experiences with him. He never budged if he was not inclined to do so; if Joe spoiled Rosie it was something he wanted to do—she could not make him. And for the first time in her life she had not successfully manipulated her father. I don't know what happened between them that day, but I knew there was a strength in Joe which could be unleashed—before Rosie provoked him. I had always thought it was only sexually related—I now knew I was mistaken. Maybe he wasn't always calm or quiet in his resolve; he could release this power in different situations. It was an uncomfortable idea. I had been able to predict his forceful behavior when it came to sex, but I wasn't sure I would be able to do that in other contexts. There was also the sticky variable of time and its unknown quantity. It took almost sixteen years before Joe reacted to Rosie.

Rosie of course never behaved in front of him as she had with me. She still had been far from perfect, but she believed her daddy was manageable. And for most of her life he had been. It was analogous to an animal trainer who worked for years thinking they were in control. What finally made an animal revert to their natural wildness and suddenly lash out? A warning for us all perhaps; they were being submissive by their own choice and we should not forget it, or we might face dire consequences. It would have been wise if Rosie had been cognizant of that. I should have remembered this myself, but I didn't. My thoughts were too focused on her poking the bear in the summer of 2019, and I had only nudged Joe a little that summer. I only received a superficial scratch.

The problem was it reopened every time I remembered the implications he had made. It bled questions: had it been a wise decision spending so much time, effort and money getting my PhD? Did I need to find a different career where I could earn real money to contribute more to our family? I knew I had to take control of my professional life and assume more of our financial burdens for my self-realization. It was outside of Joe, but he continued to be a factor, and when he returned to a normal work schedule my goals were overshadowed. For a brief period worries and stress were less intense—allowing my scratch to heal. It would not reopen again until there was a perfect environment for it to fester.

CHAPTER 29

MOVING ON

When I started to teach in community college it was challenging choosing a vacation time with Paulee because our spring breaks weren't always the same. After I started working at multiple schools, it became more than a challenge—it was impossible to synchronize with her. My own schools' breaks did not always fall on the same calendar days, let alone match Paulee's. That's when we began to take long weekends; it was the only thing we could manage. We went to Washington, D.C. the spring of 2019 for the National Cherry Blossom Festival. Paulee wanted to drive, and against my better judgment I let her; she promised to keep her cool, and accepted my compromise—if her emotions got the better of her she would let me take over.

I had worried for nothing; the ride was uneventful, but our vacation was unforgettable. It had nothing to do with the festival or the posh Thai restaurant we went to our last night. The festival was great and the restaurant was very expensive but in a few years memories of them will probably fade. And Paulee had not made it memorable by strong-arming me to dine at that overly expensive restaurant. We had both wanted to splurge on it. We usually agreed on destinations, restaurants and activities. I treasured our camaraderie and was comfortable vacationing with her. I had been perusing those very thoughts when she blew my mind. That's when the trip had been etched in my mind and will stay there forever.

She started to lecture me about Rosie; she said I controlled her too much—which was a shocker. She had experienced her godchild's difficult behavior first-hand many times. But that statement was nothing compared to her next when she said Joe should have come with us on this trip. "He would have loved the National Air and Space Museum." I had to question what was wrong with her. No joke; I was concerned she was ill, and was tempted to ask the server if they used MSG in their food, which would be unforgivable with their prices. Paulee had known Joe as long as me; she knew he refused to take vacations.

Joe would never have taken off from work to go to a museum in Washington D.C., and it was fine with me. Rosie could not be trusted. She had to have oversight since she started skipping school and staying out past curfew. I hoped my mother would be able to control her with the planned arrangement while I was gone. She juggled her schedule around Joe's to be at the house with Rosie when he wasn't home, and she planned to drive her to school on Friday morning and pick her up in the afternoon. Paulee accused me of being overly cautious, dismissing Joe's part completely.

He had taken over some of the bad cop demeanor; it was no longer only me. Joe was still way too lenient from my perspective (this was two months before she poked him) but we were more in sync about our daughter than we had ever been before. And my best friend thought we were wrong. A new reversal; Paulee was the one I more often aligned with, not Joe, and I nearly choked on my noodles when she said Rosie needed more freedom.

Paulee thinks she knows everything about teenagers because she's a high school teacher. I tell her all the time it's different when you're a mother; she disagrees so I don't know why I was surprised by what she had said. It was a predictable statement, and compared to the next bombshell she dropped it was not a shocker: "I have some news; Anthony and I are getting married as soon as school is out in June." I never expected those words to come out of her mouth.

I screamed in her face, "Why?" All the people at a nearby table turned to look at us. They probably expected to see a food fight, and would have been surprised to learn what we were talking about. Suspecting we were having a heated argument about a volatile subject would be understandable, most people would have shouted *congratulations*. My question had been more appropriate because Paulee and Anthony getting married after all these years was crazy—a news flash worthy of *Weird New Jersey*.

There were too many factors that did not forebode well for this marriage. I know mathematics is not

Paulee's discipline but wasn't she able to do simple arithmetic? The only abstract element had been not knowing if they would be compatible housemates, everything else was clear and concrete. They never lived together, were set in their ways, and both turning fifty. It was highly improbable she would let him hang his nudie posters on the walls, and he hated her cats. There were even more obstacles to count. The stats were not in favor of this marriage; but even with the odds against them, I would not have opposed it if she had told me she loved Anthony: *life is short*. That's not what she said; she told me she was marrying him because they were going into business together. She was the third investor along with Anthony and his friend Harry—they were buying a restaurant.

"Don't get me wrong, Paulee. If you want to get married I am happy for you, but why do you guys have to marry to be business partners?"

"Obviously, you do not watch *Judge Judy*, Sarah. When it comes to property and money the courts treat couples who separate much better if they're married."

"Isn't that a little cynical? It's like you're already thinking you two might split up."

"Well, what do you think a prenup is saying? And you thought that was alright for your grandfather and Marie. This is more hopeful, I'm getting married without one."

Paulee's memory was a little fuzzy. I had been neutral about the prenup. It was my mother who had insisted they have one and Pops had thought like

Paulee. He and Marie finally agreed only to keep my mother happy. Prenups were not the issue however—it was Paulee's marriage that concerned me. I had strong opinions about that and I thought she was making a big mistake. We agreed about restaurants and vacation destinations, but we weren't in agreement about her impending marriage.

She was to be married by a justice of the peace and she wanted me to be a witness. After the vows were exchanged, we would celebrate at a restaurant—the same as we did with my doctorate. I made a plea to the universe as soon as she told me her plans: *grant her better luck with her marriage and business than I had with my career.* They were putting all their savings into their business venture; she also needed to sell her condo for more capital.

Marrying, selling property, and starting a business are big moves. I urged Paulee to reconsider. I reminded her how she and Anthony argued all the time. She was not being realistic thinking she could be his wife or his business partner.

"I've told you before, Sarah. We are not arguing, that's the way we talk, okay?"

I was grasping at straws, and really freaked out when she told me she was moving to Bergen County, but I made an attempt to hold on.

"Why do you have to move to Bergen County, Paulee, and what about your job?"

"The restaurant is in Bergen County, and that's where Anthony wants to move. You act like I'm moving out of the country, Sarah. And I am looking for jobs up north. I'm not giving up teaching. I already spoke to some people I know who told me there might be openings in the district for the fall. But I'm not worrying about it. If I can't find a teaching position, I'll retire and start collecting my pension. I can manage the restaurant."

I was about to mention how her pension would be negatively affected if she left teaching early, but paused. I had to finally ask myself a question: was I thinking about Paulee or myself? She was obviously happy about everything; I was the one who wasn't thrilled. She would not be a few doors up the street from our townhouse any longer; the same as if she were out of the country. People say they will keep in touch but I knew her moving away would change our relationship. I was dependent on Paulee (more than she was on me obviously).

I laughed when she said Joe could stop in for visits when he had to go to his corporate office, which happened to be in Bergen County. I always knew she genuinely regarded him as a friend, not just the husband of a friend. It made me feel good, but I am ashamed to say a little jealous too, even though she also talked about me visiting. And she gave me other reassurances: we would keep the phone busy and our trips together would not end. This Washington, D.C. trip was not the last one. We would keep vacationing as always—"two girl buddies." I was not so sure about that. It had only been fifteen minutes earlier when she had laid down a new foundation. She changed our configuration when she said Joe should have come with us to Washington D.C.

Too much change, and I had not been able to stop it—they were determined to move forward on their plans. Anthony rented and his lease was up June 30th; they were moving in July whether Paulee's condo sold or not. Paulee wanted me to keep an eye on hers if it was still on the market at moving-time. I agreed, and she asked another favor, "Would you and Joe take my two cats, Anna and the King? All the apartments we've looked at near the restaurant don't allow pets." Our cats Bear and Ollie had died long ago, like the cats Paulee had when I first met her. She now had a white long-haired female named Anna and a male Siamese named King (the names of the principal characters from *The King and I)*. I said it would be okay; Joe wouldn't mind. He kept Ollie when Maureen left him and now I would get two when Paulee left me. I liked her cats, but I hoped her need to find a new home for them was truly about apartments and nothing to do with Anthony's dislike of felines. That had compelled me to ask one final time if she was really sure about marrying him. She insisted yes, no matter how much I objected to it.

Paulee promised she would come for Rosie's birthday in September, and she would visit her kitty babies as soon as she was settled. She also reiterated again and again that she would call so often I would not even notice that she had moved. An exaggeration if I ever heard one, and her promises were not the words that stand out the most for me. It was her saying, "It's only Bergen County, Sarah. Get over it," and I never really have. It all happened too quickly to process.

Three months flew after the Washington, D.C. trip, and I was soon waving goodbye to the newlywed Paulee as she pulled out of the court. Anna and the King had been with us for a week prior to her moving day. When she came to our house to say goodbye to them, they were already acclimated to our townhouse and the back of our couch. They looked at the gushing, tearful Paulee with disdain. If reincarnation was real, I could see Rosie coming back as a haughty cat. Her interactions with me were often luke-warm or cool just like Paulee's cats. Thinking about Rosie had momentarily distracted me from my distress about Paulee moving away.

Rosie might act like a haughty cat, but she changed for the better after she poked the bear. Joe on the other hand did not change at all; he still refused to tell me what happened between the two of them. It was annoying. I was her mother and he acted like I was some nosy neighbor who wanted to gossip. My annoyance about his secretiveness was not the most troublesome seed brewing discontent into our relationship. His digs about my effort to find work and my degree being futile kept being introduced into my memory mix. Any argument that he had not said those things directly failed to make me feel any better. It was not enough balm—his implications continued to hurt no matter how indirect they had been, and after Paulee left I had more free time to brood over them. It was better when she was his full-time advocate and could serve as a deflector. Joe's words were from weeks ago but there was a boomerang effect in my mind and they kept hitting me directly over and over again. I could not avoid them. I even studied them.

Joe is an ineffective communicator even when he wishes to speak clearly. It takes effort sometimes to figure out his true intentions, making it a necessity to re-examine his words. This generated another free-time activity. I began to look for full-time teaching positions outside of our area. It started as only a lark—I was merely curious. I remembered when I was working on my masters an education professor said: "You will find a teaching position, but you might have to move out of New Jersey." After I graduated I found my position teaching locally in a high school so easily that I dismissed what he said, and I presumed years later with that PhD diploma in hand it would be as easy finding another job—it wasn't.

Now the question was: were the professor's words still applicable? It was only a query. I wasn't looking seriously because Joe didn't want to relocate. I heard him say more than once: "I've been to a lot of places, but I rather live here than in other parts of the country." I was always tempted to ask him how he was so sure; he barely left his hotel room when he was in those "other parts of the country." I could have made a solid argument on that point alone and maybe it would have opened his mind to new possibilities. A stronger argument yet was being offered a position outside of New Jersey. I decided to present that bargaining chip; I asked him if he would relocate to another state if I found a job.

Joe could not be budged. He simply did not want to move, and especially if it meant disrupting Rosie. He countered with: "Why don't you consider looking for a full-time job teaching in high school again?" I wanted to scream: "What was the point of my PhD?" I kept my mouth shut; I was afraid he would bounce the question right back at me—*what was the point?*

It was disappointing to find several positions in other states—I didn't live in any of them. I stopped searching. It was only an academic exercise, and there was no point in depressing myself. I also needed to prepare for the classes I was hired to teach that fall, and help Rosie get ready for her senior year in high school. She needed clothes since most of hers had been donated to Goodwill, and she needed supervision with this endeavor. If left alone to her own devices the clothes she chose would probably suffer the same fate as her previous attire. If she thought time might soften her father, she was wrong. Once his mind was set on something it did not easily move. It was infuriating concerning relocation and my career advancement but when it came to Rosie's slutty clothes—I sent a thank you to the universe for his tenacity. I silently cheered him on-*stay solid as a rock, baby.*

Preparing for school was hectic. It was a shopping frenzy and not only clothes: digital tablets, notebooks, pencils, and stylus pens. The new in competition with old-school. Joe asked if all of it was necessary and Rosie said yes. I doubted it but when he would balk, I gave Rosie the money since it was for school (but made a point to accompany her). I also had to schedule a maintenance service appointment for my car to make sure it was up for all the commuting, and Rosie had to have a physical for cheerleading. I did not have many opportunities to talk to Paulee, but I would have opened up more of my time—she had none to spare. She was settling into her new apartment, launching the restaurant, and interviewing for teaching positions. It was what I had suspected would happen despite her best intentions of keeping the phone busy, and it did not ease up for her in the fall, even after finding a new job.

It's always bedlam at the beginning of any new term, but it was even more challenging for Paulee than in the past. She was an experienced teacher but in a different academic culture. She had issues with the administration early on and quickly became active in her union. There was also the restaurant after it opened to contend with. She was not directly involved with its operation but she helped Anthony if he needed her to do something. She told me she didn't mind, "after all, I'm only looking out for my investment." Her only complaint was about Anthony. "He's really high maintenance, Sarah." I held my tongue; I did not say—I told you so.

The start of the new semester was challenging for me too and none of the schools were new environments. Memorizing all my students' names in the first few days of the semester took time and could be confusing—remembering what class they were in and what briefcase went to which school. I was teaching at four different colleges; six sections when you combined all my assignments. It was equivalent to a full-time teaching load, but not comparable pay. A slew of students, a huge amount of time—hardly any money. When Paulee told me her salary I was happy for her, but felt sorry for myself. I had to make a move, but it would be impossible for almost a year—no one was moving.

I identified sometimes with those who insisted it was fabricated and a sinister machination of politicians, or a viral attack from an unfriendly country. It came upon us so fast it was unsettling. As unsettling as the fact that I found myself at times agreeing with my father-in-law—the world and I went crazy.

I had just administered my mid-term exams before the spring break; to be more accurate the semester break that followed was only at two schools. The university and one of the community colleges would not have their breaks for another two weeks. I chose to administer my mid-term exams the same week for all my classes disregarding a school's calendar—it made life easier. Who knew the week after my midterms would morph into a spring break for everyone making it even more pragmatic. I would not see any of my students in person again at any school—due to the pandemic of 2020.

We were confined to our homes for the most part, and access to many public spaces was restricted to stop the spread of the virus. I always thought our townhouse was a nice size, but when Joe, Rosie and I were trapped there its size became distorted. It was a prison and my cellmates were a grouchy complaining teenager, and an eerily quiet, reticent man. I started to look forward to hearing Rosie cursing at me under her breath—it was music to my ears, especially compared to Joe. His silence grated on my nerves.

He was always quiet but this was different—his silences were too loud to ignore. Each day he spoke less, reminding me of *The Incredible Shrinking Man*—one of my mother's favorite movies from the 1950's. I watched it with her when I was seven and it scared the life out of me. Joe gradually disappeared but was still there, like we were supposed to believe about the man in the movie who shrank smaller and smaller. Joe's transformation was as scary as science fiction except there was no fear he would be eaten by one of Paulee's cats. He ignored them, the same as he did Rosie and me.

In the early months of lockdown Joe and I went grocery shopping once a week and walked every day in the woods with Holly—and then it started. He would opt out of activities more and more until he never left the house—he shut down completely. Rosie and I walked the dog and she accompanied me to the store—Joe refused to move. He had never wanted to go anywhere very often before the world went nuts, but now he literally spent most of his time sleeping—like a bear hibernating (and even Rosie couldn't poke him). His behavior made his former self gregarious and downright chatty in comparison.

Mom said he sounded depressed; she pulled questions from a depression questionnaire to quiz me about Joe. I had no answers for many of her questions. I had no clue how he felt—he wasn't talking to me. He seemed to have no need to share with anyone. During the lockdown Paulee and I talked frequently; she was freaking out. It was not in fear of a virus; it was about the loss of all their savings—their restaurant was closed. She was teaching online like me, but it wasn't enough to make up for what they had invested in their restaurant. When I reminded her she was lucky to have her teaching job she was not very gracious: "Only one income, Sarah. You and Joe are both drawing an income so you can call yourself lucky. Don't you dare lecture me about gratitude. I'm losing every damn penny I invested in the restaurant."

It was true, Joe and I still had our jobs and he did his when he wasn't sleeping; we were fortunate not to have financial worries. My worry was Joe's mental health. It was more important than money but I wasn't going to get support from Paulee there, since losing money was her biggest concern. I needed to find support about Joe from someone else.

I returned to my mother, but her behavior was as challenging as Joe's during the lockdown. Her reaction to the virus was extreme. Every time I went to visit her she handed me a robe in her hallway and made me take off all my clothes. She insisted that she had to wash them in bleach, but never separated colors from white. I also needed to wear a mask inside for my entire visit. I did not object to the mask, but she was ruining my clothes. If I had owned more white I would have continued to visit her in-person but it's not my fashion choice; I waited until it was nice enough to sit on her deck before I returned to visit. But we connected by phone and continued to work on the depression assessment for Joe.

I answered the questions using my own observations without Joe's input. His eating patterns had changed—he was a little heavy. I thought bears gained weight before they hibernated—Joe did it in reverse; in answer to question two—no; he did not exercise. He refused to walk and I never heard him working out with his weights anymore, but he scored well on hygiene. He did not neglect it, but he stopped cutting his hair. I wasn't sure how that impacted the question. Did not cutting your hair mean you were neglecting your hygiene and a marker for depression? He kept it clean and took regular showers so I wasn't sure. The only thing I was sure about was I really knew now that he had curls. It became an amusing topic of conversation with Rosie (even if it was a marker for depression).

"Did you know that Daddy had curly hair like me?"

"Yes."

"Why didn't you tell me?"

"Well, it was more like a rumor, I never saw it. Your father has always worn his hair sheared for all the years I've known him." And at first Joe's curls were a pleasing change, until he stopped trimming. By August he looked like the Dutch scientist Antoine van Leeuwenhoek. It was not an attractive hairstyle. When he refused my offer to trim it I offered advice: "At least pull it back in your Zoom meetings, Joe."

He preferred to turn the video off. At least he was savvy with the computer—he knew the difference between the video and the mic. According to news reports some people were confused—like the guy caught without his pants on in a webcam meeting. Another had been masturbating, but I bet that was intentional and not a mistake—he was simply a new-age flasher using a digital platform. The world might have gone crazy but some things do not change.

Unpacking the next question: it was hard to measure if Joe had—*lost interest in doing things*; it was not always his choice. The golf and flying clubs were both closed so it was hard to determine if he had lost interest, or a case of them simply not being currently available to him. I was available though. I was a constant variable in our confinement, but he was no longer interested in me.

I have always maintained that I did not need a man to satisfy my sexual needs. I continue to believe that, but it's also true you can't cuddle with your vibrator.

I would snuggle up to Joe in bed at night and there was no response. He never turned around or returned my hug—like a hibernating bear. I would have elicited more of a reaction from a real one than I had from Joe.

After the lockdown was lifted I read a report that predicted there would be an exponential growth of pregnancies as a result of couples being confined together for all those months—it did not happen. These results made me feel better—maybe Joe and I were not atypical. According to this study most people had not used the pandemic confinement to have more sex, but it was only mildly reassuring. It was true we had not been so different compared to other couples sexually speaking, but Joe hadn't needed me for talk or companionship—he hadn't needed me for anything at all. Was that normal behavior? I had been locked in a house with Joe yet totally isolated from him.

When the lockdown was lifted in June Rosie continued to complain about her senior prom that had been canceled in May. It took some time before she stopped whining. I was probably not as nurturing as warranted when it was canceled and she cut me no slack. Proms are important markers in life and I had sympathized, but it had not been that obvious. I was more focused on Joe at the time. I tried to commiserate with her as soon as Joe began to come out of his hibernation, but it was too late from her perspective. I understood and even identified with her. I was thankful when Joe showed signs of renewed life but his timing was too late for me also.

After Joe completely woke up he let me cut his hair. He also went to his flying club and golfed when they reopened. I was almost giddy when Rocky came to our house for the first golf date with Joe after the lockdown was lifted. I was genuinely happy—I did not even complain about him being early (and it wasn't due to a sexual thrill). Rocky drew Joe out and I was grateful for their friendship. He appeared shocked when I invited him in for coffee. I hadn't talked to Liz for some time so I figured I could catch up a bit on their news—in addition to expressing my gratitude with coffee and a bagel. The last time I had spoken with her she shocked me. She told me they were having problems in their marriage; *did she finally see Rocky's negative side*? I never liked Rocky very much and Paulee scoffed at me when I said that, but it was true. It was also true I still got horny when I saw him. It just happened.

And the hormones were a bit excited the day he sat in my kitchen drinking coffee. I was still experiencing deprivation. Joe was ready to golf at that juncture but not ready to have relations with me. I speculated about it sometimes; was he doing it intentionally—payback for my past behaviors? I craved the attention and feel of a man. Sex toys work to reach sexual satisfaction but they do not satisfy the need for the warmth of love and a human touch. It was not Rocky I craved though—he was no threat to my marriage; and unwanted sexual itches for him were dwarfed by relief—he was helping Joe. With Rocky it was only about sex anyway. It was easy for me to satisfy an itch, but I realized something about Joe during the pandemic. He was no longer easily replaced with a sex toy.

School continued to be remote in the fall for Rosie and for me. I liked it—it was a pleasure not having to commute to several different colleges every week. Rosie on the other hand hated her online classes, even though it had been positive from my perspective. Academically speaking she had not suffered from her confinement, and to my relief and delight had been accepted at a university. She was a student at Florida International—taking online classes at home. She planned to take classes on campus for the spring and refused to continue if they were remote. She only applied to schools that had projected in-person classes for the spring. She was majoring in hospitality and tourism management. I was surprised her university continued to offer the program; the industry was suffering due to the pandemic. Is that why she was accepted—they needed students? It was an unfair speculation; she had turned her grades around in the last few months.

Joe continued to work remotely in the fall, but received word he would start in-person appointments again in January. That meant commuting and traveling out-of-state. He always complained about both, but was relieved when he received the notification from his boss. Another positive was we started having sex again—the bear woke up. Life was turning around in a positive direction for us until my mother's call after Christmas. It turned a propitious time into a gamble, and unbeknownst to me our conversation about Dee planted poisonous seeds in my head.

Dee and I only saw each other a couple of times a year compared to the past. There were even years when holiday cards were the only interaction, but that was all moot—a strong connection remained between us. That's why I was surprised I did not receive a card from her Christmas 2020 but I overlooked her omission. Some people were reluctant to send cards or even touch their mail during the pandemic. Dee being afraid to touch her mail did not sound like the Dee I knew however, and not receiving a card from her stayed lodged in my brain. I mentioned it to my mother and she told me Dee died in May.

"Why didn't you tell me?"

"Well, what good would it have done? They weren't letting people visit her in the hospital, not even her family; and you had enough on your plate in your own home."

"Did she die of the virus?"

"Oh, no, she had cancer."

She did not even hesitate; she was absolutely sure about it—so much for confidentiality. She had retired from nursing two years previously, but one of her friends who worked at the hospital told her. People talk; I have never regretted traveling a distance for therapy.

Dee was my best friend in high school but we were polar opposites, similar to Rocky and Joe. Liz's theory about them complementing one another was bunk, but it was true for Dee and me. She had added excitement to my life, I admired her risk-taking; and I was a calming force, reining her in. We were good for one another, but I never identified with her—until she died. Dee's death nudged my bout with cancer to the front of my thoughts again. It was another wake-up call about mortality.

It seemed like only yesterday when Dee and I were in high school; reflection on our limited time on this earth was not a negative endeavor. But my mind wandered into other areas best left alone, with no hint of danger—harmless thoughts. The seeds hadn't sprouted yet. I would not be aware of them until late spring. I was too occupied with uprooting Rosie and her move to Florida for school. We were planning to drive down in Joe's SUV hauling a small trailer. No shipping or booking plane tickets for us. Joe insisted on driving as usual—all the way to Miami; only stopping for restrooms and short meals. He had been annoying as a parrot repeating, "Pack snacks, I am not making a lot of stops." I never argued with him about snacks and stops, but I had made one thing clear—*I refuse to sleep in the back of the SUV at a truck stop.*

Rosie needed to be on campus the week before her classes started which worked for me. I didn't need to start my classes until the week after her. I joked with Joe about getting a rental to stay in Florida for Rosie's first semester away from home. I was still teaching online, I could work from anywhere. Jokes or sarcasm often go right past Joe, he views the world too literally. But he laughed when I said it—until we arrived at the off-campus housing. There were several girls milling around—wearing clothing very similar to what Rosie had been forced to donate. Joe took one look and said, "maybe we should consider the rental idea seriously." I reminded him this was Miami, but more importantly, these girls and Rosie were students in college, not high school. I also tried to ease his worries; based on my research FIU was not considered a party school compared to other state schools in Florida. Besides, Rosie would turn eighteen in the fall. Joe probably regretted that we had started her in school early, but I counted us as lucky she had gotten out of high school without getting an STD or pregnant. We could now only hope for the best—she was out of our control. Joe saw it differently, but agreed that he would no longer be able to oversee all of her activities.

We stayed through new student orientations and settled her into her housing, which looked more like a hotel suite than student apartments; they were also co-ed. Rosie was lucky the occupants near hers were female. If there had been one guy in the mix, Joe would not have let her stay. He was still concerned and asked why there was no adult supervisor on the premises. I repeated for the umpteenth time, "She's on her own now. You can't control her, Joe." That did not go over well.

"Are you serious, Sarah? Who do you think is paying for this?"

I felt impotent after he challenged me and I could not call him on it—I had no money to play my hand. Her schooling was expensive and my earnings were too small. If I contributed to her tuition it would be only nominal at best—I shut up. He told Rosie he would "pull the plug" if she did not pass all her classes. I wanted her to do well in school too, but I would not have phrased it that way. I had no agency to interfere however, I was not paying the bills. I let him be the leader.

"You're not here to party, Rosie. I'm serious, don't test me."

"Okay, Daddy, okay. I hear you."

"I just want to make myself very clear."

"I hear you, I'm not here to party." She sounded sincere; and she knew her father was true to his word and was no longer putty in her hands. Of course it might have been a facade, and if so she chose the wrong major at the wrong campus. Paulee had told me once how one of her acting students at graduation thanked her for teaching them how to lie better to their parents. I decided not to mention that to Joe; it would have created more worry for him. And it would have been unfair since his proclamation to Rosie had helped me worry less about her behavior unchecked. It wasn't until after she was settled that I became edgy. Not over Rosie, over my dead-end career.

Money equated power. I did not earn enough to have any agency with Rosie's education or my life—even with a full-time teaching load. Discontent grew. That's when my unhealthy thoughts did as well—sprouting right in front of my face like unchecked weeds.

CHAPTER 30

WEEDING MY GARDEN

I never fully recovered from 2020 like Joe seemingly had. He came out of his hibernation fresh and ready to return to life as we had known it. But there was a bitter residue clinging to me like sticky burrs from weeds. I continued to be resentful about his shutting me out during the pandemic, and I could not stop obsessing over my career. It had not been great before the world went crazy and it was no better after it returned to a semblance of normalcy. Any degree of normalcy was a problem. I needed a change, not a return to my status quo. Time now was also an important integral that could not be overlooked.

My daughter was starting her life with years ahead of her to realize her dreams. In contrast, my years were limited. Dee's death and my own experience with cancer made that realization more poignant. I began to re-examine my dreams and searched for new directions, but as hard as I tried I could not find a new purpose or plan. I tried to reject this rediscovery, but ultimately had to acquiesce. I did not want to change careers. I loved teaching math at the college level, but I had to find a full-time position. I needed to research those ends—not change life-long goals. That's when I started to broaden my examination to look at my whole life, even if it threatened my marriage, and I was oblivious. I convinced myself it was only exploration; and inquiry always starts with questions. Joe, being a major player in my life, would naturally shape the design of many that I formed. No alarm bells alerted me to peril.

I loved Joe, but was it love or fear that kept me in this marriage? Did I want to stay in this marriage? More importantly, how much was I willing to sacrifice to achieve my professional goals? What did I need to do? I had to find the answers.

I committed myself to researching fully just like I did for graduate work. It was no longer an idle pastime but a serious pursuit. Searching for a full-time teaching position was the driving force, but I would have been dishonest if I had denied another factor that had propelled me forward. I also held the belief that I might find a perfect soulmate in the process.

I began in earnest near the end of spring semester when new postings are listed. I was not always scientific in my methodology. I used metaphysics as one source to gather some of my findings, or sometimes to determine what the next step was in my process. I was not intent on leaving Joe so I needed a sign—the universe would direct me. I searched for positions in New Jersey and outside of the state. If offered a full-time position locally, I would accept it and stay with Joe. If not, my research would change direction, metaphysically speaking. There were no local positions available.

There were several positions out-of-state, and I was drawn to the open position at a small private college in Minnesota because of family ties to the area. It was full time with a tenure track in the mathematics department to start in the fall. I was interested, but I did not apply immediately; I was scared about what accepting a job might mean regarding Joe and our marriage. I questioned my process—didn't I have to answer the questions formed about Joe and our marriage first? I was in a stalemate until I reminded myself that investigation came before answers could be found. Fear was muddling my brain, and accepting a position was the next step in my research. I also trusted the universe that was guiding me in this direction.

And rationalizations were unneeded; the job offer was hypothetical at this juncture. That was a fact; it forced me to examine another. I wanted this job regardless of Joe and my marriage. I pressed *Send*.

When I got an interview appointment I contacted my Aunt Marion. I hoped to stay with her when I went to Minnesota. In addition to making arrangements for my stay and travel, I researched the math department of my prospective employer. I also asked my mother about her experiences in Minneapolis when she attended the University of Minnesota for anecdotal information. She was tripping merrily along memory lane until she asked, "Why are you interested in Minneapolis?" I told her I had a job interview for a teaching position at a college there.

"Minneapolis, Sarah? I thought you told me Joe never wanted to relocate."

"Maybe he'll change his mind if I'm offered the position." She had to ask me what kind of reaction I had gotten so far from him—and I couldn't lie to her. I told her I hadn't even told him about the interview yet. So much for honesty, she stopped talking.

"I don't know what you are planning, Sarah, but you better be careful."

I tried to convince her and myself it was only an interview. I hadn't made my mind up about any-thing—I had not even been offered the job; my argu-ments failed dismally. She refused to tell me anything more about her experiences in Minnesota.

Next I tried a different tactic to get information not found in a travel guide. I wanted to hear about my father's family. That had more relevance after all since her memories about living in Minneapolis were from the 1970's. Family history retains its currency as long as there's family alive.

"Can't you tell me about father's childhood and something about his family? I've never even met them. Why didn't we visit them?"

"You met them all—grandparents, aunts and uncle, Sarah."

"What, when I was four?"

"Well, you're an adult, what stopped you from going? Your sister has been visiting them since she moved out of my house."

"She has? I never knew that."

"Oh, for heaven's sake, don't you girls ever talk to one another?" (Not very much, and that's what I had been trying to tell her for years, but I didn't think it would work to my advantage if I pointed that out now).

I had never met my cousins, and did not remember having met my aunts and uncle, or my grandparents. I was only acquainted with Aunt Marion and my grandmother from their voices on the phone, and their signatures on birthday and Christmas cards. That had been the extent of our interactions in my memory from my childhood, and nothing had changed after I was an adult. Penny in comparison according to my mother had full relationships with my Minnesota relatives. It would be just like Penny to have never shared this with me on purpose—she had wanted to keep them all to herself. I was wrong. When I called her on it she was surprised: "I thought mother had surely told you I visited father's family on a regular basis." I would have thought so too since Penny had been visiting every summer since her freshman year at Stern.

For Penny they were family, but aside from Aunt Marion and Grandmother Larssen, they were strangers to me. Penny was also familiar with our family history, another distinct difference between us. She knew more than stats too; she knew where the dirty linens were stored. She told me Mom did not get along well with the Minnesota clan. That's why she never went back to visit with us when we were kids. Pops had not been the only one who had objected to our parents' marriage. My father had been engaged to the daughter of a family friend when he met our mother. There was not only a bit of gossip due to their age difference, there had also been a little scandal when he broke his engagement to marry her. I confronted my mother with what Penny told me and she became very upset. She also shocked me because I never heard her call anyone a "bitch" before; "and your Aunt Marion is crazy if she thinks I'm going to forget how she treated me. I don't care if we are a couple of old ladies now."

I was sorry I brought the subject up but my mother stopped giving me grief about the interview. Her attention shifted from me to her grievances with the Minnesota relatives for the remaining days before I flew to Minneapolis. She was so negative I grew apprehensive until Penny assured me there were no longer ill feelings on the Minnesota side—she was always treated well by everyone. She gave me contact information for all the relatives.

Aunt Marion was thrilled to have me stay with her and Grandmother Larssen. I was excited about finally seeing them face-to-face and meeting my other relatives. So much so that the interview took second place in my thoughts. Reflecting on that time I believe my psyche had kicked into a protective mode, enabling me to handle my apprehensions. If I lied to myself about the principal reason for going to Minnesota I could ignore my mother's warning about what I was doing, and I only told Joe I was visiting my father's family. It was not until I was offered the position that I had to face the truth full front, but I continued to delude myself: *Accepting the position was part of my research project.*

I planned to leave Joe for this job but not in a technical sense—no separation papers or divorce actions. And moving to Minnesota to teach mathematics was simply the next step in my study. I needed to find the answers to my questions to complete my work, and I had to complete it when I was afforded the opportunity. The universe was not promising another would materialize in the near future, and there was a time limit for completion—the same as with graduate degrees. The difference now was no advisor or university had set it—it was set by life and mortality.

The summer before fall semester, prior to finding my own place, I returned to Aunt Marion's and lived with her and my grandmother. Aunt Marion kept advising me to hold off looking for an apartment. She was sure I would soon be returning to my husband in New Jersey. A professorship with possible tenure held no prize for her at all. She was from a different generation and questioned why I would leave "a perfectly good man" who I loved for a job. She never met Joe but I agreed with her—he was a good man, so I tried to explain my research argument to her instead. That's when she told me I was having a midlife crisis. I only thought men had them—buying expensive cars or getting new, younger wives.

I never considered I was having a midlife crisis as the reason why I took the job and left Joe. It wasn't a car or a younger man I wanted—it was a career, and it was not a desire which came upon me when I hit middle-age. I've wanted it for years and I finally found it. Why Joe was removed from the equation was a question I couldn't answer for sure. I had not suffered from sexual grudges for years, thanks to Dr. Barney, and my irritation during the pandemic had faded from my view. Indignation with Joe over my career had also disappeared. I no longer cared about his implications after I found my dream job—*my degree had not been a waste of time or money*. All that said, my life with Joe was an unfinished study if I were completely honest. That's why I never extended an invitation to him; I had presumed he would not want to move to Minnesota. I also continued to question if he even was the right partner for me. The uncertainty was a necessary condition to enable me to leave him and accept the position, but my conflicting feelings made it impossible to explain my actions in a logical way. Having a midlife crisis was a solid hypothesis, but Aunt Marion's, not mine. I had been unable to form one because I was not sure why I was leaving Joe. It took Aunt Marion and other people to provide hypotheses for me.

My mother said I was "mad." She loved Joe.

Rosie cried, "You're leaving Daddy?" —(and told me I was a narcissistic bitch).

Paulee scolded, "You've never appreciated that man, Sarah. He spoiled you." I always suspected that she was more Joe's friend than mine; she did not even hesitate a minute before she said it.

They all seemed so sure of themselves. I admired them and wished I could feel as confident as they did about my reasoning for leaving.

It was tough telling Joe my plans, due to some extent to those conflicting feelings and my lack of hypothesis. The other difficulty I attribute completely to him. Joe was *being Joe* the several times I tried to tell him. He didn't seem to hear me until the day I was scheduled to fly to Minneapolis from Philadelphia International Airport. That's when I had his full attention. I explained it as well as I was able and I told him I was leaving for me, and it had nothing to do with him. I had no desire to share my research questions, and I realized what I said was probably closer to the truth—it was more about my need to leave and less about him. There was very little time to peruse this revelation because my words unleashed a force that struck me like a physical blow.

"What the hell do you mean it has nothing to do with me? It's me you're leaving."

I had never heard Joe raise his voice in anger at anyone and now he was roaring at me. I was really afraid. Joe is a large man—was he going to physically hurt me? That's what I thought because he was so angry. I backed up when he took a step towards me. I had poked the bear.

He must have seen how he frightened me because when he spoke again he sounded like the Joe I knew.

"Sarah, please don't leave. I love you."

"I love you too Joe." I moved cautiously towards him. I was still a little skittish so I approached slowly. But I could see he was my Joe, and like the first day when I met him—I gave the bear a big hug. Only this time I wrapped my arms around him very tightly and held him much longer. He hugged me back, and his warm breath found my ear when he said, "I need you, Sarah."

That's when I pulled back and I told him it was too late. I was not talking about our marriage, I did not have a solid clue about that yet. I was talking about this need he was professing—he hadn't needed me before—he chose to hibernate rather than reach out to me. He was only making a ploy to keep me from leaving. And I needed this job.

"Are you coming back, Sarah?"

"I don't know." I wasn't going to lie to him; I loved him too much to lie and I had no more words left in me. I also knew I had to go immediately or I never would because I was apprehensive. I kept asking myself— what are you doing? Why are you leaving your best friend? I turned away from him so he wouldn't see the hesitancy in my face and I walked quickly to the door to get my bags. I told him my Aunt Marion's contact information was on the fridge and I'd call him as soon as I landed in Minneapolis—as though I was headed for a vacation. It was easy to pretend until Joe had to break my delusion.

"I just want to tell you, no matter how long it takes I'll wait for you, Sarah."

When he said that I lost it; I was not taking a vacation and I was glad my back was to him so he couldn't see my tears. His words made me feel awful, but they also gave me the courage to walk out the door. I knew he would be there if I chose to return.

CHAPTER 31

DISCOVERY

Aunt Marion said I could live with her and Grandmother Larssen indefinitely: "we have plenty of room, and there's no point paying rent or being by yourself." Living with Agnes had been very challenging in the final year we were together and was still a memory. It had been difficult enough sharing a house with one female relative, I was not sure I could take two of them. I also was finally earning enough to afford rent, but the main reason I declined the invitation was superstition. There were too many similarities between my father and myself. My father had taught in the mathematics department at the University in Minnesota, and died in a car crash on the Ford Parkway bridge on his commute to work. Aunt Marion and Grandmother Larssen lived in a suburban home outside of Minneapolis. I would also have to travel on a connecting bridge to and from my job, to teach mathematics at a college in the same city. It was too creepy. I preferred to live in a place where I didn't need to drive at all. I thanked Aunt Marion for her generous offer and looked for a studio apartment in Dinkytown, an area walking distance from my campus.

I didn't leave Joe for a different man, but part of the dynamic had been to find someone I might be more compatible with. And there was a time factor—it was not infinite. I had to start my meetings to find answers to my questions if I wanted to complete this study. That's why I did not hesitate, and I made a surprising discovery after only several meetings. Of course it had been too early at that point to form conclusions with such scanty investigation, but all the data in my study was ultimately analyzed to answer my questions about Joe.

I found I disliked brainiac talk with men. There was often an unpleasant power element present like I was sparring with them; a series of word games played to show off your wit or intellect. "You're right on that point but…" —*but* was a very important word with these guys. Joe never engaged in brainiac talk but more importantly, when we talked it was for the sake of talking—we were not trying to prove anything. And my first participant stands out the most when I reflect on verbiage. His name was Ray.

Ray was a colleague from my math department. Meetings with him were the most applicable for insights on hegemony and its intersection with verbiage; and it was never more obvious than on our very first meetup on a beautiful evening in early September. We went to a bonfire sponsored by our department on the banks of the Mississippi. It was slated as a meet-and-greet, and a last hurrah for summer before fall classes and cold weather began. Ray taught the undergraduate math classes for liberal arts students. The department called them "the basket weaving courses." They were designed to enable students not strong in math skills to pass a three-credit math requirement for their degree.

Ray was challenging me on something that evening but I wasn't paying attention—there was a breathtaking sunset. It wasn't taking his breath away. He wasn't even taking notice of it, and I thought how Joe would have been taking in the sunset instead of expounding on some pithy idea. Joe was uncomplicated and got pleasure from simple things. Ray preferred power plays to sunsets. One would think he had enough ego massaging feeling superior to those liberal arts students he taught. Did he need to feel superior to everyone? Or had it only been with me?

Words were not the only thing these brainiacs used to compete with. They would use any means available—competitiveness was part of their nature. After meeting many of these men I realized competing was non-stop. They would also knife someone in the back to get ahead, even those they professed to like. If Joe did not like someone he was forthright about it. He didn't pretend he liked a person if it was not true. I sometimes complained to him about his need to always *tell the truth*; now I preferred his nerdy honesty over disingenuity. It wasn't always clear what these men I met genuinely thought about me, or anything else for that matter. Campus politics in play.

I am aware of the argument that political competitiveness speaks more of the nature of the climate rather than these men; academia is a cut-throat career. All the same, it was not an excuse for subterfuge or dishonesty. Joe was a salesman on commission, a climate as competitive as any college campus, but his focus has always been on himself. He tried to top his last performance rather than compete directly with other salesmen, and never did something underhanded to get ahead.

Examining hegemony stood out when I met these men, but verbiage was central when I compared Joe with the brainiacs for the obvious contrast. It was almost culture shock at these meetings, but it made me more objective about Joe. I was also able to evaluate him better from a distance using the proximity of these men for comparison. It was curious how he was very open with opinions about people but very closed on other topics. Joe's mother told me that he had been more talkative when he was young, and she didn't know why he became so quiet as he got older. It probably was a combination of having been molested and having a father like Mac. I was more tolerant of his quietness after I compared him to others. I didn't know the background stories of the men I met but I had more appreciation for Joe's style. It was how he calmed himself—a kind of light meditation. I would have preferred sitting with him rather than Ray that evening by the Mississippi—looking at the sunset with few words.

My examination of contrasting Joe with these men made me question myself: was it simply a matter of having had a long history with Joe that made me do it? I had to remind myself that I was compelled to compare Joe with others if I wanted to find answers to my questions. It was a major core of my research, so I continued.

Another obvious contrast was to study the attitudinal differences towards money between Joe and my participants. I noticed for example how another man named Dave was often extremely generous with his tips when we went out to eat. But it was not accurate to say he was more generous than Joe because his generosity was contractual and confined to restaurants; he walked by homeless people without a glance. Joe never did that; he always gave street people money.

Joe was frugal, but he could also be open handed. He willingly helped pay for my graduate school and school for Rosie. One might protest—that's family—it doesn't count. We are his family, but not all families were generous with one another where money is concerned. Mac refused to pay for Joe's college education, and some families fought for years over money. News sources have reported an exponential influx of disputes in recent years over inheritances amongst family members. Joe would never behave that way, but I was still irritated over his tipping. It took many years of arguments before he finally told me his reasoning behind being so cheap. He believed servers should be paid a decent salary by their employers. "If customers continue to give them big tips the industry will never change." I don't know if Joe's strategy is sound, but I liked his rationale more than Dave's, which was calculated to impress or seduce a cute server. It was a demonstrable fact—if the server was male or a less attractive female—Dave's tips were never big.

I met with many men but the last one played a pivotal role in my research. His name was Chet and taught *Global History* and *The Ancient Greeks*. He was a nice guy, and the most likable of all the men I met. But I had to end it with him when he made me realize: *what I considered meetings were dates from the other side of the table.* Maybe my mother had been on to something—was I being disingenuous? I never told these men they were participants in a study either, which was unethical on my part and flawed my research.

Ethics and misconceptions were not the only reasons I stopped seeing Chet; practicality had also been thrown into the mix. I missed Joe when Chet tried to kiss me. It also felt weird when he held my hand; his was not much bigger than mine. Joe's hands are like big paws; they made me feel petite. Chet made me feel like a cow. But size, kisses and ethics was not the decisive factor. The break came when I caught him looking down my shirt—not that this bothered me. Males have been staring at my boobs since puberty. It was not new but it triggered a memory. Would he still want me if I had only one? Or no boobs at all? Would he say like Joe—that it didn't matter?

Studying: verbiage, competitiveness, money, hands and boobs had not been frivolous; but I had sometimes wasted valuable research time on inconsequential comparisons—like how a fork was held or the quality of a sneeze. Joe was often on my mind even when I was not making comparative analyses between him and other men. Every morning when I woke up and turned to place my hand on his back and he wasn't there; or when I bought an item on sale that I knew he liked at the market, and stood dumbfounded at the checkout. I never ate anchovies.

I did not want to be with any other man, I wanted Joe. I wanted to pursue my passion but not a solo song; I no longer cared if he sang off-key. I wanted to do a duet with him. It took me a little over a year to finally come to that conclusion. I kept questioning—what if I only feel this way because I am more like my mother than I had thought? I don't like living by myself and perhaps the solution was to move in with Aunt Marion. Alone in my apartment I often found myself talking to my coffee cup or my own reflection in the mirror for want of sharing mundane conversations with someone. When I said that to Paulee she replied, "Well, you always said talking to Joe was like talking to the wall, so it should feel natural to you. I always thought it was mean when you said it, Sarah."

Maybe I was mean but it took me time to discover there are different kinds of silences; silence with Joe felt solid, silence without him was hollow. Sometimes I even questioned the silence. I laughed how the simplest of happenings triggered memories of things Joe said when we were together. Had he really talked as much as that? Or was it simply a compilation of our many years together? Whichever it was—I missed him.

I hoped it was not an argument for the cliche—*absence makes the heart grow fonder*, but there had also been an equal opportunity for—*out of sight, out of mind*. It had not happened; and throughout our marriage and entire relationship Joe has always been on my mind. The difference in the past: I was part of the study. A researcher can be a participant in her own study, but sometimes there is not enough objectivity. That had been my problem until I moved to Minnesota. I had to remove myself to form a more accurate picture.

I needed Joe and I needed my job. It was not an either-or-choice. Neither were complete without the other. There's little joy in finally obtaining a dream if there's no one I love to share it with. I wanted to share it with Joe. The configuration of my life along with its values had changed, and I believed they had also changed for Joe. The study was complete; I had the answers; it was time to form my conclusions.

Conclusion One: I would have to search for an infinity, like counting natural numbers, to find a perfect soulmate. My search would never end because perfection is an artificial construct. There is no perfect soulmate.

Conclusion two: the things that annoyed me about Joe were outnumbered by the things I missed about him. It was not an original idea. I came up with it years ago when I applied Euclid's notions to my life.

The dilemma was that the parts of my marriage always kept shifting—changing values, making it necessary to repeat my study. The configuration of my life was dynamic, it never remained constant. That's also the nature of research. Research studies have to be replicated in order to be validated and expanded to form new theories—and I was able to expand Euclid's theory: *all parts of a whole can have different values but ones that intersect are equal.*

New theory: *all parts are equal without intersecting on a negative line.* Joe was missing and he was equal to all the existing parts of my life. It might not be accurate math but it was true.

I firmly uphold my conclusions, knowing they are never absolute or definitive, but I hope I will never have the urge to repeat this study. It's with the understanding though that the very act of living is a continual flux of re-examinations. If you do not do it, you're depressed or dead.

EPILOGUE

Joe waited longer than most men would have, but I was wrong to think he'd wait until I finally figured out what I wanted. And sometimes I wish he hadn't told me he would wait. Maybe it would have kept me from walking out the door, or staying away so long. I'll never know for sure.

I never entertained the possibility of Joe re-examining his life and pursuing his own study. Although he did have encouragement. Rosie introduced him to the mother of her roommate at school, who recently lost her husband to cancer. Rosie tells me Joe is planning on selling the townhouse in Jackson and moving to North Carolina where she lives. Most of the time I'm glad Joe found someone because I love him. I want him to be happy; but there are also times when I experience the sorry-for-myself blues, especially at night when missing him hurts too much. That's when the memory plays over and over again—I'm assuring Paulee that I'd be happy if he found someone else and she replies:

"That's what you say now, Sarah."

I reminded her about our conversation recently when we were talking on the phone. I told her she had been prescient and wise when she had said that to me. I took too long to realize Joe was woven into every part of me. Now he's gone, and I'm like a fabric with only one missing thread, unraveling all the same.

Perhaps it's only these Minneapolis nights getting too cold for me again, and I miss his warm, solid body next to me. Why fool myself, he was more than just a warm body in bed—he was my rock. Often too impossible to move, but I thought he would always be there to lean on (no matter what I said or did). I overlooked the geological fact that rocks may be solid and strong but they are not impenetrable forever.

And I never gave much thought about Joe leaning on me. I was angry because he turned away when he went into hibernation. I was upset and hurt. The irony was he needed me more than ever but he was incapable of showing it, and I was incapable or unwilling to understand that. I held onto resentment when he was at his most vulnerable. I was not his rock, I did not have patience or insight—I moved in mind and body. I hurt him. Now he left me, but it's not pay-back or revenge—that's not Joe.

My thoughts are interrupted by my apartment buzzer. This building doesn't have a locked street door. None of the buildings had them when I was looking for an apartment. The neighborhood kids love to walk in, ring doorbells, and then run away. It's harmless fun but annoying. I don't feel like getting up but they buzz again. The person is persistent and the buzzing has a familiar cadence that finally draws me to the door. It triggers a memory of forgotten keys and Joe once again locking himself out of the house.

ABOUT THE AUTHOR

Marjorie Duryea has worked as an actress, director, choreographer, and educator, teaching dance and communication at the college level and in the private sector. She is a member of SAG/AFTRA and AEA and holds a masters from Monmouth University in Communication. She is the author of three other novels— A Little Blues Story from the Jersey Shore, Electra Bitches, and Dead Cat in the Cupboard.